Merely Mortal

Merely Mortal

COPING WITH DYING, DEATH AND BEREAVEMENT

Sarah Boston and Rachael Trezise

Methuen
in association with
Channel Four Television Company Ltd

First published in Great Britain 1987
by Methuen London Ltd
11 New Fetter Lane, London EC4P 4EE
Copyright © 1988 Sarah Boston and Rachael Trezise

Printed in Great Britain
by Richard Clay Ltd, Bungay, Suffolk

British Library Cataloguing in Publication Data

Boston, Sarah
  Merely mortal : coping with dying, death
  and bereavement.
  1. Death—Social aspects 2. Bereavement
  —Psychological aspects 3. Deprivation
  (Psychology)
  I. Title II. Trezise, Rachael III. Channel
  Four Television Company
  306.8'8   HQ1073

ISBN 0 413 15000 3
ISBN 0 413 15590 0 Pbk

This book is available in both a hardback and a paperback edition.
The paperback edition is sold subject to the condition that it shall not,
by way of trade or otherwise, be lent, resold, hired out,
or otherwise circulated without the publisher's prior consent
in any form of binding or cover other than that in which it is published
and without a similar condition being imposed on the subsequent
purchaser.

The lines from the Rolling Stones' 'Time Waits for No One' (© 1975)
are reproduced by kind permission of EMI Music Publishing Ltd.

The television series *Merely Mortal*
is produced for Channel 4 by Agender
Films.

*For Jo and John Boston,
Peggy and Don Trezise
and in memory of
Alan Wright*

Contents

Introduction ix

PART ONE by Sarah Boston

1 *To Talk of Death* 3
  The power of words 4
  Embarrassing conversations 7
  Social censure 11
  The words we use 14
2 *Death Is?* 23
  Medical definitions 26
  Artists' impressions 32
  Meanings of death 36
  Immortal longings 41
3 *Dying* 52
  Monster pain 61
  An end to the game of pretend 67
  The last good-bye 76
  In our own time 81
4 *After a Death* 91
  Seeing the dead 92
  Disposing of the dead 95
  Funerals 100
  Supporting roles 109
5 *Grief* 115
  The first shock 119
  The process of grief 123
  Helping 137
  Re-evaluations 149

PART TWO by Rachael Trezise

6 *The Terminally Ill*   158

7 *When Someone Dies*   165

8 *Grief and Bereavement*   196

Select Bibliography   205

Index   207

Introduction

This book arose from working on a series of documentaries for Channel Four which look at different aspects of dying, death and bereavement. We found that it was impossible to cover every area in five programmes and to give all the information that people need. The book has enabled us to explore and expand on the subject and look at how attitudes have changed. We are also able to provide in Part Two the further practical advice that we found so hard to come by.

The idea for a series grew out of Sarah's personal experience of the death of her first child and her desire to explore some of the feelings and situations that she had encountered at that time. During the making of these programmes we came across people with a variety of views and experiences but what we did discover was that most people still found it very hard to discuss the subject of death and mortality. We hope that this book, like the films, will enable people to face their own mortality as well as that of others.

Making the series and writing this book has meant that we have had to confront the subject for a long period of time. We would have found this much harder to bear without the constant support of colleagues, family and friends, whom we would like to take this opportunity to thank.

Sarah Boston and Rachael Trezise

Part One

SARAH BOSTON

CHAPTER ONE

To Talk of Death

> The British Bourgeoisie
> Is not born,
> And does not die,
> But, if it is ill,
> It has a frightened look in its eyes.
> (Sir Osbert Sitwell, 1892–1969)

The British of all classes are now born but they still do not die. The language of birth has become part of our private and public lives, but death remains evaded in private, though it is publicly displayed by the media in fact and in fiction. Death is not a proper subject of conversation in the pub, at work, in the drawing-room, round the kitchen table, in the bedroom or even late at night when the children cannot hear. It is not just that these are not appropriate situations for such conversation; there is no place or situation where it is regarded as acceptable to talk of death. It is regarded as particularly unacceptable in front of the dying or the bereaved themselves. A great silence surrounds both and both are cut off from talking about what is for them of most importance. One day it will be that which is, for each of us, the most important thing in our lives. To the silence to which we condemn others we too will also be condemned. We need to bring the language of death back into our lives so that we may use it in the hour of our need.

Before we can begin to look at dying, death and grief we have to look at the language we use to talk and write about these things. Death has not always been an unmentionable subject or one veiled by euphemisms. It is only during this century that we have developed so many ways of avoiding and silencing any talk about it. Being aware of the language and the evasive tactics we use, as well as trying to understand the reason why we use them, is a first step in opening up the subject.

The power of words

One of the reasons why we silence ourselves is because we fear that to talk about death is to court it. Somehow, quite how is a mystery, a fear has developed that the very use of the words 'dying' or 'death' will hasten our own or someone else's death. It is as though the very words have power over life or death themselves. There is, in our silence, a vain hope that if we don't talk about it *it* will go away. When we decided to make the documentary series *Merely Mortal* we realised that the making of such a series would involve much talking. There were times, though, when we began to wonder whether our talk caused the very thing we were talking about. Losing the fear of the possible power of words is not easy.

The series started because I wanted to talk about grief. My first child, Will, died at the age of nine months. Grief, I found, is a long, painful and often lonely experience. There were many things I wanted to say about it. From the desire to make one film about grief the series grew into five programmes exploring attitudes to grief, dying and death. We knew that the series had grown out of one personal experience, but what we were unprepared for were the many other personal experiences that would form an ever-present backdrop to our work. It was those experiences that began to make us wonder whether talking was indeed a dangerous thing.

Just before production started my colleague Rachael Trezise's grandmother died, and an uncle of mine died soon after production started. Although a shock when we heard about each, neither were unexpected. Both of us were sad that we had each lost someone who had been a part of our lives. We were soon to find out that for others, too, death and dying was a part of their lives. I asked a film editor to work on the first film and after I told him the subject he declined the offer as his mother was dying of cancer. He understandably felt that he could not handle the subject at that particular time, and he also knew that he would be unable to work on the film with any kind of emotional detachment. The film editor who did work on the film was sensitive to the subject for she was still trying to work through the legacy of emotions arising from the experience of seeing her brother close to death following his accidental shooting. The presenter of one of the programmes had experienced through stillbirth the death of a child, and the musician who composed the music for the series also had his own very personal as well as professional reason for contributing to it. His first child was born severely brain-damaged and she has already outlived the predictions made for her life expectancy. Indeed, once the subject of our series was known several people approached us, asking to work on it not just because they wanted a job but because some personal experience had made them aware of its importance. Sometimes people came to see us about a job but really just wanted to talk. It soon became clear that our talking about the subject enabled other people to do so. Those conversations helped to inform and enrich the series. They also confirmed us in our belief in the need for such programmes. We were in those early days of production, confident that to talk about death was not to court it and that our experiences and those others mentioned were somehow a coincidence.

The first experience that made us question our attitude was when the trainee attached to us arrived at work one morning quite disturbed by having seen someone die. She had gone swimming the previous evening and at the swimming pool a man had had a heart attack and died. It was the first dead person she had seen. She commented half seriously that she thought it no coincidence that she had had such an experience whilst working on the programme. Death, it seemed, was not safely confined to the words and images being carefully edited together. It had spilled out to the swimming pool, and perhaps in some mysterious way we were responsible for the spilling-out. Our confidence was really shaken when halfway through the series Rachael's uncle suddenly died; it left her shocked and grieving. It made us begin to fear that we had been unwise and that to talk of death was to invite it. Once the series was finished and delivered to Channel Four we felt we would be safe again. Death would no longer be part of our lives.

The curious aspect of the above events was not that they happened but that we felt in some way responsible for them happening. We harboured the suspicion that had we only kept quiet and left the subject alone, life, uninterrupted by death, could and would have continued. It was only those deaths that immediately touched us that we felt this way about; like others, we watched our TV screens and read our newspapers and felt no direct personal responsibility for the deaths reported there. Of course there is absolutely no evidence that, had we been working during that period on some other subject, any of the deaths of people close to us would not have occurred. Our talking of death had not been their cause. Words cannot literally kill, though we invest them with that power through our fear.

The origin of the fear that to talk about death is to court it is obscure. There is a feeling about it of pagan superstition, the fear of tempting the gods and fate. Its roots are clearly not in Christianity, a religion with death at the centre of its doctrine. There are records showing that although, prior to this century, people could and did talk about death some were clearly superstitious about doing so. The seventeenth-century writer Francis Bacon, himself not inhibited about the subject and the author of two essays 'On Death', noted the reluctance of many of his contemporaries to make a will. This reluctance he claimed was because 'When their will is made, they think themselves nearer a grave than before: now they, out of the wisdom of thousands, think to scare destiny, from which there is no appeal, by not making a will, or to live longer by their protestation of their unwillingness to die.'

Bacon's claim has a very contemporary echo to it. Indeed, Patrick Holden in an interview for the programme 'Born to Die' commented, 'We are all going to die . . . and it's foolish to shut your eyes to the fact it's going to happen, but some people think that the fact of making a will in some ways brings death nearer.' Making a will is both to recognise death yourself and to recognise it publicly inasmuch as at least one person has to witness the signature. Many people today think, just like their seventeenth-century predecessors, that somehow the act of making a will, of thinking, writing or talking about death, is to 'bring themselves nearer a grave than before'. We also, like our predecessors, hope that by remaining silent we will 'scare destiny'.

Whilst the origins of this fear are obscure, if we are to begin to be able to confront death and our own deaths we have to confront it. We have to divest words of the power we have invested in them. To talk about death does not shorten our lives. Remaining silent will not lengthen our lives. Recognising our mortality might give our lives, both personally and in a wider social and political context, more meaning.

Embarrassing conversations

Although talking about death while we were making the series *Merely Mortal* did not cause any deaths, what it did do was to reveal how much it is part of all our lives. Like so many hidden experiences, once you bring them out into the open you find they are common – in the case of death very common. All those people who worked with us were not employed because of the experiences they had had. Indeed, many we had worked with before. They would not normally have thought their experiences appropriate for discussion at work. Our talking broke the silence. The programmes merely made it a legitimate subject of conversation. Death and dying are part of life and around us all the time. What we brought out was normality, not abnormality.

Those who worked on the series had been warned of its subject and therefore had accepted that their work would involve at least listening if not talking. This was not the case for the many who were confronted 'out of the blue' with the subject of our work and were therefore unprepared as to how to respond. In fact the responses provided an interesting insight into attitudes, and one which we had not anticipated. It also showed how our fear of social reaction inhibits us from talking about death. Although our experience could by no means be assessed as a scientifically based sociological study, we did in the course of the production have to reveal the subject to a wide range of people, including bank managers, insurers, laboratory workers, publishers, friends and relatives, besides those who took part in or worked on it. Sometimes we even had to explain it to the recipients of one of our company cheques which had printed on them 'Agender Films/Death/Channel Four', 'Death' being the code-name Channel Four had given to the series for the purposes of their computer. It was a convenient short version of our working title *Death in our Time*. Our final title, *Merely Mortal*, came out of a decision that to have the word 'death' in the series title would be a 'switch-off' for the audience (this was in contrast to our previous series about attitudes to sex, where we decided that the word 'sex' in the title would cause the audience to 'switch on'). We also wanted in the series title words that diffused rather than increased the drama of death. The decision about the title was thus taken in anticipation of social responses to specific words. Of course, had the series been fictional, there would have been an entirely different set of considerations which might well have led us to include the word 'death' in the title as likely to be not only acceptable but also appealing to a section of the audience.

Of all members of the team working on the series I had had the most direct experience of social embarrassment and its power to inhibit talk of death. Any parent who has experienced the death of a child dreads the innocent question, 'How many children do you have?' Still, eleven years after the death of my child, I pause before answering. I pause because I know that saying 'I have two but one died' will cause my questioner embarrassment and confusion. Both these emotions are painfully evident in their failure to know how to respond or what to say. On the other hand if I reply, out of consideration for the feelings of my questioner, simply that I have one child it makes me feel a deep sense of betrayal to myself and my first child. It is as though I am denying the existence that he had. Since I strongly refuse to do that I have had to learn to deal with social embarrassment. However, I had thought that such embarrassment was particular to such a personal situation. It became clear to all of us working on the programme that it surrounds the subject in general and is only heightened by personal experiences.

During the course of making the series we were regularly asked, 'What are you working on?' Our answer was usually simply, 'We're doing a series about attitudes to dying, death and bereavement.' There were times when even we ducked answering the question and would admit only to doing a documentary series. These occasions usually came about either because we felt that the person innocently asking the question would be unable to cope with the reply, or that the social situation was such that to speak of such things would be to cause an unwelcome change of mood. Sometimes it was because we didn't want to be involved in yet another conversation about the subject. Mostly, however, we would answer straightforwardly. The responses were rarely simple. There were those, more frequently men than women, who would make some remark like, 'There can't be many laughs in that', and quickly change the subject. Another response would be to make a joke about it, revealing how much humour is used to avoid directly confronting the subject. Sometimes a response to our answer would be deflected with 'Hasn't there been something on television about it before?' To put them at their ease we would make a light comment like, 'It's hardly an original subject.'

It was curious how often people did not seem to hear, or if they did ignored, the 'dying and death' part of our answer and would assume that the whole series was about bereavement. That was the aspect of the series that people most talked about. Very often they would respond by telling us about their own experiences of bereavement. One man had been to three funerals in the past six months, another talked of how his wife's father had died the same day as their second child was born. We heard a long and fascinating description by one of the death of his grandfather in the back of a car, and a woman told of the death of her friend's mother in their flat. In one or two cases the bereavement was recent and still causing the person much pain, and our raising the subject made it possible for them to talk of their feelings.

Usually we could predict on the basis of gender the kind of response we would get. Men, we found, were in general much less comfortable about having the subject raised at all than women. This was borne out by a seminar on the subject arranged by the Mental Health Films Council which I attended. The Council hold regular seminars on different aspects of mental health, and this was the only one they had ever held to which only women turned up. Unintentionally, the traditional roles of men and women were highlighted right from the first session, when we watched a video where a man (expert) was being interviewed by another man about how the bereaved could be helped and counselled. The all-women audience, most of whom were nurses or health visitors working with the terminally ill and their families, showed considerable impatience with the theory and immediately discussed the difficulties they faced in practice.

In general, we found that those men prepared to talk about the subject did so in their professional capacity as counsellors, stonemasons, undertakers etc. Others used their professional knowledge to deal with the subject. An example of the latter was the owner of a second-hand bookshop which Rachael Trezise visited. Browsing through the shop, she had picked out some books which she thought might be useful. The owner, seeing them, inquired about the reason for her interest. After one of her experienced pauses for thought as to whether she should explain the reason, she decided to do so. His response was purely professional, and he immediately 'dealt' with the subject by suggesting and looking for other books that she might buy. In contrast, I could cite a number of examples of 'professional' women whom I approached for their advice, and almost invariably the session would start with a personal discussion.

One of the responses we received on telling people the subject of the programme was 'how interesting'. It was always a great relief to hear this, since it enabled at least some kind of conversation about the series to take place. Among those who responded in this way, the questions were usually about how we were making the series and about the hospice movement, bereavement counselling and the costs of undertakers. It was as though those who could talk about death could only do so when such a discussion was distanced from personal feeling. To talk of professional services is safe. What clearly is not safe, and what was almost totally absent from the responses, the questions and the conversations we had, was any discussion by individuals about their feelings and attitudes towards their own death. This reticence about talking personally reflected another inhibition that has developed. Besides fearing that to talk about death is to court it, and that to talk about death is embarrassing, a fear has developed that to talk about death, and in particular one's own, is to attract the social censure of being regarded as morbid.

Social censure

BBC Radio 4 decided on Monday, 10 November 1986 to *Start The Week* with a discussion about death. The aim was, in the words of the programme's presenter Richard Baker, to try to put 'death in his place'. Most of the discussion avoided this aim, talking instead about obituaries, epitaphs, funerals, coffins and gravestones. Only the Roman Catholic priest talked of his attitude towards his own death, his firm belief in an afterlife being supported by one other person. In the middle of the programme someone commented that it was only the priest, out of the nine people taking part in the studio discussion, who seemed at ease with the subject. Quickly, the one doctor participating firmly interjected that he thought the discussion 'morbid' and claimed that people 'don't really like discussing death'.

According to the *Oxford Dictionary* this word first came into use in the seventeenth century, simply to describe disease. By the nineteenth century it had acquired another meaning relating to the mind, not just the body. The dictionary defines the second meaning as 'of mind, ideas, etc.: Unwholesome, sickly. Hence of persons: Given to morbid feelings or fancies. 1834'. In the nineteenth century, when the second meaning of morbid came into use, this clearly referred only to people who had an 'unhealthy' propensity to dwell on disease and death. From the evidence of literature and other records, there appears to have been a clear distinction between a healthy acceptance of death and an unhealthy dwelling upon it. Someone who spoke of their own death would not have been regarded as morbid but merely as sensible and realistic. That distinction has now gone, as has the common understanding of the two usages of the word. The second, nineteenth-century definition of morbid is now the one that is commonly used and understood. It is used about people who talk about death, and in particular those who talk of their own death. To talk of this at all is no longer seen as the sign of a healthy, sensible person but as a sign of an 'unhealthy' mind. Social censure has become yet another way of silencing us.

Anyone making films, talking or writing about the subject of death runs the risk of being labelled morbid. Ian Crichton opened his book *The Art of Dying*, published in 1976, with the observation: '"That's morbid" is the usual response when people hear you are writing a book about death and dying. But this expression of disgust and fear, with its accompanying grimace, may be a good reason for the book's existence.' We, a decade later, experienced the same reaction and justified our interest in the subject for the same reason. Like Ian Crichton we risked being labelled morbid, the risk being at its greatest when we asked people about their attitudes to their own death. Having decided that the first programme in the series should be about attitudes to dying and death, and that it should be based on the experiences of ordinary people who for reasons of disease or age had had to confront their mortality, there was no way of avoiding the issue. However, realising the sensitivity of most people, not just those who face imminent death, about talking about the subject, we were careful and tentative in our research.

In most cases people were approached through an intermediary who knew them well. This, we felt, would enable the person being approached to say no without feeling that they had been pressured. For instance, in the case of the Marie Curie Home, where we subsequently filmed, we asked the Matron, who after discussion with the nurses approached one or two people they felt would be open to being questioned. Where there was no obvious intermediary a letter was a way of broaching the subject, and again it enabled the recipient easily to say no. Because of the time pressures of making a film there were one or two people whom I ended up approaching 'cold'. Phoning some stranger up, explaining to them the content of the film and then asking them if they would be prepared to be filmed talking about their attitudes and feelings was hard. I had an uneasy feeling before and after making such phone calls that, even if the person phoned said no, my phone call had perhaps disturbed their day, raising a subject that most of us would prefer not to think about.

When interviewing people, I usually approached the

subject tangentially, circling initially around the central question. With older people it seemed easier to start with general social changes and whether they felt or had observed changes in their lifetime. Quite often I realised at different points in the conversation that the conversation could be pursued no further. A few were disarmingly open, the interviewee leading me rather than the other way round. Mostly, people were uneasy about talking of their attitudes to death. The unease seemed to arise from embarrassment, mine in raising the subject and theirs in responding, and from a general attitude that such matters are of private concern to the individual. Privacy should of course be respected, but if our desire for privacy is based on the fear of being labelled 'morbid' if we talk, then we have to examine the reasons for this desire.

Our British embarrassment, our view that death is a private matter and our silence are peculiar to our culture and century. Although other societies have used a variety of words, secular and sacred, to talk of death they have all talked. We have not in the twentieth century been able to avoid the subject completely, but what we have done is to develop a new and evasive language.

The words we use

Many of the words that have been recorded over the years are informed by religious belief. Christianity has been the dominant belief in the West, and for Christian believers death is inextricably tied up with beliefs in judgement, the soul, salvation, heaven, hell and eternal life. As it is central to Christian belief, death has always been part of the dialogue.

In secular circles it is harder to find out what language was used, though euphemisms for dying and death have been used for a long time. In the sixteenth century Sir Philip Sidney in a poem about grief entitled 'A Farewell' complained about the use of the word 'depart' to describe death. As a 'weakly' word he regarded 'depart' as inappropriate to describe death's 'ugly dart'. Shakespeare used a variety of phrases and words for death; 'shuffled off his mortal coil', 'come to dust', 'exits' are but a few. A contemporary, the poet John Donne, opened a poem with the line 'As virtuous men pass mildly away', clearly seeing the phrase 'pass mildly away' as an evocative way of describing the gentle death of virtuous men. Thomas Hardy wrote in 'Friends Beyond':

> William Dewey, Tranter Reuben, Farmer Ledlow late at plough, Robert's kin, and John's and Ned's
> And the Squire, and Lady Susan, lie in Mellstock churchyard now!
> 'Gone' I call them, gone for good, that group of local hearts and heads . . .

Mrs Micawber tells David in Dickens's *David Copperfield* that her mama 'had departed this life' and that her papa had 'expired'.

The use of such words to describe death and dying was, however, clearly for descriptive and poetic purposes rather than evasion. John Donne was not afraid to start a poem with the arresting line, 'Death be not proud'; Shakespeare frequently used the words 'die', 'dying', 'death'; Shelley simply stated, 'I weep for Adonais – he is dead.' Thomas Hardy, a Victorian, could report in his poem 'Her Death And After' that, 'Next night she died.' Even Dickens, who used the full range of Victorian euphemisms when appropriate, also used direct language. Mrs Micawber's way of telling David that both her parents had died was in response to his simple question, 'Are they dead, ma'am?' Whilst it is hard to know how people actually spoke, the literary evidence leads one to assume that people were not afraid to say someone had died or that they were dying. What emerges from letters, biographies and fiction is that they had the choice of using the simple, straightforward words or other more descriptive words.

Today, we have limited that choice, particularly in our personal usage. So, although newspaper headlines regularly include the words 'dead' and 'died', and television newscasters also bring into our homes almost daily these words, people avoid such language in talking of their personal experiences. It is publicly possible to use blunt language but privately it is avoided and feared. The words 'death', 'dying' and 'died' slipped during this century from common private usage to be replaced by such words as departed, be taken, passed away, passed on, gone away and last sleep. Kick the bucket, peg out, cop it, snuff it, bite the dust, number's up, pop your clogs, turn up your toes and the Cockney slang 'brown bread' for dead are just some of the more common colloquial expressions. These expressions are more frequently used when talking about death at an emotional remove, in other words a husband is unlikely to speak of his wife biting the dust, though might use the phrase about someone else's wife in their absence. Some of the colloquial expressions are particularly used in military situations, where soldiers are more likely to say that their friend copped it or that his number was up than that he died. The civilian euphemisms for death are for the most part singularly inappropriate to describe death in action. Although, like our predecessors, we have a rich range of words at our command, we have allowed the 'real' words to slip from usage so that for many it has become unacceptable to use them at all.

It is interesting to look at when such words and phrases came into the ascendancy. Gravestones provide an indication of language change; the wording on them reflects quite baldly changing social attitudes. Prior to the mid-nineteenth century people either 'died' or 'departed this life'. Usually this statement was related to the precise whereabouts of the body or mortal remains of the person. The following wording from a gravestone in Arlington, Devon, 'Here lieth interred the body of Robert Chichester, Deceased on 16th May 1622', was typical of the period, as was the stone to Sir John Dodderidge in Exeter Cathedral, who in 1628 'Departed this life and according to his desire his body was interred here.' Death and bodily decay were encompassed very often within one sentence, such as, 'Underneath are laid the mortal remains of . . . who died.' Long before cremation became an accepted method of disposal of the dead reference to the body had disappeared. By the mid-nineteenth century death had become linguistically sanitised, and references to bodies interred and mortal remains were omitted from gravestones. It was as though people did not want to be confronted with the facts of bodily decay and decomposition. After 1850 it is very rare to find a gravestone or plaque like the one from 1813 in Exeter Cathedral which simply said, 'Near this tablet is deposited all that was mortal of Anna Eliza Stanhope.'

With the disappearance of words relating to the body came the appearance of other words for 'died'. Apart from the phrase 'departed this life', it is very rare, though not unknown, to find any other words on gravestones until the latter part of the nineteenth century. During that period phrases such as 'entered into rest', 'at rest' and 'fell asleep' began to creep into usage. Nonconformists appear to have taken more quickly to the new language, such phrases as 'fell asleep in Jesus' being used in their cemeteries as early as the 1870s and 1880s. Although the language of death was changing during the late nineteenth century, the big linguistic divide was unquestionably the First World War. Before it, euphemisms for the word 'died' were the exception and after it they became the rule. The twenties saw a growth in the usage of many other phrases, the commonest being 'passed away', a phrase that was very rare before. In my local London cemetery I could find only one pre-First World War 'passed away' and have found few other examples of its usage prior to 1920. The fact that the BBC Radio announced in 1936 that King George V had 'passed peacefully away' shows just how far the phrase had become accepted, and indeed on that occasion it replaced the word 'died'. From the thirties onwards it is very common to find gravestones saying 'passed away', 'passed on', 'departed this life', 'fell asleep', 'called home' and 'at rest'. The latter phrase was described by P. D. James in *An Unsuitable Job for a Woman* as 'the commonest epitaph of a generation to whom rest must have seemed the ultimate luxury, the supreme benediction'.

Sometimes people 'died' in different ways on one gravestone. It is not uncommon, for example, to find that, whilst one member of a family 'passed away', another 'fell asleep' or, as one gravestone recorded, the father in 1905 'entered into rest'. In 1937 his wife 'passed away' and in 1964 the daughter 'died'. Apart from those stating that a person was killed in action, most of the phrases reflect a desire to communicate that the death was peaceful. Sometimes such a desire clearly conflicted with the reality of the death, as in the case of the man who, according to his gravestone, 'entered into rest suddenly'. Surprisingly, given that our society is based on clearly defined gender roles, there is no obvious difference in the choice of euphemism according to sex. One gravestone did, however, conjure up an image of gender stereotypes after death, claiming that in 1921 the wife 'entered the homeland' whilst her husband, dying three years later, 'entered into life'.

As in all other aspects of life there are clearly fashions in the wording on gravestones, and these fashions are often local, probably influenced by stonemasons and their catalogues of inscriptions. However, despite local variations, there has been an overall change in the language used, and that change reflects our attitudes to death and what we want to, or are able to, say publicly about it. Gravestones are public statements. Although the Victorians loved euphemisms they did not use them extensively on gravestones, whereas we, who often pride ourselves that we have liberated ourselves from so many of the inhibitions of the Victorian era, recoil from using the word 'died' on a gravestone. It is perhaps not surprising that part of the legacy of a war that had caused so much death, followed by the other wars and holocausts of this century, was the desire of people to change the language of death. The diminishing number of Christian believers, and the consequent uncertainty for many about an afterlife, have also influenced the words used. Language reflects thought, and clearly our Western way of thinking about death has changed.

Changing the language or, rather, losing certain words from the language does not affect only writers and the range of words available for poetic expression – it profoundly affects us all. There are times when clear and precise language is of deep importance. Euphemisms and evasions can cause confusion at a time when clarity is needed. The use of them can be particularly harmful for children, who do not have a grasp of the subtleties of language. They cannot distinguish the difference between 'gone away' on a holiday, to work or shopping or 'gone away' for ever as in death. Children who are told that a dead person has gone away, even if they have been told that he or she has gone very far away for a long time, will expect that some day he or she will come back. To complicate it further for a child, when the dead 'gone away' person does not come back they begin to fear that any other person who has gone away may not come back. They fear that the person who has gone away shopping, or gone to work, will not come back; they can also worry that their behaviour has caused the person to go away, and feel deep guilt. Children, not surprisingly, become confused by the way adults lose people. A child assumes that a lost person can be found, and unless it is clearly explained to them they do not understand that 'loss' can also mean death. Far from being protective, the use of such euphemisms for death can further destroy the certainties and securities of a child's world.

Phrases such as 'last sleep' and 'sleep forever' can also cause confusion and fear in a child. Sleep for a child is something you go to and wake up from. It is something you are urged and encouraged to do nightly by adults; it may be something you resist, but even for the child afraid of the dark sleep in itself is not frightening. It can, however, become deeply feared. If sleep is something you might not wake up from then the child thinks it is better not to sleep. Going to sleep turns into a waking nightmare. A child cannot and should not have to differentiate between sleep and 'the last sleep'. Other phrases can cause equal misunderstanding. 'Gone to Heaven' or 'to God' can be as confusing as 'gone away'. Alexandre Dumas in his *Memoirs* described his confusion as a small boy after being told in 1806 that his father was dead and that God, who 'lives in the sky', had 'taken him'. To try to get even with God Dumas went and got a gun which had been promised to him when he grew up. On his way upstairs with the gun he met his mother who asked him where he was going. The small boy replied:

> 'I'm going to the sky!'
> 'What? You're going to the sky?'
> 'Yes, don't stop me.'
> 'And what are you going to do in the sky my poor child?'
> 'I'm going to kill God, who killed Father.'
> My mother clutched me in her arms, squeezing enough to suffocate me.
> 'Oh, don't say such things my child,' she cried. 'We're quite unhappy enough already.'

Heaven to a twentieth-century child could be some kind of theme park not unlike Disneyland. Indeed, my nine-year-old daughter wrote in her diary the single word 'paradise' to describe her visit to Disneyland.

It is hard enough for anyone, adult or child, to grasp the reality of the meaning of death when confronted with the death of someone close to them. Clear language can help to start the process of grasping that reality. But it is hard to suddenly begin using that language when it is needed, if such words have never been part of the vocabulary. To be able to use them when we need them we need to have used them before. If we cannot talk to children about the dead bird in the garden or the death of Bambi's mother, we will not be prepared to talk to them about the death of someone important in their lives. If as children we have been unable to talk, then as adults it is hard for us to acquire the ability to do so.

To Talk of Death

Many adults regard conversation about death as not suitable for children, and others fear that talking about it may be seen as raising a potentially contentious issue. This latter fear I had not been prepared for when I approached the head of a junior school to ask if a class of children could write some poems about death. From the artwork displayed in the school I knew that one class had done a project about the cemetery which lay on the other side of the school wall. The subject could not be a total taboo. The head, having heard the reason for my interest, agreed to ask one class of nine-year-olds to write some poems. He then quickly and adamantly asserted that asking a class quite straightforwardly to write a poem about death without any discussion on the subject was all that he was prepared to do. I was a little thrown by the firmness with which he told me this, as I had not asked for any discussion. After I reassured him that all I was interested in were some poems, he then explained that he feared that if there was any class discussion about the subject it might not only cause children to be disturbed, but that parents might also be disturbed. Disturbed parents would complain, and then he would have a lot of explaining to do.

Of course the subject, if handled insensitively by a teacher who did not know of any experiences of death or dying the children might have had, could cause upset. But the head's fear of possible parental complaints should the subject be discussed revealed a great deal about our social attitudes to talking about death. Many people would argue that it is a discussion that should not take place at all. But the children did write poems about death, and revealed that they were not frightened to confront the subject and call death by its name.

The legacy of not talking about death or of talking about it only in euphemistic language extends far beyond the confusions created in a child's mind. It affects the treatment of the dying and is the cause of the linguistic evasions that so often surround a dying person. The Big Question surrounding the treatment of a dying person is 'should the doctor tell?' and it is a question returned to later in this book. If, however, we were to bring the language of death back into our lives and thus remove many of the fears surrounding the use of that language, much of the tension surrounding the Big Question would be diffused. Linguistic evasions affect the bereaved, who are often left isolated because people cannot talk or, often more importantly, listen to them about their bereavement. These evasions affect our attitude to life, for if we cannot acknowledge that life ends with death what then is the meaning of life? To try and understand why we have lost the ability to talk of death we have to explore our fear of it.

CHAPTER TWO

Death Is?

Death 1. The act or fact of dying; the final cessation of the vital functions of an animal or plant. Often personified.
(*Shorter Oxford English Dictionary*)

It may seem stupid to pose the question 'what is death?'. After all, it is assumed that everyone except babies knows what death is. It is simply the point at which one stops living or, as the dictionary defines it, 'the final cessation of the vital functions'. Yet if we look at religion, history, medicine, literature, art and language death is, and has been, seen and portrayed in a variety of ways. Death is not simply not living – we have given it a range of meanings which have a deep influence on our attitude, our fear and/or acceptance and indeed our definition of it. But, whatever the other meanings we give death, explored later, death is and always has been the final cessation of the vital functions.

Most people learn at some point during their childhood that death is the irrecoverable end to life. How we learn that fact as children is influenced very much by life experience and how we are taught about death. In Bangladesh, a country in which one child in four does not reach the age of five, children that do are much more likely to understand at a younger age the biological reality of death than their Western counterparts. Nowadays, in the West, a child's first experience of death (other than what they see on TV, films or read in books) is more likely to be the death of a pet, bird or animal than of a person. The poems on death written for me by a class of nine-year-olds confirmed this likelihood. Not one poem was about the death of a person whom the child had known. Only two dealt with human death. Of those, one poignantly imagined 'dying all alone' with 'no friends, no family, nobody to hold your hand', and the other started with the line, 'Death feels like you're asleep' and ended philosophically with, 'But everyone has to die'. All the other poems were about the death of animals or birds, many of which had been killed by cars. The following extract from a poem shows how the child had grasped the reality of death.

> My pet, gone for ever
> My pet will never come back,
> My pet dead, I'm so sad,
> My pet buried.
> MY PET DEAD.

One poem dealt with the physicality of death and decomposition and the child's reaction to that. The young poet wrote of being 'shocked' to see a bird 'rotting' with blood 'dropping down'. 'I know,' the poem ended, 'he will be just bones when I come home. And it was true.'

It is a relatively recent fact that children have so little experience of human death. Barely a century ago most children would have known at quite a young age someone, and very likely a close relative, who had died. Not only would they have known someone who had died but they might well have witnessed that death, for children were not excluded from the room of a dying person; and if they had not witnessed the death they would probably have seen the dead body laid out. Rousseau, writing in *Emile* about education in the eighteenth century, reminded teachers that, 'Of all the children who are born, scarcely one half reach adolescence, and it is very likely your pupil will not live to be a man.'

In 1840, when the first official statistics on life expectancy in Britain were published, it was revealed that a boy could expect to live for 40 years and a girl for 42. It is now 77.6 years for girls and 71.6 for boys. The single most important change in average life expectancy has been the decrease in

Death Is?

infant mortality. People now expect a baby to live, whereas a hundred years ago they regarded it as particularly good fortune if a child survived beyond infancy. How a child now learns about death is influenced both by their own experience of it and also by the way they are taught. Parents who stop to explain about the dead bird lying in the road can help their child to understand the biological reality of death. Conversely, if they try to hurry past, telling their child not to look, then the child is likely to pick up the message that death is something secretive and embarrassing.

Understanding the meaning of death is not easy for adults, let alone for children, but adults can help children to comprehend its meaning. The very young child struggling to understand and assert her/his individual identity and existence finds it hard, not surprisingly, to comprehend the end of that existence or of any other person's existence. Research has shown that most children under the age of five are confused about death and that, for the very young, death and life are not seen as mutually exclusive. Small children can talk about someone being 'very badly killed' and not find anything odd about what they have said. My own daughter, when quite small, asked quite directly and seriously after looking at the numbers (dates) on gravestones, 'Are those the dead people's phone numbers?' Because we had always talked to her about her brother who had died before she was born, we assumed that she had understood the finality of death. From her question it was clear that she was confused. Children can easily interpret adult statements wrongly in their attempts to understand death. Sylvia Anthony in *The Discovery of Death in Childhood and After* wrote of one small boy, aged four years and ten months, who thought that 'we all turn into statues when we die, owing to the fact that he first met Queen Victoria as a statue in Kensington Gardens and then was told that she had been dead some time.' Both cases show how adults forget how difficult it is for a child to understand death and its biological reality.

Francis Bacon wrote, 'Men fear Death, as children fear to

go in the dark: and as that natural fear in children is increased with tales so is the other.' He might have added that for children tales of death increase their fear as much if not more than they do for adults. A balance can be achieved between evasion, confusing and frightening in itself, and causing children sleepless nights of terror from exposure to macabre tales. Between the ages of five and nine most children sort out the confusion. With differing degrees of help or hindrance from adults they learn the facts of death and that it is the 'final cessation of the vital functions'. Defining and deciding exactly when that has happened is more problematical.

Medical definitions

The responsibility of deciding when someone is dead is that of the living. It is a responsibility we have to give to others and yet fear they may fail in it, because medical definitions of death are under question and because we fear the possible ignorance or irresponsibility of others. Fear of the latter, that we may be pronounced dead erroneously and perhaps buried alive, has haunted people for centuries. Advances in medicine have not allayed that fear and have complicated medical definitions of death.

The fear of being erroneously pronounced dead is not without some rational base. Everyone, including doctors, makes mistakes. Philippe Ariès in *The Hour of our Death* records a number of cases of mistaken diagnosis. They include that of a man who was assumed dead and thrown shrouded into a grave, where 'he regained consciousness about eleven o'clock at night, tore off his shroud, knocked at the porter's hut, got him to unlock the gate and went home', and another case of a woman who 'struggled out of her shroud' after a thief had tried to cut her finger off to steal her ring. Wars produce similar stories of people who had a lucky escape through being presumed dead by their enemy. Sometimes it was their own side who left them for dead. In 1967 a case hit the newspaper headlines of an American soldier in Vietnam who was pronounced dead and sent to the mortuary, where the embalmer noticed that he was still alive.

Such stories of misdiagnosed death in peacetime, whilst not so common today, are not unknown. In 1965 Taylor's *Principles and Practices of Medical Jurisprudence* recorded several cases of error made by doctors in certifying a person dead. In 1970 Dr Roger Chapman, Sheffield's Deputy Medical Officer for Health, argued that there would be fewer mistakes and that it would help to allay the fear of mistakes if all mortuaries were equipped with cardiac oscilloscopes so that even minute electrical impulses from the heart could be detected. An earlier, somewhat less sophisticated, version of a life alarm system was installed in a mortuary in Frankfurt-am-Main, where strings were attached to the corpses's fingers so that a bell would ring if there was any movement.

Gothic novels and horror films explore and play on our fear of being buried alive. Black comedy also recognises it by frequently using such situations as a 'dead' person knocking on his coffin or sitting up on the mortuary slab. In an episode of the television series 'Allo, 'Allo a German army officer searching for members of the Resistance asked if there was a dead body in a coffin. Although the coffin actually contained earth from tunnelling, the man covering up for the Resistance replied, 'I hope so. We put a screwdriver in there in case we made a mistake.' The remark was a typical example of how humour recognises our fear but at the same time tries to reassure us. The living, however, need proper reassurance that errors will not be made and that they will not have to use a screwdriver. Reassurance has been and is sought through a variety of ways. Before it became the practice for doctors to pronounce someone dead people often instructed, usually in their wills, the living to perform certain 'tests' on their body before they could be buried. These tests were usually that their body should be watched over for a period of time, not less than twenty-four hours but sometimes as long as three days, before it could be moved and buried. Sometimes the tests required were physical, the most common being a demand that the soles of the feet be scratched or cut to ascertain that death really had occurred. Although people no longer feel a need to make such stipulations in their wills, some are still fearful of error. A counsellor working with the terminally ill told me of how she had very recently to reassure a dying teenage girl that she would not be buried alive.

Today we rely on the law and in what we have to hope is the infallibility of doctors. In the UK the law requires that a qualified medical practitioner certifies a death. No dead body can be legally disposed of without a death certificate, and the death certificate can only be issued by a coroner or a qualified medical practitioner. Curiously, the law does not in all cases require that the qualified medical practitioner examine the dead body. If a doctor has attended someone during their last illness they can sign the death certificate without examining the body, but they must make that known on the certificate. Relying on the diagnosis of an unqualified person or on the evidence of a casual glance can, however, be very risky. A recent example of an error made in such a case was that of a doctor who acted primarily on the testimony of a young boy who had been sent to the surgery to get a death certificate because his grandpa was dead. The doctor went to the house, saw the man apparently dead in bed, wrote out a death certificate and only on returning to his surgery did he remember that he had not seen the patient in the previous two weeks and dutifully informed the coroner. Investigating the death, the coroner went to the house and found the 'deceased' sitting up in bed and curious as to why a coroner should be visiting him. In the absence of a law insisting that a body be examined before it is certified dead, anyone wanting to reassure a dying person or themselves should demand such an examination.

For qualified medical practitioners diagnosis of death is not always as clear cut or simple as the definition of death given by the *Oxford Dictionary* would lead one to assume.

Death Is?

Modern medical developments have helped in some ways to diagnose death, but in some cases they have made it much harder and more complicated. Doctors themselves are no longer agreed on a definition of death. Modern techniques are an improvement on the times when death was diagnosed by the absence of 'mist' on a mirror and/or a heartbeat. Shakespeare's King Lear asked for a looking glass to try, by seeing whether Cordelia's breath would 'mist or stain the stone', to ascertain whether she was dead. If the results of the mirror test were uncertain then the onset of putrefaction was a more certain sign of death. Nowadays, if there is no evidence of breathing or heartbeat (the classical definitions of death) and there is doubt about diagnosis, more sophisticated methods than the mirror test can be used. Doubt is likely to arise in cases where someone is in a deep coma, or after certain forms of poisoning when the breathing may be so shallow as to be undetectable and the pulse so weak that it cannot be felt at the wrist or even heard through a stethoscope. In such cases the doctor has to look for other signs of death such as the relaxing and sagging of the facial muscles or the changes which occur in the eyes following death. If there is still doubt, the heartbeat can be tested by the use of an electrocardiogram (ECG) and the brain tested for signs of life by an electroencephalogram (EEG). The problem is that the sophisticated methods we have developed for sustaining life and diagnosing death have confused the definition of death.

Medically, there are four kinds of death which are usually but not always interrelated. Firstly, there is what is commonly understood as death which is when a person 'ceases to be'; this is known as *somatic* death. In medical terms, the cessation of breath and heartbeat is diagnosed as *clinical* (often called 'heart') death. Following clinical death is *cellular* (sometimes called 'molecular') death, which is when the cells in the body die. Cells can and do die before clinical death. Indeed quite a number of cells in our bodies can have died, having been killed off by disease, before we are clinically dead. It takes varying amounts of time for the cells to die after the cessation of the heart beating and of breathing. Brain cells die within four minutes of the heart stopping beating, for they cannot survive any longer without the vital materials feeding them through the bloodstream. Muscles, on the other hand, die much more slowly, and will respond to electrical stimuli for up to two hours after clinical death. The stiffening of the body, *rigor mortis*, following death is in fact the result of the action of cells (cellular metabolism).

Apart from 'cellular death' being a clear sign of death, little interest was taken in it as a definition until the advent of organ transplantation. The organs of the body which experience cellular death the fastest are those specialised organs – heart, kidney, liver – which are most demanded for transplants. It is obviously of great importance that such organs are removed from the body immediately after clinical death, and thus defining the moment of death is crucial if an organ is to be removed for transplanting. In the case of a transplant, death has to be pronounced by two fully registered medical practitioners, one of whom must have been qualified for five years and both of whom must be totally independent of the doctors undertaking the transplant. An organ cannot be removed from a dead body unless the person has, prior to death, consented to its removal; in the absence of that written consent permission must be given by the nearest relative after the death. If there are no traceable relatives, and there is no involvement of a coroner, the hospital management committee has legal charge of the body and may permit an autopsy for removal of organs.

Carrying a donor card, if you wish any or all of your organs to be removed, can both ensure that your wishes are carried out and save any relatives a potentially agonising and difficult decision at a time of shock and stress. If you are sure you do not wish any organs to be removed after your death, making that clear to your nearest relative or doctor can also ensure that your wishes are followed. Although the requirements for pronouncing someone dead

Death Is?

are more stringent in transplant cases, the problem of diagnosis is not necessarily any easier.

The United Nations define death as the permanent disappearance of every sign of life. The Harvard Medical School makes that general statement more precisely by listing the tests required to be performed before reaching a conclusion that every sign of life has permanently disappeared. These tests include 'making sure that there is no sign of life', that the body does not respond to various stimuli repeated after an interval of time, that if the patient is on a respirator which is switched off there is no evidence of the patient spontaneously trying to breathe, and that the electroencephalogram registers no brain life. If doubt persists, they recommend repeating all these tests after twenty-four hours. One might assume that all this should prove definitively one way or another whether someone is dead, but it is known that in cases of barbiturate poisoning, when the central nervous system becomes depressed, or in certain cases of hypothermia even these tests may be unreliable. Emphasis also has to be put on the *permanent* disappearance of every sign of life; someone may 'die' briefly following a cardiac arrest before being resuscitated. Although in the vast majority of cases diagnosing death is simple, there are times when it can be extremely difficult. That difficulty has been increased by a new medical category of death: *brain* death.

This fourth medical definition of death is a product of modern medicine. Before people could be kept alive by artificial respirators brain death always followed heart death. Now brain death can precede it. It is in these cases that the dilemma of diagnosing someone as dead becomes an ethical problem of concern to all of society and not just a problem of diagnosis for the medical profession. A person can be kept alive artificially by the use of a respirator and other life-support systems even though they are brain dead. Brain death is checked by the use of an electroencephalogram, and if there is no sign of brain activity then the person is pronounced brain dead. The question then is whether their cellular life should continue to be maintained artificially when they have ceased to exist in any recognisable sense as an individual person. Briefly, it is a question of whether the life-support machine should be turned off and if so who takes that decision. Is it a decision that should be taken by qualified medical practitioners, by the relatives or by society through legal guidelines covering such situations? At the moment there is no unanimity as to how that decision should be made.

In general, there is agreement that if the brain has ceased to function, and that spontaneous circulation and breathing have ceased, then death has occurred and these three factors meet the United Nations definition of death. Given agreement of the definition and agreement in a particular case that the diagnosis is correct, there still remains the decision as to whether life-support systems should be switched off. At present that decision is taken by doctors, usually in consultation with relatives. Relatives should obviously be involved in the decision, but they may have a financial interest in the timing of that decision. Hospitals, particularly those starved of resources, may also have a financial interest in the decision. Doctors argue both for and against the decision resting with them, and the law has avoided taking on the responsibility of providing legal guidelines.

Although such cases usually hit the headlines, they are in fact few and far between. In the majority of cases diagnosing death is simple, involving neither ethical dilemmas nor sophisticated medical technology. People calling in a doctor to diagnose the death of a friend or relative would be wise to make sure that the doctor does indeed examine the body, and that if there is any doubt further tests, besides clinical examination (looking, listening and feeling), should be carried out.

Artists' impressions

Death is a monster
If I could see it
It would be black as night.

Death Is?

> Death is safe,
> It can't be killed.
>   (Nine-year-old child, 1986)

Children frequently think of death having a physical form, be it a monster, a skeleton or a white shape. John Dunton, writing in 1705, recalled that as a child he saw death as a 'walking skeleton, with a dart in his right and an hourglass in his left hand'. Twentieth-century children still often see death as a shape or form, though often a less defined one than that of their predecessors. It is hardly surprising that children should, in their imaginations, give death a form, since artists in the West have for centuries done so. The skeleton, usually portrayed with long bony fingers and a full set of teeth that appear to be grinning, is the main image that has been used; a good example of its symbolic use through the centuries is the image on the death card in a pack of tarot cards.

One of the most specific representations of death is a statue sculptured in the sixteenth century, now in the Musée de l'Oeuvre Notre Dame, Strasbourg. This is of a human figure standing up wearing ragged clothes. The head is a skull and a few fleshless rib bones are showing where the rags do not cover the chest. In his, for it is undeniably male, right hand death holds an hourglass. As a statue this figure of death is unusual. Artists have usually portrayed the figure of death in paintings or drawings, rather than making it quite as tangible as is inevitable in sculpture. The skeletal figure of death in art is frequently shown hovering in anticipation, but sometimes it is depicted in the more active role of surprising, grabbing or dragging off its victims. The most famous sequence of drawings depicting the work of death is the forty-one woodcuts done by Hans Holbein the Younger in the sixteenth century, called 'The Dance of Death'. Holbein showed death as a skeleton dragging off women and children, and visiting all – including the Pope, the Emperor, the peasant and the beggar. In his woodcut 'Death and the Plowman' death is a strange, skinny, featureless, ragged figure running by the plowman with a stick.

Many other artists have used the symbolic skeleton for death, and its use as such has continued to the present day. Death is thus represented, whether by Dürer (fifteenth century), Holbein (sixteenth century), Munch (nineteenth century) or Rouault (twentieth century), as a figure in itself, quite separate from the devil or angels who might be standing in the wings ready to receive the dead person. The clearest representation of that difference can be seen in a mass-produced early nineteenth-century lithograph entitled 'The Dying Man Prepared to Meet God'. The lithograph is the classic bedroom scene of a dying person, with the family (including children) around the bed, either weeping or looking distressed. A priest is at the bedside with his right hand pointing upwards to the source of the shaft of white light coming down towards the dying man, and pointing downwards with his left hand to the devil who is poking his horned head out of some flames on the floor. The dying man is thus poised between heaven and hell, quite a common theme in paintings. There is, however, in this lithograph another figure in the room lurking behind the pillows of the dying man. It is the figure of death, once again portrayed as a skeleton holding an hourglass in one hand and a sword in the other.

Although death is usually portrayed as a skeleton, it has been portrayed as a variety of figures, always with some semblance of human form. Even the black shrouded figures of death are clearly, underneath their shrouds, human forms. The image of death as a person is not confined to children and artists. Two American undergraduates quoted in *The Psychology of Death* by Robert Kastenbaum and Ruth Aisenberg, 1972, visualised death very clearly. For one he was 'fairly tall, having clear-cut features'. His Mr Death had a straight nose, sparkling eyes, a light complexion and wore a dark suit. The other undergraduate saw death as 'a quiet person and kind of scary', picturing 'him' 'being millions of years old but only looking about forty'. Like the artists who gave death a distinctive gender, these undergraduates saw it as male. It is rare for death to be portrayed as female. The nineteenth-century poet W. E. Henley, who described death as both male and female – 'She's the tenant of the room, He's the ruffian on the stair' – is quite unusual. Often death is, as in the lithograph of 'The Dying Man Prepared to Meet God', a neutral figure. Death just *is*, without social or religious meaning.

Sometimes the figure of death takes on other connotations. Death can have religious significance through being depicted as having the characteristics of an angel or the devil. It can also, for example in the portrayal of death as the grim reaper scything down the poor, be used as social comment. In the twentieth century the image of death as a skeleton has been used particularly by artists wishing to convey the reality of war. For instance, in a prophetic drawing by Frans Masereel, 1940, a long winding line of people are being led by the classic figure of death – a skeleton.

In all these depictions of death what is perhaps most interesting has been the desire by artists to give it a form. They try to make tangible the intangible. Their effect on the imagination is not neutral – rarely is death portrayed as a gentle, friendly figure. One such portrayal is a woodcut by Alfred Rethel, 1850, in which death appears as a skeleton clothed in a hooded monk-like robe. The woodcut is called 'Death as a Friend', and in it death is gently ringing a bell for an old man sitting peacefully by an open window in an armchair. The images of death as someone unwelcome or frightening are far more common. These depictions, particularly those of long-fingered, grinning skeletons dragging people off, cannot but have helped to increase the fear of death, but even the more inactive figures hovering around provide an uncomfortable image. Of all the attempts to define death as an active figure those made by artists probably most feed the imagination. They play on the remnants of the images of death we constructed as children.

Artists are not the only ones to have given death a form

and an active part to play. Dramatists have cast parts for Death, and Holbein's sequence of woodcuts was in fact based on groups of touring players who dressed up as skeletons and enacted 'The Dance of Death'. It was, surprising as it seems to us today, a form of popular entertainment. In *Everyman* the unknown author, writing about the year 1500, also gave a part to Death. The brothers Grimm included in their collection of *Fairy Tales* one called 'Death's Messengers' in which Death is all but slain by a giant. He is saved by a compassionate young man and thus the world is saved from becoming 'so full of people that they won't have room to stand beside each other'. Even the twentieth-century author Russell Hoban constructed an argument between his character Kleinzeit and Death. The argument starts with Death hammering on the door and Kleinzeit refusing to let it in. Kleinzeit wins the first round but Death retorts, 'I'll get you later, see if I don't'. On going out of his door Kleinzeit meets Death, 'black and hairy and ugly, no bigger than a medium-sized chimpanzee with dirty fingernails', and the dialogue between the two continues. Whilst Hoban's vision of Death as like a chimpanzee with 'steady work' and 'job security' is unusual, the dialogue he has with it is one which is immediately familiar. The idea of Death as a character with whom we can have a dialogue is an old one. It may be that humanising death in art or drama is a way of working out our relationship with our own mortality. That relationship is one about which there is wide disagreement.

Meanings of death

Almost all the people we interviewed for the first programme in our series *Merely Mortal* described death as a 'fact of life' and asserted that 'we are all born to die'. It was from the latter phrase that the title of the programme 'Born to Die' was taken. Whilst at one level there is general agreement and acceptance about death being a fact of life, for each individual that fact had greatly differing meanings. For one interviewee it 'is a fact and it has to be faced, but you see to me death is only an intermission and then there's everlasting life'. Another, with an open mind at the age of eighty-eight, commented that if death means 'oblivion, well, I shan't know anything about that, shall I? And if it's something intensely more interesting I go forward with hope.' Yet another interviewee said, 'I don't believe in an afterlife. I think that's one belief system that people use in order not to think about death, that they'll die and then they'll go to heaven or whatever. No, I can't believe in that. I think that death in some ways is final but in another sense it's not, because people that you leave behind have always got something of you.'

These three differing views of death are reflective of the range of contemporary beliefs. That there is such a wide range shows how people now, in the absence of one dominant religious belief, find their own meanings. People seem to draw on many traditions and religions to construct their own personal beliefs.

Freud claimed that 'death is an abstract concept with a negative content', but others have made death a concrete concept with a whole range of content. St Paul's concept of death as 'the wages of sin' was hardly abstract. Francis Bacon's image was equally concrete but more benign. 'Death,' he wrote, 'is a friend of ours, and he that is not ready to entertain him, is not at home.' The seventeenth-century Francis Bacon would have argued long and hard about what death is with the twentieth-century writer Arnold Toynbee, who claimed that for man death is 'incongruous and humiliating'.

Death has been many other things to many other people. Depending on one's belief, death has been seen as a beginning, a transition or an end. For the believers in heaven and hell death is the moment of judgement or the passage to purgatory before the final reckoning. As such it is a scary event. Children exhorted by the seventeenth-century John Norris to 'act over frequently in your Minds, the Solemnity of your own Funerals; and entertain your Imaginations with all the lively scenes of Mortality' and also to meditate 'upon the fewness of those that shall be saved' must have had a deep fear of death. Indeed, a contemporary of John Norris, John Dunton, recalling his own childhood wrote of his 'servile fear of hell . . . a place full of the blackest and most frightful terrors'. More recently, a woman recalling her childhood before the First World War said, 'That's what I believed in [heaven and hell] and I was scared because I was pretty sure that I was going to be one of the goats.'

For those who believe in eternal life without fear of judgement, death is the gateway. In particular it is most often seen as the gateway to meeting up with others who have died, and a place to which others will follow. Clearly the belief, if firmly held, that death is a gateway to an eternal meeting-place gives many people solace. That solace is eloquently expressed in the following poem written in 1985 by a man very close to death.

> Today I feel like nothing on earth:
> I had the last rites this morning.
> My legs hurt and my back hurts.
> Last night I heard her voice calling me.
> They are all there – but I heard her voice.
> My father and mother are there,
> My three brothers and two sisters –
> All happy and smiling – I hope to join them.
> We will be together.
> It is four years since I lost my wife.
> No reason why we can't go on being happy:
> That's all that matters –
> To be with her.

The human condition on earth influences definitions of death. Individuals who contemplate suicide see death as a way out of their particular emotional or physical suffering. Apart from suicide, death is nowadays only seen in the Western world as a release from suffering when it ends a long, painful illness. For the poor of previous centuries it was a release from the suffering of this life. Death in itself was a release, but one made sweeter for those who believed

Death Is?

in an afterlife which had to be better than life on earth. Nowhere is that sense of release and belief in a better life articulated more clearly than in the spiritual songs of the black slaves of America. In the spiritual 'Deep River' the first and last verse express the expectation of a better and free life.

> Oh don't you want to go to that gospel feast
> That promised land where all is peace.
>
> Oh, when I get to heaven, I'll walk about,
> There's nobody there for to turn me out.

A more secular version of the hope of release from the unending toil of this world is expressed anonymously in 'The Tired Woman's Epitaph'.

> Here lies a poor woman that always was tired,
> She lived in a house where help was not hired.
> Her last words on earth were: 'Dear friends, I am going
> Where washing ain't done, nor sweeping, nor sewing;
> But everything there is exact to my wishes
> For where they don't eat there's no washing dishes.
> I'll be where loud anthems will always be ringing
> But, having no voice, I'll be clear of the singing.
> Don't mourn for me now; don't mourn for me never.
> I'm going to do nothing for ever and ever.'

A milder comment on the quality of life compared to death was made by Mark Twain in Pudd'nhead Wilson. 'All say,' Twain observed, 'how hard it is that we have to die,' which he found 'a strange complaint to come from the mouths of people who have had to live'. Affluence has enabled the rich to buy on earth what the poor had imagined they would have in heaven. The one commodity the affluent have not been able to buy is eternal life either for the living or for the dead. What affluence has provided is a longer life for many and more things to give up at death.

War has given rise to a quite separate tradition of beliefs. At one extreme were the Japanese Kamikaze pilots who chose death and, judging from letters written shortly before their final mission, it was clearly something they looked forward to. Such comments as 'My chance will come. Death and I are waiting' or 'Please congratulate me, I have been given a splendid opportunity to die' make the reader realise that some saw death as a chosen honour. In many ways the Kamikaze pilots' attitudes are but an extension of the whole tradition of the nobility of dying for one's country. It was a sentiment much expressed in the early days of the First World War. The other attitude provoked by the First World War as the reality of so much killing became clear was the utter futility of so much death. With hundreds of thousands of dead and dying strewn across northern France, death lost its heroic meaning. Wilfred Owen summed up that loss in the opening line of his 'Anthem for Doomed Youth', in which he asks 'What passing bells for these who die like cattle?'

In contrast to Freud's assertion of the negativity of death, many have seen death very positively. It is and has been seen as the meaning of life without which life would have no meaning. The French writer Baudelaire claimed that:

> It is death that consoles and makes us live, alas!
> Death is the goal of life, death is our only hope,
> Which like an elixir cheers and intoxicates
> And gives us heart to live another day.

While some people attribute to death all the meaning of life, there are writers in the late twentieth century who have tried to define death as nothingness. Guildenstern in Tom Stoppard's play *Rosencrantz and Guildenstern are Dead* attempts to describe that nothingness. 'Death,' he explains, 'isn't romantic ... death is not anything ... death is ... not. It's the absence of presence, nothing more ... the endless time of never coming back. ... A gap you can't see, and when the wind blows through it, it makes no sound.' Some twentieth-century commentators have seen this reduction of death to nothingness as a sign of progress. These two opposing viewpoints of death, that it contains all life's meaning or that it is nothingness, are summed up by one historian, Paul Robinson (American), commenting on the views of another historian, Philippe Ariès (French). In reviewing the latter's book, *The Hour of Our Death*, Robinson wrote in 1981: 'Perhaps more fundamentally I disagree with Ariès's proposition that death is one of the great existential truths whose reality we must constantly reaffirm. The neglect of death – its reduction "to the insignificance of an ordinary event" – is, I would argue, a measure of our psychic maturity.'

Between 'all meaning' and 'nothingness' there is the very personal meaning of death. 'There is ... no death.... There is only ... me ... me ... who is going to die.' André Malraux, in that line from *The Royal Way*, touches a reality for us all, whatever our beliefs, our lives or our definition of death.

Immortal longings

At a press conference for the British Heart Foundation someone asked Len Murray (retired General Secretary of the Trades Union Congress) how he felt now about his life expectancy following heart surgery. 'Immortal,' was his jovial reply. After that press conference we interviewed on film another man who had had heart surgery and asked him whether he shared Len Murray's optimism. 'Well, we are all immortal, aren't we?' he replied and added, 'None of us are going to die. Nobody ever considers the fact that they are going to die. In my own case with a transplant one's lifespan becomes a little bit more problematical because one talks about life survival after a transplant.' Of course both men, like all of us, know that we are not immortal, but we in the twentieth century try to live out our lives, both in private and in public, in an attempt to evade that knowledge.

It is as though that knowledge, like the facts of life for the Victorians, is an obscenity. Even deeper, there is the unexpressed attitude that death represents failure for the human race. The idea of failure goes back a long way at least as far as the book of Genesis in the Bible; Adam and

Eve became mortal through their failings and their sin, and the idea of sin causing death has never been far from the surface, as the reaction by many to deaths from AIDS reveals. The logical conclusion of seeing death as a moral failure is that if we are morally perfect then we will not die. Christianity promised eternal life to those who did not sin, but even for those who do not believe in Christianity there is a hope that by leading the right kind of life we will ensure for ourselves continued existence.

Unfortunately, death keeps raising its ugly head and nowhere more dramatically in recent years than when, as Rory Mundane described it in the *Guardian* (20 February 1986), 'the big D went prime time' and millions of people in the world watched as 'the Grim Reaper scythed seven astronauts right out of the sky'. Rory Mundane argued that the event was so traumatic because the reality, there on our TV screen, was so much at odds with Western society which for the past few years 'has pretended that life was not inherently fatal. The theory has been put about that if only you could cut out the booze and the fags, say goodbye to animal fats, exercise constantly, control stress and subsist entirely on Perrier, nuts and bran, one could hang on to the ripe old age of about 150. And by then there would be every chance that some new wonder drug would have been found that would delay the Big Sleep even longer.' Life is of course, even without scientific mistakes that cause rockets to blow up, inherently fatal. To remind us of that Rory Mundane suggested that 'this year's key table accessory is a skull', and that people should make 'a *memento mori* part of your mental furniture.'

Most people would react with horror at the idea of having a skull sitting on their coffee table or a painting of one on their living-room walls, but such was not always the case. Indeed, it was believed that people should be reminded. The two symbols mainly used as a *memento mori* were those of the skull and the hourglass; both were used as symbols of mortality. One of the most arresting paintings on that theme was by Frans Hals in the early seventeenth century,

Death Is?

called 'Young Man Holding a Skull'. The painting is of a young man clearly in the prime of life sporting a prominent red hat with a large matching feather in it. The only thing that shows it is not merely a portrait of a dashing young gentleman is the fact that he is holding a skull in his left hand.

Other artists used the skull in a similarly symbolic way. The most famous painting with such a message was Hans Holbein the Younger's 'Ambassadors Jean de Dinterville and Georges de Selve'. In this painting of two ambassadors the skull is hidden in the centre of the picture and can only be made out from a particular angle. Portrayed as such, it is a reminder of the hidden presence of death in life. As well as being included in portraits, skulls were also the centrepiece of a number of still lifes. The mirror image was also a common theme. 'The Burgkmaier Spouses', painted by Lucas Furtenagel in 1529, is an intensely human painting of a middle-aged couple holding a mirror, and their mirror image is of two skulls. Unlike the use of active skeletons to depict the figure of death, the use of skulls is purely symbolic; they are merely present in paintings as a reminder. It is a symbol that twentieth-century sensitivities find hard to take.

The other powerful but less gruesome symbol used for centuries was that of the hourglass. Its practical use was to measure time before the widespread ownership of watches and clocks, but it also had a commonly understood symbolic function. The grains of sand running through represented the human lifespan – a lifespan that had a measured beginning, middle and end. Many artists placed the hourglass in drawings and paintings as a symbolic reminder of mortality. Not only did the figure of death frequently hold an hourglass, but in paintings not directly related to death an hourglass would often be included in the scene, not as a clock to tell the time, but as a symbol of the finite nature of human life.

Contemporary art no longer includes such symbols of mortality. It is unimaginable that a contemporary pop artist, film star, sports person or politician would have a portrait or photo made of themselves holding a skull. It would be thought an image in bad taste and one that would neither sell nor get votes. People no longer have hourglasses on their mantelpieces or bookshelves to remind them that their life is running through to an inevitable end.

At least one advertiser has used the image recently, however, though the meaning of the image was ambiguous. The advertisement sent through the post to me was for an insurance scheme that would pay out money during periods of hospitalisation and was in the form of a leaflet. On the front was the image of an hourglass with four pillars, rather than the symbolic three, making it look like an egg-timer. The image was repeated throughout the leaflet with the sands at different stages of running through. The image was clearly not designed to remind the reader that they might die but that they might well at some point have to spend a period of time in hospital. It is perhaps not surprising that advertisers would neither get the image quite right nor wish to use the classic symbolism of the hourglass. There is not a big market in mortality.

Although modern literature is full of accounts of death (who-dunnits, spy stories and war stories in particular), few writers include in their imagery references to mortality. For writers that do 'time' is, and has been, the main metaphor used to echo the visual image of the hourglass. W. H. Auden's 'Birthday Poem', with the lines 'O let not Time deceive you, You cannot conquer Time', is a rare twentieth-century reminder of mortality, but one that continued a long tradition. One of the most famous poems in that tradition was Andrew Marvell's 'To His Coy Mistress', in which Marvell tries to seduce his coy mistress with the following argument:

> But at the back I always hear
> Time's wingèd chariot hurrying near;
> And yonder all before us lie
> Deserts of vast eternity.
> Thy beauty shall no more be found,

> Nor, in thy marble vault, shall sound
> My echoing song: then worms shall try
> That long preserved virginity,
> And your quaint honour turn to dust,
> And into ashes all my lust:
> The grave's a fine and private place,
> But none, I think, do there embrace.

Remarkable as the poem is for its literary qualities, the message would have been by no means unique; literature of the seventeenth century was full of references to the fact that life was finite. The reverse is true of the song written by Mick Jagger and Keith Richards of the Rolling Stones called 'Time Waits for No One'. The lyrics can hardly qualify as great literature but they are notable in that they mention mortality in an age which does not normally publicly admit to such a fact. We are very rarely told in any form, let alone in the words of a popular song, to:

> Drink in your summer
> Gather your corn
> The dreams of the night time
> Will vanish by dawn
> And time waits for no one
> And it won't wait for me.

An earlier song called 'Time is on my Side', sung by the Rolling Stones but not written by them, better reflects the attitudes of the twentieth century.

The interesting question is why we have rejected during the twentieth century the need to be reminded of our mortality, and indeed what is the effect on us of our rejection? There appear to be many causes, and in the absence of any study which has analysed the reasons one can only hazard guesses. Unquestionably, the First World War was a dividing line in terms of attitude. That can be seen not only in the language used about death before and since, but in the changes in funerals, mourning rituals and the whole way the subject of death has been dealt with both in real life and in literature. The First World War also saw the beginning of the twentieth-century capacity to kill. This century has witnessed slaughter on a terrifying scale; it has also developed the means to wipe out the human race. Yet although on one hand we have developed such power to end life, on the other we still cannot control mortality. All that we have managed to do is to give some of the world a longer life expectancy, but one that is little longer on average than the biblical three score years and ten.

The decline in the numbers of those believing in religion has also had its effect, though the effect is not quite as clear as is often assumed. Many of those who do not accept the traditional Christian view of death retain vestiges of that belief by holding on to a belief in some kind of afterlife. Other religions have also influenced twentieth-century attitudes. The existence of a wider range of beliefs in Britain, based mainly on different ethnic groups, has also affected the wider community. Ideas filter outwards. A belief in reincarnation, for instance, is quite widely held even if in a less defined form than that propounded by some Eastern religions. In the West a belief in the cycle of life often takes the form of regeneration rather than reincarnation. That belief in regeneration is usually in terms of a biological continuity something along the lines of the song 'On Ilkley Moor Baht'at'. In the song, a moral tale about the dire consequences of courting Mary Jane on Ilkley Moor without a hat, regeneration is accepted. Death from cold initiates the following cycle:

> Then we shall ha to bury thee,
> Then t'worms will come an' ate thee up,
> Then t'ducks'll come an' ate up t'worms,
> Then we shall go an' ate up t'ducks,
> Then we shall all 'av etten thee,
> That's where we gets our oahn back.

The same idea of 'living on' in this world through leaving behind memories is also held by many people. What the decline in the dominance of Christianity has done, amongst other things, is to remove from people's lives many reminders of death in the rituals and symbols of the Bible and other Christian writings. The Spanish film director Luis Buñuel wrote, in his autobiography called *My Last Breath*, of the influence such symbols had had on his attitude: 'The thought of death has been familiar to me for a long time. From the time that skeletons were carried through the streets of Calanda during the Holy Week procession, death has been an integral part of my life. I've never wished to forget or deny it, but there's not much to say about it when you're an atheist.' We now reject the parading of skeletons through streets as primitive, but we have not replaced them with other symbols.

Modern medicine has also contributed much to our attitude that death is an embarrassing fact of human life about which we do not wish to be reminded. Indeed, it has done much to try to conceal death from the living and the dying. The way a death is dealt with in a hospital reflects this attitude. The curtains are immediately pulled around the bed of the dead person and are drawn round the beds of the others in the ward so that they may not see the body being hurriedly and surreptitiously removed to the hospital mortuary. Everything is then scrubbed clean, all evidence of the departed person in terms of personal belongings is packed speedily into a grey hospital plastic bag and the curtains around all the beds are opened again. The clean, made-up empty bed stands there as the only evidence that someone occupied it and died in it.

Norbert Elias in his book *The Loneliness of Dying* wrote: 'Never before in the history of humanity have the dying been removed so hygienically behind the scenes of social life; never before have human corpses been expedited so odourlessly and with such technical perfection from the deathbed to the grave.' Hospitals have done much to hide death; before their growth, most people died at home. Death was something people witnessed and was often a family affair which included children. It has not been so much the existence of hospitals that has caused the hiding-away of death but the attitude of those deciding on hospital policy. That attitude is informed by the medical profession. For them death is a failure. Their job is to prolong and/or save life. Their training and conditioned reactions make it even harder for them to accept death as the natural end to a long life. Richard Lamerton described in his book *Care of the Dying* how as a junior physician in a hospital he answered an urgent 'cardiac arrest' call and instantly launched in, helped by a houseman, to resuscitate with violent drugs and blasts of electric current a ninety-year-old woman. The old lady's heart had stopped as, he wrote, 'hearts are apt to do, around ninety!' Inappropriate as, he felt afterwards, their behaviour had been, there had been nothing in their medical training to guide them on how to react to a cardiac arrest except in the way that they did.

The more medicine achieves in terms of saving life, the more death is seen as a failure. The fact that modern medical practitioners are so embarrassed by death has meant that they have been unable to treat the dying with any kind of acceptance. A dying person is either sent home from hospital, a reflection of doctors' attitude that their role is ended, or is nursed as an embarrassment in a corner of the ward. It was as a reaction to this kind of treatment that the hospice movement came into being. It has fought and continues to fight to bring an acceptance of death back into our lives, arguing that only if we accept death can we help the dying.

Those most obviously to benefit from an acceptance of death are the dying, something discussed in the next chapter. But perhaps such an acceptance could benefit us all, both personally and as social beings. What touched us in the course of making the programme 'Born to Die' was that everyone in it, chosen because for one reason or another they had had to confront their own mortality, had clearly found that that confrontation profoundly affected their lives. Initially that was not something we looked for. Our choice of people was based on an attempt to air attitudes to death and not to single out 'the dying' from the living. We thought that people who had had to confront their mortality either because of disease, career (i.e. the armed forces) or because of age would have more to contribute than most of us who, as we know, prefer not to think of such things. 'Born to Die' and 'Some Mother's Son' were films that started out with being about death and ended up, we felt, with being about life. Each person we interviewed affirmed how much they valued life after having confronted death. That confrontation had brought about changes to them and their lives, some of which were quite small and others quite dramatic.

For example, following a heart transplant Patrick Holden changed his value system, this led to his changing jobs and he now works for a charity. A young woman, Audrey Brown, with sickle cell disease, having come to terms with the fact that she could die, has committed herself to living life to the full and to helping others with the same disease to live the most fulfilling lives they can. Clive Baulch, having in the army inflicted death and witnessed the death in action of a close friend, revalued his own life and that of others and became a pacifist. Claude Moore, in his late seventies, who works with Caribbean pensioners, said of his realisation that he will die, 'I pass this way but once myself and I like to do whatever I can because I don't know what tomorrow will be.' Coming to terms with the approach of death through age also causes re-evaluations. 'It teaches you,' Katharine Moore said, 'to live in the present. I do feel I've got to enjoy this while I can still do it. I've got to live every moment as well as I can.' Those most aware of valuing each day are the people who know that they are dying. The poem 'Then and Now', written by Hazel Goldbrom, one of the interviewees in the film, expresses poignantly that re-evaluation.

> As I sit upon my chair
> I recall glad days when free as air
> I woke. Before me lay a day
> Which I controlled in my own way.
> In either way then I was free
> To do the things making my life me.

> But now I know as I awake
> That each day's meaning I must make.
> I can't be free as I would be
> To see the things that I would see.
>
> I have to put into my days
> Something with meaning in all my ways
> And simply because I sit upon my chair
> I will not let my time escape as air.

The evidence of our interviewees is by no means unique. The writings and actions of many others reveal that same changed perspective on life which the confrontation with death can bring. The following are just two examples. Wolfgang Amadeus Mozart, writing to his father on 4 April 1787, claimed that death 'is the key which unlocks the door to true happiness'. He then explained: 'I never lie down at night without reflecting that – young as I am – I may not live to see another day. Yet no one of all my acquaintances could say that in company I am morose or disgruntled. For this blessing I daily thank my Creator and wish with all my heart that each of my fellow-creatures could enjoy it.' Mozart's letter, written four years before his death at the age of thirty-five, is a powerful affirmation of the way acceptance of death enriched his life.

Another testimony to that enrichment is that of the black American woman Audre Lorde, who spoke for many when she wrote in 1980 in *The Cancer Journals*: 'Living a self-conscious life, under the pressure of time, I work with the consciousness of death at my shoulder, not constantly, but often enough to leave a mark upon all of my life's decisions and actions. And it does not matter whether this death comes next week or thirty years from now; this consciousness gives my life another breadth. It helps shape the words I speak, the ways I love, my politic of action, the strength of my vision and purpose, the depth of my appreciation of living.'

We all live under the pressure of time and yet do not let

that inform our lives. Mortality is not part of our mental furniture. Making it a part could help us to learn, as Audre Lorde argues we must, 'to count the living with that same particular attention with which we number the dead'.

CHAPTER THREE

Dying

> We need to reclaim our right to preside over our dying so that, as Edwin Shneidan says, it fits [us].
> (Jory Graham, 1983)

Even if we do not fear death itself, most of us fear dying. We fear the possible physical pain that may precede death and the emotional pain of knowing that our days are numbered. We fear, as the young poet described earlier, 'dying all alone' with 'no friends, no family, nobody to hold your hand'. We fear dying before our time, though however long we live most of us feel death comes before its time. We fear preparing for death and yet fear dying unprepared. We fear saying the last good-bye. We fear being kept alive when we are no longer of the living. The thought of dying inculcates in most of us a range of emotions, but fear is unquestionably the strongest. Fear of dying is not unique to the twentieth century, but during this century we have created conditions which have increased our fear rather than helped to allay it. Social changes, developments in medicine, the attitude of doctors and a conspiracy of silence have all contributed to heightening the level of fear. Above all, we have lost control of our dying and our sense of being able to support others dying. This loss of control is particularly frightening.

There is considerable evidence that people, apart from situations of sudden violent death, did indeed preside over their dying. 'Death,' Philippe Ariès wrote in *Western Attitudes Towards Death*, 'was a ritual organized by the dying person himself, who presided over it and knew its protocol.' The dying person would have known the protocol from having witnessed other deaths. Death as a public affair was something everyone learnt about from childhood. Throughout the centuries artists have depicted death-bed scenes and always the dying person, very much in the centre, is surrounded by family and friends. Literature prior to the twentieth century is likewise full of descriptions of death-bed scenes, and again in these it is always a public affair. The two descriptions that imprinted themselves on my mind as a child were that of Mr Barkis in Dickens's *David Copperfield* and Helen Burns in Charlotte Brontë's *Jane Eyre*. Mr Barkis was surrounded by caring friends, whereas Helen just had the company of Jane. But in neither case did the person die alone.

From witnessing other deaths people also learnt that the dying person did indeed control and preside over their own deaths. The dying, to use a twentieth-century phrase, 'called the shots'. They would say their good-byes and give their last messages. Their affairs would be sorted out and those with property to leave would ensure that their last will and testament was drawn up and signed or marked. There is evidence, too, that they controlled to a certain degree the timing of their dying. People knew when they were ready to die. Ariès illustrates the point with numerous cases, one of which was that of a seventy-four-year-old peasant woman who contracted cholera. The village priest came to give her the last rites, but she sent him away saying, 'Not yet, M. le Curé; I'll let you know when the time comes.' Two days later she *was* ready and called for him. Religious as well as social ritual placed control in the hands of the dying. Jewish ritual rested on the dying person calling for the Rabbi and then speaking to him the *Vidui*, the confessional. Having asked for God's forgiveness and having reaffirmed faith in the one God, the dying would speak the last words, 'Into Your hands do I now commit my soul,' and then turn their faces to the wall. Christians were expected to lie on their backs facing heaven, pray and, if Roman Catholic, request the last rites.

In all the above protocol and ritual doctors had very little part to play. Once it was clear that someone was dying doctors kept their distance. In 1818, a French author on medical science wrote: 'When a doctor cannot save a man's life, he avoids being in his home after he has died, and all practitioners seem totally convinced of the axiom that it is not seemly for a doctor to visit the dead.' As with birth, doctors left administering to the dying to others. However, as doctors gained more control over people's physical lives from the late nineteenth century onwards, they began to control both birth and death. Increasingly, both experiences were moved into hospitals. Medical developments were often used more to control than to help. In the case of birth too many drugs were used and with the dying often too few. From both events family and friends were excluded and they became lonely and frightening experiences. Geoffrey Gorer made a study in the early sixties of *Death, Grief and Mourning in Contemporary Britain*. Although the study was primarily about grief and mourning, Gorer looked at when and how the deaths occurred. About half the deaths had taken place in hospital and 44 per cent of the rest had taken place at home, but within that overall statistic Gorer found considerable regional, class and religious variations. The Scottish and Roman Catholics were, he found, more likely to die in hospital, whilst someone from a clerical or unskilled working family in the Midlands was more likely to die at home.

Regardless of place, Gorer found that: 'Most people, it would seem, now die alone, except for medical attendants; less than a quarter of the bereaved were present when their relative died, and nearly two-thirds of those present were women.' In this too Gorer found a class variation. Quite simply, the higher up the social class the more likely one was to die alone. His picture of death in Britain in the sixties is cold, depersonalised and frightening. The most chilling line in the whole description is, 'Nearly all the children died in hospital, alone.' One can only question the kind of society we have created in which we have become so frightened and alienated from dying and death that we allow children to die alone in hospital. Indeed, my own child died in 1975 alone in hospital with only medical attendants. My only consolation is that he died following major heart surgery from which, I have to believe, he never regained consciousness. We saw Will shortly before his death and the doctors were then clearly aware that he could die. Looking back, I cannot think why they did not ask whether we wished to stay with him. Even in the high-tech environment of an intensive-care unit a place could have been found for us to have sat by him and held his hand.

What Gorer's study did not do was look at the *experience* of dying in the early sixties. Other surveys done in the fifties and sixties did, and found that it was unnecessarily painful – physically as well as emotionally. One study made by the Marie Curie Memorial Foundation found that one-fifth of dying patients in hospitals in the 1950s were in severe unrelieved pain and two-thirds of cancer patients being looked after at home had severe or moderate suffering. Others also found that far too little was done to relieve pain. It emerged that, regardless of a patient's response to a drug, nurses dutifully gave them at four-hourly intervals as instructed by the doctors. Doctors all too frequently showed little concern about pain control except to believe that patients should be protected from becoming addicted. In his book *Care of the Dying*, first published in 1973, Richard Lamerton cited many examples of the way lack of nursing care, not just in terms of pain relief, caused suffering. Terminally ill patients with bed sores, thrush of the mouth and constipation were not uncommon, the latter in some cases being the cause of death. Arguing for the use of more enemas, Lamerton claimed that: 'Far more die of constipation than ever did of enemas. Indeed we actually had four patients referred to us in one month who were dying until given an enema.' The surveys and the testimony of concerned nurses and doctors also revealed that the treatment of the terminally ill was often uncaring and, in some cases, negligent.

It is interesting to observe that during the past two decades most of the crusading work that has been done in trying to change medical attitudes and practices has been in the field of childbirth and in the care of the dying. In both cases the thrust of the crusade has been to wrest control back into the hands of those giving birth or dying and to reassert the fact that both are natural processes. It has been a crusade which, except on the extreme fringes, has not aimed to exclude the medical profession but rather to harness the developments of medical science and the skills of the medical profession to the physical and emotional needs of the patient. Ironically, it seems that at the point at which dying could have been made a better experience through the development of pain-controlling drugs, hygiene, professional nursing and generally greater medical knowledge it was made worse. At the point when medicine began to gain more power and control through making real breakthroughs in the treatment of many diseases, the dying, who symbolised medical failure, became ignored.

Although there is no question, as the historian Ariès and others have recorded, that dying before this century was a more socially accepted and therefore more socially supported affair, what their studies tend to omit is the dark side of dying before the developments of modern medicine. The death chamber must have in many cases smelt foul even to those used to the smell of bodily odours. Death came more quickly without modern medicine, but some people must have experienced great pain, with no drugs for relief, although then as now many people clearly found a pain-free calm in the period immediately before their death. One has only to read descriptions of the deaths of women from infection following childbirth in Edward Shorter's *A History of Women's Bodies* to realise that dying was not always a beautiful affair. A typical example of one such death was recorded by an Edinburgh doctor in 1774. Two days after giving birth the woman experienced 'pains in the lower part of her abdomen'. During the following six days the woman suffered extreme pain 'in the region of the uterus',

Dying

a high fever, a pulse rate of 160 to the minute and 'on many parts of her body small red tumours under the skin, moveable and painful'. By the sixth day, despite the swellings and 'breathing very quick', she was coherent and without pain – a state in which she remained until her death the following day.

The Tolstoy short story 'The Death of Ivan Ilych' is often quoted as a literary example of someone who comes in the end to accept, without fear, death. Those who quote the end fail to include the description of the extreme pain suffered by Ivan Ilych in the days when medicine brought little relief. 'But the pain, why this pain? If it would only cease just for a moment!' is the cry of Ivan Ilych as he swallows his medicine, fully aware that it 'won't help'. Even those not in extreme pain probably suffered a whole range of physical discomforts which modern nursing can greatly minimise. In trying to convey the benefits both to the dying and the bereaved of the way that society handled death in the past there has been a tendency to romanticise it, to forget what must have been the smell, the pain and the distress of witnessing that painful death.

During this century doctors have increasingly taken control of our dying, but they are very often unsympathetic in the execution of that power. Lay people have been made to feel impotent in relation to the dying, and all too often give up their role to the professionals. The only role left for the non-professionals has been reduced to the nursing skills traditionally associated with women, but their confidence, even in that skill, has been eroded. Social attitudes that shunned the dying were both the cause and the result of the dying being isolated. It was through the realisation that the dying were condemned to an unnecessarily bad experience that the hospice movement was born. (In this book the term 'hospice movement' is used as a convenient name to cover all those who since the 1950s have worked to try to improve the care of the dying.)

The idea of the dying needing special care was not new. In the mid-nineteenth century Mary Aikenhead founded in

Dublin an order of nuns, the Irish Sisters of Charity, one of whose duties was to care for the dying. It soon became clear that a special place was needed in which they could be nursed, and for that purpose Mary Aikenhead gave her own house in Dublin. It was she who used the name 'hospice'. The word originated in the Middle Ages, when hospices existed to provide travellers with food and refuge to fuel them physically and spiritually for their journey. Expanding their work, the Irish Sisters of Charity opened at the beginning of this century St Joseph's Hospice in London. A similar movement was also started in the late nineteenth century in the USA, where an order of Dominican nuns established a number of homes in which the terminally ill could be nursed.

The hospice movement as we know it in Britain today, though drawing on these roots, was really started in the 1950s by two main campaigners. The Marie Curie Foundation, in its commitment to fighting the suffering caused by cancer, realised that there was a need not just for skilled nursing but also for special residential homes which could save 'much mental suffering, stress and strain for the relatives'. Acting on their recognition of that need, they set about raising money to establish, over the years, a number of residential homes. The other campaigner was Cicely Saunders. She, as a social worker, discussed with a dying Polish refugee called David Tasma the needs of the dying, and out of their discussions came the idea of establishing a special home where those needs could be met. When in 1948 David Tasma died, he left Cicely Saunders £500 'to be a window in your Home'. From that point on, the care of the dying became her life's work. After gaining medical training and experience through working at St Joseph's Hospice, she opened St Christopher's Hospice in 1967 as a special place where her ideas could be fully put into practice. St Christopher's did indeed become a special place, and was visited by many people not just from Britain but also from Europe and America in order to learn about Cicely Saunders's concept of total care for the dying.

Hospices sprang out of religious conviction embodying, as one person described them, 'a rather rare combination of spirituality and hard medicine'. The movement has grown and brought about the establishment of more hospices based on that combination. Other people, however, have realised that not all the dying are religious and that there is a need for the provision of good care for all and not just for those who are being prepared for a spiritual journey. Drawing on the ideas and experience of those working in the hospice movement, others began, and continue, to work to try and bring about a change in the care of the dying throughout Britain. It has been realised that there is need not just for more services but for a greater variety. Hospices have been and are being established which are not religious and in which, as in the Marie Curie Homes, an individual's belief or non-belief is respected.

Many hospitals, too, have become more caring and have begun to change their attitudes and practices. Some hospitals have established separate wards for the dying, which is a first step towards recognition of their needs. Of course, many still die at home. They die at home not just because they are sent home by hospitals but because they and their relatives or friends wish them to be there. Caring for a dying person can be physically arduous and emotionally stressful. Recognition of the need to support home-carers has led to the growth of a range of help.

Many hospices and other homes for the terminally ill encourage people to use them for short stays. The short stay may be to get a person 'sorted out' in terms of pain control and other physical needs. It can also be used to give a break to those caring for someone at home. Hazel Goldbrom in 'Born to Die' described how Eden Hall, a Marie Curie home, fulfilled at different times both these services for her and her friend Priscilla. 'We know that whenever I get really ill or if Priscilla can't cope with problems, because obviously there is a limit to everybody's ability to cope with problems, Eden Hall will come to our rescue and it always does. We just have to pick up the telephone and if I'm ill

Eden Hall will take me; if Priscilla can't cope Eden Hall will take me as soon as they have a bed. Because of that I'm able to live outside as well as inside. I have a life of my own still.'

The setting up of day-care hospices is also being considered in some areas. The fact that they would be cheaper to run is by no means the only argument in their favour. They would enable a dying person to keep their ties with home and all that is familiar about home for as long as possible and would give home-carers a break. When necessary they could ease the passage from home to being under full-time hospice care. Other support and help is also available. The Marie Curie Foundation and the Macmillan Service provide skilled nurses to help those looking after someone at home. Home-care units have been established in some NHS areas to provide support for the terminally ill. These units usually consist of a team of nurses, a doctor and a social worker, all of whom visit the patient and those caring for the patient at home. Such support can often make the crucial difference between relatives being able to nurse someone at home and feeling unable to cope and therefore having to have them admitted to a hospice or hospital.

Unlike the movement to change the experience of giving birth, which was founded and campaigned for by women themselves, the hospice movement was founded and continues to be campaigned for mainly by caring professionals. It is hard for the dying to campaign for themselves, though, as some individual testimonies show, not impossible. The danger of the professional input to the hospice movement, caring as those profesionals may be, is of their taking over and controlling yet again our dying. One dying person, Jory Graham, wrote in her book *In the Company of Others*: 'My one reservation about the hospice movement is that, in trying to achieve uniform standards for hospice care, the planners may unwittingly try to program the dying.' She criticises those who try to convert our dying into 'pseudo-scientific stages labelled "bargaining" or "denial"', arguing that dying is 'not comparable to a flu that follows a well-defined course'. She goes on to state what is well for all to remember that, 'dying and its anguish are wholly individual'. Writing as someone terminally ill, Jory Graham recognises very clearly the needs of the dying and the changes in attitude necessary for those needs to be met. The hospice movement has and is doing much to change those attitudes and meet those needs. Although dying is an individual affair, there are many things which can be done by lay people and professionals to help the individual both physically and emotionally. We can draw on our knowledge of the past about the social recognition and support given to the dying and use the developments of modern medicine *for* the dying. By knowing what can be done we can allay many of our fears. With help we can, as Jory Graham wishes, 'reclaim our right to preside over our dying'.

Monster pain

> Pain is a monster.
> We all know pain,
> We've all had pain.
>
> Pain is worse than a house at night
> And any evil spell.
>
> Pain is such a silent mover
> So watch out for Monster Pain.
>   (Jessie Buscombe, 1986, aged eight)

Claude Moore, when asked in the programme 'Born to Die' whether he was afraid of dying, replied, 'No, I'm not afraid of dying. What I'm afraid of is maybe the suffering that might precede that death.' His fear is one that is shared by most people. Enough people have witnessed or heard about the terrible pain suffered by the dying to fear that they too will some day suffer the same.

A few years ago a friend of mine phoned me in deep anguish. Her husband was dying and she was nursing him at home, the hospital having come to the end of any treatment. As a family they had acknowledged that he was dying and had discussed it between themselves and with their young son. The source of her anguish expressed during that phone call was having to witness his physical pain. 'No one,' I vividly remember her saying, 'should ever have to suffer such pain.' She might have added that no one should ever have to suffer the distress of witnessing someone in so much pain for a prolonged period of time. Had I known then what I know now about pain control and the support she could have had I would have given her some practical help. Sadly, I didn't know and all I could try to do was to be a sympathetic listener. The fact that I remembered so vividly that particular phrase was not just because those sort of human experiences are memorable, but because I inwardly shuddered with fear. Fear that one day I might have to witness someone I loved suffer such pain or that I myself might. The outrageous aspect of their experience was that there was no need for him to have had to suffer that prolonged pain, nor for my friend to have had to witness it. No one, as she rightly said, should have to suffer that much.

Pain control has been one, if not *the* central concern of the hospice movement. It is central not just because no one need, given modern drugs and their considered administration, suffer such pain but because so many other aspects of caring for the dying stem from pain control. Pain can be all-consuming, physically and emotionally stripping a person of their ability to 'preside over their dying'. Further, as Richard Lamerton wrote, 'A patient distressed by pain and terrified of dying becomes rapidly exhausted and dies quickly and badly.' In contrast, 'with the proper use of opiate analgesia he will be peaceful and comfortable, living longer and dying with dignity'. We fear pain and pain creates in us fear. It is distressing for all to witness. 'How people die,' Cicely Saunders so rightly stated, 'remains in the memories of those who live on, and for them as for the patient we need to be aware of the nature and the management of terminal pain and distress.' Only too well aware of the distress caused by pain, Cicely Saunders set about, with

Dying

crusading commitment, changing attitudes and using medical advances to control pain for the benefit of the dying.

Changing medical attitudes was, and still sadly is, as important as the research into the drugs used and individual responses to those drugs. Of attitudes to the dying Richard Lamerton commented: 'Doctors who otherwise pride themselves on careful diagnosis followed by rational and precise treatment so often sink into a mire of mythology and emotion when faced with a dying patient. Science goes to the wind and superstition takes over.' From their behaviour it seemed until recently as though doctors accepted the irrational cultural beliefs of our Judaeo-Christian heritage that pain is punishment for sin and that the patient achieves nobility through enduring suffering without complaint. Nowhere was the superstition and prejudice more evident than in their attitude to the use of drugs for pain control. Opiates, the drugs mainly used, were regarded as dangerous and addictive. They would not, the medical argument went, sanction the creation of hallucinating, dying junkies dependent on larger and larger doses. Many held the attitude that opiates should only be used as a last resort and it was feared that they could be lethal. Because of this attitude little attention was paid to the actual effect of opiates when used for pain relief, or to the individual's need for and response to them. Doctors' attitudes did much to inhibit progress in their use. That attitude is now being changed, and at last more research is being done into pain control.

The following, said to us by Hazel Goldbrom when interviewed for 'Born to Die', is perhaps a more reassuring testament to the possibilities of pain control than any reassurance given by professionals:

> I had a lot of pain before I came to Eden Hall, but when I first came here I asked one of the nurses about pain and she said to me, 'There's only one thing we don't allow at Eden Hall and that's pain.' I found that to be true, because the whole philosophy of the place is that it doesn't really matter how many drugs one has to take as far as becoming addicted

is concerned because we're not people who are going to live for a very long life. Therefore we do become physically addicted to drugs, even though mentally we're not addicted. But the drugs are very, very carefully monitored and as our pain increases so the drug increases and sometimes the drug increases before our pain increases. I must say quite honestly that we do not suffer and I've seen people die here, many people that I've known die here, and not one of them has died in pain and not one of them has died in tears.

The testimony of one terminally ill cancer patient gives reality to the assertion by a group of American doctors that 'with care and patience, the physician can render practically any cancer patient pain-free'. Having got over the obstacle of believing that using opiates will cause addiction, the emphasis must be placed on 'with care and patience'. In exercising care doctors have to forget their conditioned reflexes about prescribing. Drugs used for pain control cannot be administered in fixed doses at fixed intervals. They have to be given not according to set rules but according to each individual's need. Pain is of all things individual – no one else feels it. Given with care, opiates should neither cause someone to hallucinate nor should they cause someone to be 'so drugged up' that they are barely conscious. They do and can cause some dulling of alertness but they do not stop people functioning. Someone in pain, on the other hand, functions with extreme difficulty.

We have to forget the idea that suffering is noble – pain often strips people of their nobility and dignity and is extremely distressing to witness. One of the reasons why so many people give up trying to nurse a relative or friend at home is because of the distress to all that pain causes. Doctors and nurses can help those at home by teaching home-carers how to administer drugs. Having worked out a patient's needs, relatives can be taught how to give injections if necessary. One family we interviewed, who nursed their mother through a long terminal illness, found that being given the ability to administer drugs themselves helped greatly to minimise her pain and their distress. Whether patients or the relatives and friends of patients, we should remember that, as Jory Graham argued, we have 'the right to be free of pain'. We know that, even though pain cannot be totally eliminated, it can be greatly minimised. That knowledge should not only greatly reduce our fear but also increase our demands for that right.

Although pain, particularly that caused by cancer, is the main fear, there are other distressing physical conditions associated with mortal illness. Many people particularly fear death from respiratory failure. Fighting for breath is a common distressing feature of such cases. It is frightening to experience and to witness, but fortunately these attacks can often be relieved by morphia. The 'death rattle' is another feared condition, caused partially by saliva trickling down the throat and partially by the lungs waterlogging as the lungs fill. Injections of a drug called atropine and repositioning the patients can help to make them more comfortable. In these cases, as in most others, good skilled nursing can eliminate or minimise most physical discomforts.

Summing up what can be done, John Hinton in his book *Dying* wrote: 'With good care, the pain of most fatal conditions, including cancer, can usually be relieved. The breathlessness from failing heart or lungs too often remains an unsolved problem in the terminal phase.' However, getting good care, as Hinton found, is not always easy and those in ordinary hospitals and those at home without the help of skilled nursing are the most likely to suffer. A study carried out at St Christopher's of 100 patients dying consecutively in 1978–9 revealed that 98 out of the 100 patients died peacefully and it should be noted that these patients were ones referred to the hospice 'for the control of symptoms found difficult elsewhere'. Further study of the nursing notes revealed that 60 of the patients were peaceful for twenty-four hours or longer before their death, 27 experienced distress between four and twenty-four hours before, and only 13 experienced distress during their final four hours.

An important factor, besides medication and nursing, is the fact that so few suffered distress during their final hours must have been that only 6 died alone and all the rest had family and/or nursing staff with them. Nothing is more distressing or frightening than being alone, too weak to call or ring for help. Anyone who has been in that situation in a hospital can easily imagine how much more terrifying it must be when dying. There can be no doubt that the presence of someone with a dying person must greatly reduce fear, panic and distress. Of patients' state of consciousness, observations made at various times during the final twenty-four hours showed that 10 patients were recorded as 'alert', 23 were recorded as 'unrousable', 'unresponsive' or 'unconscious', and the remaining 67 were recorded as 'drowsy', 'rousable', or 'semi-conscious'. If, with good care as this study shows, a peaceful death can be given to most people, then that quality of care should be available for all who need it.

Little can be done to allay the fears we have of pain from sudden death. The only consolation is that the period of pain preceding sudden death is brief. Some people take solace from the stories of those who claim to have 'died' and returned to life. Their stories are comforting in that they are always of peace and light. However, as Cicely Saunders comments, 'Whether these are in fact experiences of "death" rather than of some form of altered consciousness appears unproven, indeed unprovable.' She goes on to say wisely that although these stories 'have helped some patients to lose their fear of death, in no way are they proof of immortality; that seems to remain a matter of faith'. Many people say that a sudden death is the one they would choose because they fear not just the possible physical pain of dying, but the emotional pain of saying good-bye. Sudden death not only makes it harder for the bereaved to come to terms with their loss, but it eliminates the possibility of the dying 'presiding over their death'.

Dying

Luis Buñuel, as an old man, wrote in *My Last Breath*: 'Sometimes I think, the quicker, the better – like the death of my friend Max Aub, who died all of a sudden during a card game. But most of the time I prefer a slower death, one that's expected, that will let me revisit my life for the last good-bye.' Being able to say the last good-bye is only possible if the knowledge that they are dying is made public to all concerned, including the dying themselves.

An end to the game of pretend

Death, in the Grimms' fairy tale 'Death's Messengers', to show his gratitude to the young man who had saved him from being incapacitated promised, 'I will not fall on you unexpectedly, but will send my messengers to you before I come and take you away.' Given that Death could 'spare no one' and could not, as he explained, make 'an exception' even of his saviour, sending a messenger was the greatest gift he could offer. The gift was appreciated by the young man, who recognised that, 'It is something gained that I shall know when you come.' Not only does the story seem to us a curious one to be read to children, but its content is at odds with twentieth-century attitudes and behaviour. We do not see a messenger of death as a gift, but the opposite, often going to considerable lengths to deny people the knowledge that they are dying. Katharine Moore expressed well the twentieth-century attitude of silence when she said: 'There is this strange conspiracy not to let people who are dying know that they are dying. It's supposed to be so dreadful. Whereas of course it comes to everybody. The people who are afraid to tell somebody that they're dying treat it as a strange calamity which is happening to this person alone, instead of something which will happen to them inevitably. I think it confers a sort of loneliness on the person who is dying, who is nearly always aware of it.'

For many, knowing that they are dying is a question of acknowledging that they are getting older and that their life will inevitably come to an end. This is the gentle way of coming to terms with dying. Recently a friend of ours came to stay the night. He is now in his early sixties and still leads an extremely active life. After I told him about the series *Merely Mortal* he told me that during the past two years, for the first time, he had realised that life would not go on for ever. He was aware of having less energy, of minor physical complaints and that his wife had recently had her first serious illness of their married life. Hopefully, both of them will have much more time slowly, through aging, to get used to the idea of dying. A quarter of a century older than him, Katharine Moore told us:

> One's vitality gets lowered on the physical side and you can't help knowing – I'm eighty-eight now and it's unlikely that I'll be here say in five, six, seven, eight years – and one already gets the feeling, 'Oh well, I shan't be here then,' which in some ways is a comfort, I'm afraid. But also I think age makes you face the fact that death is going to happen to you, that you're not going to be here any longer, and that's queer. I talk a lot about it being a natural thing and one has to accept it and it's happening to everybody, but it's a queer feeling. However much you have had to face death – and I've had to face it a lot during my life – it's still very funny to think it is going to happen to you. It's entertaining in a sort of a way.

Katharine Moore takes comfort from the fact that what many of her loved ones and friends have 'passed through, I shall pass through'. But her fear, and that of many others, is 'pain and helplessness'. Besides fearing pain there is an equally strong fear of losing the physical ability to care for oneself and of losing one's mental awareness. This anxiety is by no means unique to this century. Francis Bacon some three hundred years ago in his essay 'On Death' wrote, 'I make not love to the continuance of days, but to the goodness of them,' and indicated that he was 'not earnest to see the evening of my age; that extremity of itself being a disease and a mere return to infancy'. He died at the age of sixty-five, a good age for his times, but was saved from 'that extremity' he feared.

Although aging is often a preparation for dying, one cannot technically die of old age. Death certificates in Britain unfortunately require a doctor to give the *cause* of death – most other countries usually only require the *fact* of death to be certified – and old age is not regarded as an acceptable cause. Richard Lamerton in *Care of the Dying* reproduces a death certificate on which he had written under 'CAUSE OF DEATH 1 (a)' 'She died of old age.' The case was of an old woman under his care who had had no particular fatal illness but 'had just faded out peacefully and normally'. The certificate was returned to Richard Lamerton by the registrar, who informed him that if he did not fill in an acceptable diagnosis the coroner would have to be called in to perform an autopsy. To save the family the distress of going through the process of having a coroner called in he changed the form and gave, in inverted commas, a diagnosis. The adverse affect of having to give the medical cause of death is that statistics about mortality increase our fear that we will die of something. According to the statistics, heart diseases, cancer, bronchitis, pneumonia and cerebrovascular diseases are the main causes of death of people over eighty. Since we cannot statistically die of 'old age', we feel that in fact we cannot do so. Medically there is no natural end to our lives. That fact compounds the view, or hope, that since death is caused by a specific disease or diseases it is a medical failure and not a natural phenomenon.

Whether dying over the age of eighty or before, there is still for most people a point when their condition (or deterioration through age) is such that it can be called terminal. It is the point when, bar miracles, death is the only end. Pat Seed described that point in her book *One Day at a Time*. She had just had a second session of radiotherapy when her consultant asked if she would come into the office to talk to him. In his office sitting facing him across the desk she was told by him that: 'Things didn't look too good for me. He was sorry to have to give me such bad news, but in fact he had to tell me that I was dying. Dying? *Dying?* Every now and then, life deals us a blow which sends us reeling. This one pole-axed me. Knowing that you have cancer, you also know that there is always a possibility that it might kill you. But to have it spelled out for you, not as a possibility, but as *certainty* . . .'

Pole-axed, she asked him how long she had and he replied that he 'couldn't say with certainty'. Pat Seed recounts how at the time she expressed sympathy with the doctor in his difficult task of having to break bad news. Having agreed with her about the difficulty of his task, the doctor said, 'Of course, one couldn't tell every patient in your circumstances but I know you'd rather have the truth, Pat, than be fobbed off with plausible explanations.' When cancer had been initially diagnosed Pat Seed had signalled to her GP that she wanted the truth and he responded by saying, 'You don't know what a relief that is. There are times when I stand outside a house, trying to remember whether it is a home where the patient knows and the family doesn't – or vice versa.'

Clearly, Pat Seed's doctors assessed people and decided whether they would be able to receive 'the truth'. 'It is to be remembered,' as John Hinton pointed out, 'that while doctors are trying to judge their patients' capacity to stand unpleasant news, many patients are equally making their intuitive judgements of whether their doctor can bear sincere but difficult questions.' The debate about whether a doctor should tell or not is partly about whether the doctor is able to deal with the situation.

Doctors are ill-equipped and ill-trained in communication. In 1984 Robert Buckman wrote an article entitled 'Breaking bad news: why is it still so difficult?' The article looks at 'the anxieties and fears we [doctors] have which make it difficult to start the conversation; and those factors that drive us into taking responsibility for the disease itself, making it even more difficult once the conversation has been started'. It is an interesting article in that it explores many important aspects of medical behaviour and questions them. The reasons, Robert Buckman claims, why doctors fear giving bad news are to do with their professional status and the training which they receive. As professionals they fear that they will be blamed or seen as failures. 'Because', as an interviewee on the BBC Radio 4 programme 'In Sure and Certain Hope' said, 'medical science has developed so rapidly we think that doctors can cure anything.' Doctors feel that pressure of expectation and patients, when that expectation is not met, feel like the interviewee, 'terribly outraged. . . . I felt terribly cheated of all that doctors say they can now do.' More openness can reduce the expectation by patients that doctors are miracle workers, and doctors, by admitting to the limitations of medical science, can learn to see their inability to cure some cases as a limitation rather than a failure.

Another problem which doctors have to deal with is the fact that their training leads them to regard the expression of emotion by themselves or by others as an embarrassing disturbance in the smooth and orderly running of their work. If a patient cries, doctors tend to think they have failed to do the right thing to prevent it. 'It is not easy,' Robert Buckman writes, 'to suggest that a patient's crying is not in itself a disaster (for the doctor or the patient) or that the tears may actually have done the patient some good, when confronted by nurses or other doctors who, from the kindest motives, don't want the patients to be "disturbed".' What patients know is that they are expected to control their emotions or risk the penalties of being labelled 'hysterical' if they do break down. There is great pressure on patients, from doctors, to 'take the news' well or at least to do their crying somewhere other than in the consulting room or hospital ward. No one would assume that it is easy for doctors to break bad news, but Robert Buckman suggests that with training in communication skills and some changes in attitude doctors will at least be better equipped to do so.

The most fundamental change of attitude required is over

the question of their right to control information. Doctors have traditionally believed that they have the right to control information about our bodies. Our medical records are kept secret from us and we are only given such information as doctors deem we are able to take or understand. The question of control of information is central to all medical ethics, but is particularly pertinent to the dying. The patient has the right to know. What they do with that knowledge and how they deal with it is again their right. We have a right to know because, as a nurse who had lied to many patients and then found she had pancreatic cancer said, 'When truth is gone, everything is gone.' Without the truth, we cannot as patients give informed consent to any treatment. Knowledge of whether we are terminally ill or not may radically affect our decision as to whether we would accept certain treatments or not.

Over 90 per cent of healthy people, when asked in surveys if they would like to know whether they have a terminal illness, have replied that they would. If doctors *listened* to patients they would quickly, with few errors, detect that small minority who do not want to know, and they would hear the questions of the majority who do. As Cicely Saunders wrote, 'No one should have information forced upon them, but any continuing communication with a patient is likely to open up this subject sooner or later.' Continuing communication enables the establishment of mutual trust, and in a situation of trust questions can be asked and answered honestly. Telling is not, or should often not be, a 'one-off, one-way' situation but rather a slow exploration of a patient's condition. Patients can then offer their own knowledge and express their hopes and fears. The doctor can give hope, advice and admit to the inadequacies of medical knowledge without fearing that such an admission reflects on professional competence. Although doctors fear that patients will blame them for the truth, the blame is even greater if patients find out that the doctor is lying. Lying corrodes rather than strengthens any possible relation of trust between the doctor, the patient and others concerned. Lying may give short-term solace to doctor and patient, but sooner or later most lies are found out. Of the consequences of not telling Robert Buckman writes: 'Exerting control over this information may not alter things clinically, but it does offer the chance of behaving in a sort of doctorly way. This disguised therapeutic impotence originates from the very best of motives, and it's very difficult to realise while you are doing it that you may not be helping the patient and family at all.'

The kind of damage lying and deceit can cause to the patient and the family was well summed up by Gorer. Of the people who died from cancer in Gorer's study he found that in almost all of the cases 'the survivor was told by the doctor or hospital that their relative was incurable; but without exception the dying man or woman was kept in ignorance'. One widow interviewed by Gorer said, 'My doctor said *he* wasn't going to tell him, and the hospital wouldn't either; so if I tell him, he's not going to have much faith in the hospital, is he? It's just one of those things. I told him awful lies.' Of the effect of such deceit on the two interviewees quoted Gorer said, 'What had been good marriages (as the remainder of the interviews show) were reduced to unkindness or falsity by the doctor's professional (or, one might think in the case of the second case, pusillanimous) unwillingness to tell his patient the truth.' As in the case of the two widows quoted by Gorer, many people feel that if a doctor does not tell a patient then they have no right to either. There is a belief that if a patient does not know that they are dying they are likely, somehow, to die more easily. More often that argument is made by those who find it easier to deal with a dying person if they hide from them their knowledge.

Ironically, more often than not, the dying person knows that they are dying despite all the attempts made by doctors and relatives to shield them from that knowledge. In 1977 the *Chicago Tribune* carried an article by the science writer Ronald Kotaluk. It was about the tragic death of a twelve-year-old girl called Lisa and the fact that after her death her parents found some comfort in the fact that Lisa 'had been spared the agony of knowing' during her three-year illness that she had an incurable cancer. However, her mother in going through Lisa's things found her diary, which revealed that she had had complete knowledge of her illness but did not want to upset her parents by letting them know that she knew she was dying. Kotaluk commented on the situation, 'All those years of lying and pretending had been wasted. Instead of sharing one of life's deepest tragedies, they had played a game of pretend.' We have to stop thinking that it is in anyone's interest – doctors, relatives, friends or patients – to play a game of pretend.

Those most harmed by the game of pretend are the dying themselves. If they are dying in ignorance then doctors and relatives are cheating them of the chance to 'preside over their dying' in whatever manner they wish. If, like Lisa, they feel compelled to hide their knowledge they are not only cheated but are also condemned to isolation. Of the latter situation Jory Graham wrote: 'Denial and refusal of the right to talk about one's own life-threatening disease is the ultimate cruelty. It is solitary confinement, as bleak and unremitting as is any prison where, you realize, it is used as punishment for wrong-doing. . . . No one should ever be condemned to such total isolation. No rationalisation exists to support such punishment.'

Many dying people complain of the social isolation to which they are condemned. One interviewee in the Radio 4 programme 'In Sure and Certain Hope' said, 'Some people are so scared of facing me and my condition – I don't know what it is, I don't usually have time to ask them – that they will cross over the road rather than meet me.' It was a situation she found extremely 'distressing' even though she understood that the action of such people was caused by 'their fear' and not by the fact of her terminal illness.

Dying is an individual affair and the control of the knowledge about dying should be in the hands of the dying person themselves. They have a right to say, 'No, I do not want that knowledge,' and if, as most do, they want that knowledge they not only have a right to it but they should have the right to use it as they so wish. It is not only doctors who should listen to patients but other professionals, relatives and friends as well. If a dying person wishes to deal with the knowledge of their own dying by not talking about it, it is their right, hard as it may be sometimes for friends and relatives to respect. Mabel Heron, who helped nurse her dying sister, when asked in the programme 'Born to Die' if the family had talked to her sister about the fact that she was dying replied, 'Well, she knew and we knew but no one ever spoke about it. I think she tried to hide it from us to save us grief, and we were doing the same to her. So it was just avoided all the time. But she definitely knew she was, you could tell that.'

Mabel had tried once or twice to talk to her sister and on one occasion had brought a scapula so that they could pray together. Her sister remarked, 'Your scapula's doing me no good at all,' about which Mabel commented, 'That's just what she said, wasn't it? But that was it – no more.' Mabel gave her sister the chance to talk and, sensitively realising that she did not want to do so, let it rest. It was not a question of lying or deceit, but one of respecting the way in which a dying person wished to deal with their own situation. To force someone to talk can be as harmful as refusing to talk with them when they have clearly indicated that they would like to do so.

If everyone realised that the rights belong to the dying person then there would be no problem. There is a danger, though, that the changes made during the past two decades in improving the care of the dying have given rise to a body of theory about dying. In 1984 Cicely Saunders wrote a paper called 'On Dying Well', the content of which is a summation of the ideas behind the hospice movement. The title, however, implies more than I think she realises. From her perspective it puts much of the onus of a 'good' death on to the professionals caring for the dying, and there is no question that her work and the work of others have helped many to have a 'good' death.

However, from the perspective of a lay person the title implies that dying for us will be some kind of 'test' which we pass if we die 'well' and fail if we die badly. Passing the test involves our coming to terms with our dying and making others know that we have done so, finishing our unfinished business and dying with dignity. Not only are we put to the test, but those 'tests' have been formalised by the American Elizabeth Kübler-Ross into five stages. We are expected to pass each stage and move on to the next, finally reaching 'acceptance'. If we do not pass through the stages in the right order – denial and isolation; anger; bargaining; depression; acceptance – we will somehow be seen as having failed psychologically to deal with our own dying. Although Elizabeth Kübler-Ross first wrote about the 'stages' of dying in order to try and broaden an understanding of the emotions experienced by dying people, her words have sadly become in some cases the tablets of stone on which teaching about dying is based. Once again, other people are trying to control dying. The following poem written by a dying woman should act as a reminder that standards of behaviour should not be set for the dying, but only standards of care.

> *Not Cruel But True*
> No, that poem isn't cruel. It's true:
> > 'Do not go gentle into that good night,
> > Rage, rage against the dying of the light.'
> That is how I feel today.
> I know I shouldn't and I'm letting people down
> But I don't want the light to die.

The last good-bye

Given the knowledge that we are dying, we can then exercise our own control over that knowledge. Knowing that we are dying does give us the opportunity, if we so wish, as Luis Buñuel pointed out, to say a 'last good-bye'. Sudden death is not only more traumatic for the bereaved but it deprives the dying of consciously leaving this world.

It is interesting that many now would choose a sudden death, whereas in the Middle Ages it was greatly feared. Not only did sudden death deprive a person of taking leave, but there was the Christian fear that it was an expression of the wrath of God. Philippe Ariès in his book *The Hour of our Death* quotes a thirteenth-century bishop who, in addressing the question of sudden death, wrote: 'If a man dies suddenly while taking part in a game such as ball or bowls, he *may* be buried in a cemetery, because he was not trying to hurt anyone.' (The benefit of the doubt was not always extended to other victims of sudden death.) Our desire for sudden death is not just a reflection of our fear of physical pain but our fear of emotional pain. To have to carry the burden of the knowledge that we are dying is something that most people assume would be emotionally almost unbearable. However, in reality, many dying people find that that knowledge enables them, in a variety of ways, to organise their affairs and take leave of this world.

So often when someone dies the bereaved are left with the haunting memory of 'if only'. If knowledge of dying is shared, painful as the sharing of that knowledge may be, it does enable people to finish 'unfinished business'. The latter is a phrase that has come into use to describe the process of sorting out personal relationships and other affairs. John Hinton, who has spent much of his working life concerned with the dying, wrote about this process:

> Making the practical preparations for their approaching death can be an important and sometimes an emotionally rewarding task for the dying. They wish to leave no unfinished problems for their families. They complete the major tasks, like winding up their business affairs and making sure their will is in order. They often take great care over the minor arrangements – where they put things and who is to have the small properties – so that there should be no subsequent disagreements. Often the dying take great pleasure in knowing that all is handed over in good order to their successors.

Such organisational work can often be the final gesture of care and concern by a dying person to those that they love. Christopher Booker wrote in the *Daily Telegraph* a memorable article entitled 'Prepared for the End'. In it he cited the cases of three people he had known whose preparation for their own deaths had left a deep impression on him. The first was that of an old, deaf man who lived on his own. One day the man phoned his son, whom he hadn't seen for twenty years, and asked him to come to his flat. The normally untidy flat was 'in apple-pie order. There was a neat pile of letters ready to be posted, including every bill paid.' The son drove his father to the hospital, 'giving them a chance for a long conversation', and before the day was out the man was dead. Christopher Booker wrote of the case: 'It was an unforgettable episode, because of the extraordinary, transfiguring dignity with which that old man, out of the chaos and loneliness of his last years, rose perfectly prepared to meet his death.'

An equally moving account was that of the way his own father prepared for death. Knowing that he was dying of cancer, his father spent his last few weeks finishing unfinished business. That included not just sorting out his financial affairs but also mending a 'long-standing family rift', having long, careful conversations with his two children and phoning up his daughter-in-law and son-in-law 'for what amounted to a farewell'. 'Every word was considered and significant. And by the time he died everyone in the family was lifted up and inspired by the way he had played his part as head of the family during those last weeks. The way he had taken charge in face of his impending death left a profound impression which still remains with us all to this day.' Such preparation does clearly give solace to both the dying and the bereaved. It can also confer a dignity on the process of dying. Christopher Booker, like others, was deeply touched by witnessing that dignity. I remember visiting an aunt of mine in hospital the day before she died. Her serene calm and the way she spoke of how she had organised her affairs left on me a deep and lasting impression.

An aspect of organising death that concerns many dying

people is their funeral. The other case cited by Christopher Booker in his article was that of his aunt, who had not only organised her affairs but also organised her funeral. 'She left handwritten instructions as to precisely what sort of funeral she should be given, written in the humorous, down-to-earth way that had always characterised her approach to everything in life.' Since she wanted a particular priest who had been taken ill, she told him 'to hurry and get better because she wanted him to take her funeral'. The final touch to her arrangements was the ham that she had saved to be served for tea after her funeral service.

By contrast, some people, like Claude Moore in 'Born to Die', take the view that: 'Anybody who wants to pay for my funeral can do so, but I'm not paying for it. I'm not responsible for that.' His statement represents the attitude of those who feel that their own funeral is of little importance or concern to them. For them life ends with death and the manner of disposal of their body is the responsibility of the living. Others may well have strong feelings but are unable to express them. Removing the stigma of being 'morbid' can help people to state what they would like and be comforted by knowing their wishes will be met. Hazel Goldbrom, speaking in the same programme, explained her wishes:

> I've also made arrangements for my funeral. I've asked a particular one of Jehovah's Witnesses to take the funeral and I've made three copies of the letter exactly how I want the funeral to be taken because I feel very strongly on the subject. I don't want a coffin present at my funeral because I want it to be life-orientated, not death-orientated, and we speak very much about death. Priscilla [Hazel's friend] and I speak about it, the boys [Priscilla's sons] know that I am going to die. We all speak about it. It's not secret.

Hazel Goldbrom clearly finds peace in the fact that her funeral will be as she wishes. Jory Graham, terminally ill with cancer like Hazel, also found great comfort in organising her death. In her book *In the Company of Others* she lists the instructions she has given about her death. They include giving her physician the right to perform an autopsy and denying any funeral director the right to embalm. She wishes her body to be cremated and her ashes buried 'in a place of my choosing'. Like Hazel, she wrote down instructions for a memorial service but also wrote her own obituary and the wording she wanted on her headstone. The reason, Jory Graham explains, for doing all this is 'so that no one will have to guess my wishes, and because making these simple decisions gives me a firm sense of directing parts of my own dying — for I may not have control over the rest'.

Perhaps the hardest part of saying the 'last good-bye' is having to say good-bye to those one loves. Age makes the task easier. For someone like Katharine Moore who, at the age of eighty-eight, has witnessed the death of most of the people she has loved, there are fewer painful good-byes. Most have already been said. Younger people not only have to say good-bye, but have to deal with the pain their death is causing others. Pat Seed, who was able to tell not only her husband about her terminal illness but also 'the world' through being interviewed on radio, understandably baulked at telling her mother the truth. When her mother asked, having read about her daughter in a newspaper, 'What's all this about you being a dying woman?' Pat Seed, a newspaper reporter herself, replied, 'It's only newspaper talk,' and deflected the conversation by suggesting, 'Let's put the kettle on and make a cuppa.' That incident happened in the summer and it took her until Christmas, when she was temporarily feeling and looking better, to be able to tell her mother 'the true facts'. There is no question that to tell those one loves a painful truth is very hard, but once done that knowledge can be shared. The dying person is not left isolated and those to be bereaved can also benefit from the knowledge.

In the final stages communication can often just be physical. There are many cases of people who have, when sitting by a dying loved one, said afterwards that the person 'just squeezed my hand and gave me a faint smile' and that was understood by both as the final good-bye. In other cases the dying person presides in a more articulate way, giving final messages, instructions or comments. In the past, close family members would remain at the bedside during the final stage. In the section on 'Last Words' in the *Oxford Book of Death* the editor D. J. Enright admits that of those he has selected 'if they are not literally authentic, they are authentically in character' and that 'no doubt in the past ghost-writers have taken a hand and embellishments have crept in over the years'.

However, regardless of their literary authenticity the interesting thing is that people were expected to say 'last words' and the saying of them is predicated on the knowledge that they are about to die and that someone is there to listen to them. Although many people drift out of life, the majority, as shown in the survey done by St Christopher's Hospice, have periods of consciousness during their final twenty-four hours. It is in these periods that the last good-bye can be said. Generally, hearing is the last sense a dying person loses. That fact should be a warning to all those around a deathbed who talk about the dying person in the assumption that because they are semi-conscious they cannot hear. All too often they *can* hear, but have not the breath or strength to talk. The bonus of the fact that many retain their hearing to the end is that much comfort can be given through a soothing voice, as well as the physical comfort that can be given by holding a hand.

In our own time

There is much evidence that people, given the chance, exercise within certain obvious confinements control over the timing of their death. That control, something not possible in sudden death, is dependent on the medical profession allowing it. We find it strange to read about the peasant woman who told her priest, 'I am ready now to die.' Indeed, we think that anyone who says such a thing must be mentally unstable or has some secret reason for not wanting to continue living. The only socially acceptable reason for someone not wanting to live is if they are in unremitting, intolerable pain. But part of reclaiming our right to preside over our dying must be to exercise as much control as possible over that timing.

Elizabeth Kübler-Ross used the term 'bargaining' for what I would prefer to call control of timing. It is an important difference, for she likens 'bargaining' to the behaviour of a child who has been denied something and who then, to get its own way, offers to be good and do helpful things. 'The bargaining,' she writes, 'is really an attempt to postpone; it has to include a prize offered for "good behaviour", it also sets a self-imposed deadline . . . and it includes an implicit promise that the patient will not ask for more if this postponement is granted.' Apparently none of her patients 'kept their promise', and again she likens them to children who say, ' "I will never fight my sister again if you let me go." Needless to add, the little boy will fight his sister again.' Control of timing, in contrast, is the mature reaction to reality. Many people keep themselves alive for something important – the birth of a grandchild, a wedding, a visit from a relative, to see spring or to settle their affairs. Having achieved their desire, they are ready to die. Pat Seed, after being told that she was dying, set out to raise a million pounds to buy Manchester's Christie Hospital a CAT scanner, a machine which can diagnose cancer in its earliest stages. She achieved her goal before dying. Although she may not have consciously said to herself, 'This I must do before I am ready to die,' in reading her book *One Day at a Time* one has a distinct sense of that goal. Her behaviour could hardly be likened to that of a child.

There is a literary example of people knowing that the time is right. In Dickens's *David Copperfield* Mr Peggotty tells David that Barkis 'is going out with the tide', and then explains to David, who is unaware of local dying habits, 'People can't die along the coast except when the tide's nigh out.' The two wait and watch by Barkis's bedside until

Mr Peggotty touches David's arm and whispers 'with much awe and reverence, "They are both going out fast."' Barkis's famous last words were, 'Barkis is willin'.' 'And,' Dickens writes, 'being low water, he went out with the tide.' In that phrase Dickens gives the sense of dying being at one with, not an outrage to, nature. Perhaps Dickens had used literary licence which Richard Lamerton does not in describing the foreknowledge and control of timing his grandmother exercised at her death. In his book *Care of the Dying* he remembers how in 1960, when his grandmother realised she had breast cancer, she took out all her savings and went on a shopping spree: 'My mother was puzzled, but accompanied her as she bought shoes, silk stockings, lacy underwear, a smart costume, matching hat and handbag and a pair of white gloves. They were all carefully stored in drawers and cupboards (with mothballs, I'm afraid!) and the mystery deepened. Then, on the day of her death, she asked to be fully decked out in the whole outfit "because I'm going before God today".' Like Richard Lamerton's grandmother, the examples cited by Christopher Booker of his aunt and the old man were both clearly cases of people who knew (the old man knowing to the day) when they were going to die.

Unfortunately, modern medicine has greatly complicated the question of controlling the timing of our death. 'Science,' Miguel de Unamuno wrote, 'says, "We must live," and seeks the means of prolonging, increasing, facilitating and amplifying life, of making it tolerable and acceptable; wisdom says, "We must die," and seeks how to make us die well.' The medical profession in their attitude towards death have been torn between science and wisdom. The training of doctors is based on 'science', while the hospice movement was born out of 'wisdom'. The latter argues *for* an acceptance of the right time to die and *against* either hastening the termination of life (euthanasia) or the unnecessary prolongation of life. As regards the latter, it can be very difficult for doctors to decide at which point active treatment should be stopped but care continued. Almost all books written on the subject are written by doctors who assume that this decision is the burden of doctors alone. It is a burden doctors have placed upon themselves by, for the most part, refusing to base their practices on informed consent. In some situations, such as whether to resuscitate a cardiac-arrest patient, the patients themselves cannot make that decision, but in many cases the dying themselves could, and indeed should, be given the opportunity for choice. The patients themselves can decide whether they want further major surgery which would give them a little extra time, or whether they would prefer not to undergo the trauma when it would not greatly alter the outcome. Some treatments, chemotherapy for instance, can have such unpleasant side-effects that patients may well decide they would rather have less, but qualitatively better, time. Sadly, all too rarely are patients consulted about their treatment, the choices of treatment or whether treatment should be stopped.

One man with only a few weeks to live did decide to challenge the doctor's right to make such decisions on his behalf. In 1984 Peter Holtom went into hospital for what he thought would be minor surgery. When they opened him up the surgeon found irreversible stomach cancer and decided, whilst his patient was unconscious, to perform extensive surgery. Afterwards Peter Holtom argued that the surgeon had had no right to make that decision for him. In a television interview he said: 'The doctor's view of what are my best interests are not the same as my own view of my best interests and he had no right to make this assumption. By doing so he has deprived me of the right to make the decisions I need to make for myself and my family.' Peter Holtom, like many many others in Britain, had not given his informed consent to treatment. In theory informed consent obliges doctors to inform patients both of alternatives and of risks and side-effects to any treatment. Patients can then, informed, give their consent to the treatment they choose.

As an ethical basis for practice the doctrine of informed

consent is now enshrined in US Federal Law and is also practised in Canada. However, in Britain the patient still has few rights, for in this country informed consent is not a central tenet of medical ethics. Indeed in 1985, in the case of Mrs Amy Sidaway who claimed that she would never have agreed to an operation had she been informed that there was a risk of her being left partially paralysed, the Law Lords ruled that the doctor was not obliged to inform her of all the potential risks. Lord Diplock said: 'The only effect that mention of risk can have on the patient's mind, if it has any at all, can be in the direction of deterring the patient from undergoing the treatment which in the expert opinion of the doctor it is in the patient's interests to undergo.'

One might ask how doctors know what is in their patient's best interest. An individual doctor has one opinion and another is likely to have a completely different one. Medicine is not an exact science. Speaking passionately for the right of informed consent, Jory Graham wrote: 'The patient is the master of his or her own person. Informed consent is not just a theory, nor is it a token gesture, a toy to be withheld by those who play God. It is each patient's absolute right, assigned by ethics, justice, the law, and our humanitarian traditions. With his expectations, with his pain, with his life, and with his money, the patient is the one who will pay. To him who pays belongs the right to call the tune.'

Patients should learn to call the tune and exercise control over their destinies. NHS patients pay for their treatment even though the cash relationship with the doctor is not as immediate or direct as in the USA. We should remember when confronted by the power and authority of the medical profession, as Carolyn Faulder wrote in *Whose Body Is It?*, that 'Our bodies belong to us. They are who we are. The person we are reposes in their material form.' Doctors should learn to respect the ownership by each individual of their own body and not trespass, without permission, on human property that does not belong to them. Informed consent is no more than a respect for the individual patient. Based on that respect crucial decisions could then be made by patient and doctor, and doctors would no longer need to burden themselves with the onerous task of 'playing God'. It is surprising that doctors, who complain about the fact that they have to carry so much responsibility, do not usually share that responsibility willingly with the patient. People's fears, which are great, that they will have their life prolonged unnecessarily could be greatly allayed by the realisation that they can exercise some control over that decision.

As a reaction to loss of control and the ability of modern medicine to keep us alive in what we feel can be a sub-human state, the debate about euthanasia has arisen. The debate for most people is not now about the right to choose to end one's life. Suicide is no longer a crime in Britain and has not been since the Suicide Act of 1961, though for believers in certain religions it remains unacceptable. Roman Catholics, for instance, regard it as a mortal sin. What complicates the euthanasia debate is that ending one's life when one is senile or terminally ill usually requires the assistance of someone else. Legally, although suicide is not a crime it is illegal to assist a suicide. Euthanasia is therefore technically illegal.

One of the most coherent arguments against the need for euthanasia is made by supporters of the hospice movement. Richard Lamerton sums up the argument in these words: 'Once a patient feels welcome, and not a burden to others; once his pain is controlled and other symptoms have been at least reduced to manageable proportions, then the cry for euthanasia disappears. It is not that the question of euthanasia is right or wrong, desirable or repugnant, practicable or unworkable. It is just that it is irrelevant.'

Strong as this argument is, it still does not allay the fears of those who, like Luis Buñuel, see a 'horrible death' as one 'that's kept at bay by the miracles of modern medicine – a death that never ends'. Many would share his sentiment that, 'In the name of Hippocrates, doctors have invented the most exquisite form of torture ever known to man: survival.' Those who support euthanasia see it as the only answer to that exquisite torture. It is the answer of the desperate. Requests for euthanasia usually come either from dying people themselves or from relatives who feel that such an act would be a 'mercy'. 'It seems a terrible indictment,' John Hinton commented, 'that the main argument for euthanasia is that many suffer unduly because there is a lack of preparation and provision for the total care of the dying.'

Although euthanasia is and always has been technically illegal, it has and does happen in practice. The practice varies from the most overt – giving someone a lethal dose – to the covert, which is usually when active measures to keep someone alive are ceased. The decision to hasten the end of someone's life is normally taken by relatives and doctors in agreement, though sometimes it is taken by either party on their own. Traditionally, the medical profession has argued for doctors to have the right to use their discretion and against the imposition of any legal guidelines. The most astounding example of that medical position was recently revealed when the notebooks of Lord Dawson of Penn, King George V's doctor, were made public. On 27 November 1986, fifty years after the King's death, the *Guardian* reported that 'the celebrated medical bulletin, "The King's life is moving peacefully towards its close", was the prelude to death by euthanasia – with the timing arranged in part to catch the morning newspapers'. According to Lord Dawson's notebooks, the decision to give the King a lethal mixture of morphine and cocaine was not made to relieve pain (the only grounds the British Medical Association now regard as ethically acceptable) but to shorten 'the final scene'.

'Hours of waiting,' wrote Lord Dawson, 'just for the mechanical end when all that is really life has departed only exhausts the onlookers and keeps them so strained that they cannot avail themselves of the solace of thought, communion or prayer.' Finally, Lord Dawson justified the timing of his action on the grounds that the death should 'receive its first announcement in the morning papers rather than the less appropriate evening journals'. Later that year, 1936, in the House of Lords Lord Dawson spoke against a bill on voluntary euthanasia: 'This is something that belongs to the wisdom and conscience of the medical profession.' In the intervening fifty years many have questioned the wisdom and conscience of the medical profession and their right to have control over such decisions. Lord Dawson's actions would not now be found acceptable.

The argument continues despite the fact that it has not had governmental attention since 1969, when a Bill was debated in the House of Lords. Then, as in 1936, the advocates of voluntary euthanasia lost their argument. Although many supported the bill, what emerged was the difficulty of making any acceptable legal framework that would guard against abuse. One man, Derek Humphrey, believes that the framing of legal guidelines is possible and argues his case in a book, *The Right to Die – Understanding Euthanasia*. In an interview about the book he told Polly Toynbee:

> We want to introduce a power of attorney for health care, in the same way as you can make a power of attorney for financial matters. While sane and fit, you could choose to sign a paper giving someone else the right to act for you, in your interests, should you become no longer able to make decisions for yourself. As long as it is open, and legal, with proper guidelines, I don't see there needs to be any problem.

Part of his argument is based on the experience of Holland, which has a form of voluntary euthanasia. There a pact can be made between doctor and patient, but the family is not permitted either to suggest or veto the act.

The British Voluntary Euthanasia Society now issue cards for those who wish to carry them. Like donor cards, they are designed so that their members can carry around, in case of need, an expression of their wishes. The cards ask for the person to fill in the name of the next of kin and, like donor cards, there is a space for members to sign a statement of permission for the medical use of organs after death. However, unlike donor cards, members carrying this card can also sign the following statement: 'If there is no reasonable prospect of recovery I do *not* wish to be resuscitated or my life to be artificially prolonged.' Those who are not reassured by the arguments of the hospice movement and find unacceptable the possible 'exquisite torture' of survival might well consider carrying such a card. It has no legal standing, but at least it indicates the individual's wishes. In a situation where doctors and relatives are unsure what to do they would at least have the guidance of the person most concerned.

One can proffer no simple answer to the question of euthanasia. Even the Pope has found the question a dilemma. The Catholic Church has always opposed any form of euthanasia on the grounds that the disposal of life is in God's hands. However, a recent document issued by the Pope revealed that, as Norman St John Stevas pointed out in the *Standard* on 29 January 1987, 'On the principle the Pope is unyielding but on the practice he is more flexible. That document makes it clear that there is no obligation to use any means to prolong human life.' Summing up the Pope's position, Norman St John Stevas said, 'In short, the Pope is balancing the right to live by declaring there is also a right to die in peace.'

It is that balancing act which is so problematical ethically, legally and medically. No doubt the desire for euthanasia would be greatly reduced if doctors, as Buñuel wrote, 'would only let us die when the moment comes, and help us to go more easily'. The more people who are allowed to die 'when the moment comes' and the more, through good care, they are 'helped to go easily', the fewer people will think euthanasia an answer. The fewer too will be the requests for it. Hopefully, the solution to the debate lies in its becoming increasingly less relevant. Whilst some will always see suicide as a way out of what for them has become an intolerable life, a change in attitude by all can make dying a more acceptable experience and one less feared. Norbert Elias in *The Loneliness of Dying* wrote realistically and eloquently about the need for change:

> What people can do to secure for each other easy and peaceful ways of dying has yet to be discovered. The friendship of those who live on, the feeling of dying people that they do not embarrass the living, is certainly part of it. And social repression, the veil of unease that frequently surrounds the whole sphere of dying in our days, is of little help to people. Perhaps we ought to speak more openly and clearly about death, even if it is by ceasing to present it as a mystery. Death hides no secret. It opens no door. It is the end of a person. What survives is what he or she has given to other people, what stays in their memory. If humanity disappears, everything that any human being has ever done, everything for which people have lived and fought each other, including all secular and supernatural systems of belief, becomes meaningless.

CHAPTER FOUR

After a Death

> At one point we got on the theme of immortality, in which she believed without being sure of its precise form. 'There is no death,' she said. 'No, my dear lady, but there are funerals.'
>
> (*Comfort Me With Apples*, Peter De Vries, b. 1910)

Thomas Mann wrote: 'A man's death is more the survivors' affair than his own.' Dealing with death is, both legally and emotionally, the responsibility and burden of the survivors. It is a situation in which the law, money, beliefs, emotions and social ritual are all involved. Most of us are ill-informed and ill-equipped to deal with death. The law is confusing. Costs can be very high. It is only a minority now that have religious beliefs which dictate ritual actions and behaviour following a death. In the absence of a religious or social ritual the bereaved are usually left to muddle through as best they can. The desire of our society to turn its back on death has not only had a profound effect on the treatment of the dying, but it has also had an equally profound effect on attitudes to bereavement.

Death as an embarrassment to our society is nowhere more evident than when someone dies. Dead bodies are secretly scuttled out of houses and hospitals to a mortuary. Friends and relatives of the bereaved do not know what their role should be or what they should do. Doctors are embarrassed and usually offer little more help and support than tranquillisers or sleeping pills. At the centre are the bereaved, who have to deal with the legalities, the costs, their own emotions and the absence of any supporting social rituals. Although it is easier for the purposes of a book to break down the period immediately following a death into separate sections, in real life they interact, each affecting the other. The importance of the period immediately after a death is that crucial decisions have to be made which can affect the rest of one's life. If this period is handled in a way that meets the needs of the bereaved, it can help to start the process of grief and the coming-to-terms with death and loss. Decisions often have to be made quickly after a death by people who are in a state of shock. There are many ways in which the bereaved can be helped to make the right decisions – 'right' meaning right for them in that the choices made meet their emotional needs. The choices are not entirely free, for some are tied up with costs and legal requirements, but within those confines there are usually still many important choices to make.

Seeing the dead

Unless the bereaved are with someone when they die, or find that person dead, then one of the first choices to be made is whether they wish to see the dead body. It is a choice created by the twentieth century when many deaths do not occur in the home. The choice is further complicated by whether the bereaved wish to see the body immediately after death, or would prefer not to see it until later in a chapel of rest at an undertaker's. Given that there is no generally accepted ritual any more about viewing the dead, individuals have to make their own choice and usually there is no one around to help guide them. The only time seeing the body may be forced on the bereaved is for purposes of identification, and this is almost always a deeply traumatic experience.

Like so many other rituals surrounding death, the laying-out of the body for people to view meets an important human need. Most people are in a state of shock and disbelief immediately after a death. They use phrases like, 'It hasn't sunk in yet', 'It's not real', 'I still expect them to . . .', 'I feel numb' and, particularly in the case of sudden death, 'I can't believe it'. In that state of shock the visual image is that of someone alive as last seen, and it is

After a Death

extremely hard to create a visual image of them dead. Many feel that they want to hold on to that visual image and that to see someone dead will eradicate the living memory. Seeing someone dead is often the first important step in comprehending the reality of their death. Dead people look different from the living. Except in the case of death through a mutilating accident, dead people retain their physical characteristics, and yet without life those physical characteristics are subtly but definitely altered. It is important that people are prepared for that alteration, and yet it is that very alteration which helps the bereaved to see the person as dead.

Those that are present at a death usually witness that alteration in the gentlest and most acceptable way. It is worth remembering that most people who were with someone when they died were, later, glad that they had been. Although the actual death, however much expected, comes as a shock, the acceptance of that death is made easier for having witnessed it. Hospitals tend not to encourage relatives to stay with the dying or to view the dead before they have been removed to the mortuary, though they usually extend the choice to the bereaved. After the death of my own son we were asked by the hospital if we wished to see him. Of the decision to see him I wrote in *Will, My Son*: 'I was hesitant but Ed was sure that he did. We both went. It was the final reality, a reality so devastatingly real it seemed unreal. But it is that final reality, that final memory that is imprinted on me irradicably. That is death.'

Hospices, recognising that their role is to help the bereaved as well as the dying, take a different view from that of hospitals, which is now filtering through to hospitals. Knowing of the need for the bereaved to confront that 'final reality', whilst not forcing anyone to view a dead body, they encourage it. By accepting death and treating the dead body with dignity, as opposed to something to be scuttled out under cover, they try to create an atmosphere which enables the bereaved to feel that they are welcome at the bedside of the dead.

Those unable to see the deceased at or immediately after their death can choose either to see them laid out at the undertaker's or to have the body laid out at home prior to the funeral. Often religion or accepted social ritual will dictate whether either of these happen. In Britain the working-class tradition of having the dead person brought to the house and laid out in a coffin in the front parlour before the funeral was at one time very common. It enabled the family and friends to pay their final respects but, more importantly, it enabled the bereaved to sit quietly and, in the confines of their own home, confront the reality of death. Many regard the tradition as macabre and, instead, visit the dead body at the undertaker's. Undertakers always ask if the bereaved wish to view a body and meet the wishes of those who do.

Many adults do wish to see the dead person, but few adults recognise that children may need that experience to help them accept and understand the reality of the death of someone important to them. Although there are descriptions of children who were terrified by having to file past a relative laid out in a coffin, on the whole, for children and adults, death becomes more comprehensible for having witnessed it. Many of our fears as adults about dying and death stem from the fact that we were too 'protected' from it as children. In the programme 'Born to Die' Christine McGee described how her mother had died in their family's front room, where the family had nursed her throughout a long terminal illness. After the death, instead of instantly getting the body removed before the children came home from school, they left it there. The children came home from school, they all ate fish and chips for tea and could see and say good-bye to their grandmother before the undertakers came and removed the body. Although Christine had feared the effect it might have on the children afterwards, she commented: 'It turned out perfect.'

After a Death

Disposing of the dead

One of the first decisions to be made following a death is the manner of disposal of the body. It is legally required that the body is disposed of, but before that can be done certain other requirements have to be met. There is in fact a maze of laws relating to inquests, burial, cremation and disinterment of the dead. This body of law has built up since the 1850s, when the government began to regulate procedures and collect statistics. For most of us there are only a few important legal requirements. These are that within five days of a death it be registered with the local Registrar of Births and Deaths, and that a doctor provide the registrar with a certificate stating the cause of death. Where there is no doubt about the cause, after registration a certificate for the disposal of the body will be issued. If there is any doubt the coroner is called in and a certificate for the disposal of the body cannot be issued until the coroner's inquiry has been completed. (Details of these legal requirements can be found at the end of this book.) Whatever the wishes of the bereaved, these formalities cannot be avoided; they simply have to be done.

They can, however, be done by others (for a list see pp. 170–1). Registering a death can be an extremely upsetting task for the bereaved and it can also be, particularly for the old or disabled, physically difficult. The offices of the Registrars of Births and Deaths are not always situated in places easily accessible to all. The task of registration is something that can be done by others. This is not only of practical help but many bereaved, in the first five days, would prefer emotionally not to have to sign on the dotted line. To have to do so forces them to sign to a reality of death that they are still struggling to comprehend.

All societies have rules about disposing of the dead. For all the infinite variety of rituals surrounding death, there are and have been two main methods of disposal: burial – whether in the ground, in the sea or in tombs – and burning. The exceptions are few: for example, leaving the dead body to birds of prey was once practised in Mexico, Mongolia, East Africa and among the ancient Persians. Religions have often dictated which of these methods are practised and in what precise way they are performed. In the West, burial was the accepted form of disposal from the early days of the Roman Empire until the late nineteenth century, when cremation became an alternative. Christians buried their dead in the belief that a decent burial was a necessary pre-condition to ensuring that the spirit rose from the dead. The place of burial, however, varied. Initially, they inherited the practices of their pagan counterparts who, fearing the spirits of the dead, buried them at some distance from the living. Cemeteries and burial grounds were thus always outside the city walls. Attitudes changed and it became the practice to bury the dead in and around churches. The rich tended to have their burial place in the church, the poor in the churchyard.

This method of disposal did not present any problem until the cities grew and the churchyards became grossly overcrowded. The poor rarely had an individual grave and the churchyards increasingly became places in which bodies were piled up on top of each other, exposing the living to disease and revealing what seems to us a shocking disrespect for the dead. 'We saw several graves open and the bones thick on the top', was one description by Samuel Steward of a seventeenth-century cemetery. Another was by John Evelyn, who wrote in his diary that cemeteries were 'filled up with earth, or rather the congestion of dead bodies one above the other, to the very top of the walls, and some above the walls'. The city cemetery was clearly a very different place from that which Thomas Gray described in his 'Elegy Written in a Country Churchyard', where,

> Beneath those rugged elms, that yew-tree's shade,
> Where heaves the turf in many a mould'ring heap,
> Each in his narrow cell for ever laid,
> The rude Forefathers of the hamlet sleep.

After a Death

The situation in the cities was to get much worse before anything was done. It was not the Church nor the government which set about providing decent and hygienic places to bury the dead, but private companies. In 1830 the General Cemetery Company was founded to meet growing demand. In 1831 they bought their first site in Kensal Green, now in London, then in the country. The thirty-nine acres of the site to the north of the canal were consecrated by the Bishop of London, but the fifteen acres to the south were reserved for non-believers. Londoners had a place to bury their dead, but at a cost. Providing cemeteries proved profitable to the Company and they expanded to open what became the most famous of all Victorian cemeteries, Highgate. More private cemeteries were opened in London and in other cities.

One of the most innovative companies, the London Necropolis and National Mausoleum Company, opened Brookwood Cemetery primarily for Londoners. Their idea was to transport the funeral cortège by special train from Waterloo Station to Brookwood. For that purpose they opened three stations – one for ordinary passengers, one for Anglican funerals and one for 'Dissenters, Roman Catholics, Parsees and others'. On the trains passengers, including the dead, were further divided by class. Money bought first-class travel for the dead. In the 1850s a parliamentary report criticised the speculative element of private companies, and this was followed by the government enacting that local Boards of Health could also establish cemeteries. Since then the situation regarding burial has remained basically unchanged. The choice is usually dictated by belief, expressed wish, availability of space, location and/or cost and is between churchyards and local authority or privately owned cemeteries.

Cremation, although a very old form of disposal, was for many centuries not practised or accepted in Britain. Christianity, with its emphasis on resurrection, favoured burial and the Church therefore opposed cremation even though they could not themselves provide decent burials in many places, particularly in the cities. Italian law, which required that anything washed up by the sea had to be burnt on the shore as a precaution against disease, provided in 1822 a case of cremation which fuelled many imaginations. The drowned bodies of Shelley and his friend Williams were washed up on the shore near Viareggio and were therefore burnt; the skeleton of Shelley was then taken and buried in a Protestant cemetery in Rome. This was no doubt a fitting place for a poet who had written: 'The cemetery is an open space among the ruins, covered in winter with violets and daisies. It might make one in love with death, to think that one should be buried in so sweet a place.' Throwing his ashes to the wind would not have been acceptable, however.

It was to be almost three-quarters of a century after the deaths of Shelley and Williams before cremation was legally accepted in Britain. The main campaigner for it was Sir Henry Thompson, Queen Victoria's surgeon. He had been impressed by a model of cremating apparatus that he had seen at an exhibition in Vienna. The main arguments put forward at the time in favour of cremation were that it provided a sanitary form of disposal, particularly in the cities where land for burial was scarce and cemeteries 'covered in winter with violets and daisies' rare. A society, the Cremation Society of England, was formed to further the cause of campaigning for cremation. Members of the Society signed a declaration stating: 'We, the undersigned, disapprove the present system of burying the dead, and we desire to substitute some mode which shall rapidly resolve the body into its component elements by a process which cannot offend the living, and shall render the remains perfectly innocuous. Until some better method is devised we desire to adopt that usually known as cremation.'

Despite their arguments, the Home Office refused to change its position until in the early 1880s a judge ruled in a case of cremation that it was legal provided that the process caused no nuisance to others. Finally, in 1885 in Woking the first person was legally cremated. Since then cremation has slowly gained acceptability. Some religions still prohibit cremation whilst others – Hindus, for example – have always disposed of their dead by burning. During this century some religions have changed their policy to permit it; in 1963 the Pope proclaimed that it was no longer prohibited for Roman Catholics.

For those not bound by religious doctrine the question of the manner of disposal of their body is one of choice. For the bereaved the choice is made considerably easier if they know what the wishes of the dead person had been. Those wishes can have been expressed verbally, discussed or written down. If they are written down it is important that the bereaved know where to quickly and easily find them. Including them in a will does not guarantee that the information will be communicated at the relevant time. Wills are often not read until after a funeral and other instructions may not be found. Simone de Beauvoir in *A Very Easy Death*, having described her mother's funeral service in a chapel in which the catafalque was devoid of flowers because the undertakers had left them in the hearse, wrote that afterward, 'In a blotting-pad that I had brought back from the clinic I found two lines on a narrow piece of paper, written by Maman in a hand as stiff and firm as when she was twenty: "I should like a very simple funeral. No flowers or wreaths. But a great many prayers." Well, we had carried out her last wishes, and all the more faithfully since the flowers had been forgotten.'

In the case of religious believers, those wishes may be implicitly known through the doctrines of the religion and therefore do not need to be explicitly communicated. In the absence of such information, except with the death of a small child or in a case where the choice is dictated by protocol, most people wish to do what they feel the dead person would have liked. A funeral is in a sense the last act the living do for the dead, and in doing it they feel they are carrying out the 'last wishes'; this feels right for most, and what feels right gives consolation. Sadly, however, all too frequently people argue about what the dead person would have liked, and when it is left to family and friends to make the choice much anguish can be caused. Families split and argue about cremation or burial, religious service or not and whether to have a large funeral or small. Forgotten often, in the arguments, is that disposing of the dead is an important event for close relatives. It is their needs which should be primarily considered and where possible met.

It is interesting to note that we use the phrase 'to bury the dead' both literally and metaphorically. It is necessary both to physically bury the dead (or dispose of the body in an acceptable way) and to emotionally bury them. Funerals provide, or should provide, both the physical disposal in a dignified manner and an emotional chance to start the process of metaphorically burying the dead.

Funerals

In disposing of the body all that the law requires is that it be disposed of in an acceptable manner and in an acceptable place following the formalities of registration and the issuing of a certificate of disposal (see p. 173). Social, religious and emotional requirements are much greater. A funeral is much more than the disposing of a body. It is the formal mark of the end of someone's life. As such it can be anything from the performing of the most basic necessities of burial or cremation to a funeral with all the pomp and ceremony of the last King, George VI. As with the manner of disposal of the body, the choice is greatly helped if they know the wishes of the dead person. Of the funeral of Christopher Booker's aunt who died leaving precise instructions he said: 'By the time we all gathered at the little village church of Ugglebandy last Wednesday afternoon, with the sun shining down on the snow-covered moors she loved, nothing was a greater source of strength to her grieving family than the all-pervading sense that she had been completely ready for this month.' Not only had her instructions revealed that she was prepared to die, but those left living could take consolation from the fact that they had fulfilled her final wishes. For the dying there is no guarantee that their wishes will be met, but expressing them can be of great help. It relieves the bereaved of the burden of choice, can quash potential family arguments and can assist greatly in making those involved in the funeral feel that they are doing 'the right thing'.

Central to funerals is the need for the living to, in all senses, bury the dead. Amidst all the paraphernalia of funerals that central need and function can be lost. Social requirements often dictate what kind of funeral is expected. Some of these requirements can be of great support to the bereaved and others can place enormous emotional and financial strain on them. It was Puritan reaction to the undignified casualness of many seventeenth- and eighteenth-century funerals that led to a demand for decent and dignified ones. During the nineteenth century demand for such funerals became almost a national obsession, with decency and dignity often equated with the size and cost of the funeral. Katharine Moore remembered funeral parades before the First World War and 'the funeral horses with their long tails going through the streets. They were taught specially to go slowly and to step high.' She remembered also the 'deep black-edged notepaper that everyone used' and that 'widows had to wear black for a year and then they were allowed to wear a little mauve and grey and they had great bands of crêpe on their skirts and hat'.

The expectation that people should have a 'good funeral' was shared by all classes. Working-class families, if they had not saved for a funeral, could find themselves heavily in debt afterwards. It was, however, quite common for people to save money for their own funeral. John Morley in *Death, Heaven and the Victorians* wrote that in the mid-nineteenth century 'From a total of £24 million deposited with savings banks, £6 to £8 million was saved in order to meet funeral expenses.' One of the funds established by friendly societies and trade unions was the death benefit, whereby members saved to enable them to draw benefit to help meet the costs of a funeral; trade unions still provide death benefit. Other schemes were also established, and still exist, whereby people can save up for or put money aside for the cost of their own or someone else's funeral.

It was during the nineteenth century that elaborate funerals became the fashion and it was not surprising that the funeral business boomed. People were often under pressure to spend more on the coffin, the cortège, the place of burial, the funeral gathering, the headstone, mourning clothes, mourning stationery, etc. than they could really afford. Undertakers exploited people's emotional vulnerability and the social pressures for a good funeral. Charles Dickens described in *Household Words* the selling approach of undertakers in the 1850s:

> 'Hearse and four, Sir;' says he. 'No, a pair will be sufficient.' 'I beg your pardon, Sir, but when we buried Mr Grundy at number twenty, there were four on 'em, Sir; I think it right to mention it.' 'Well perhaps there had better be four.' 'Thank you, Sir. Two coaches and four, Sir, shall we say?' 'No, coaches and pair.' 'You'll excuse my mentioning it, Sir, but pairs to the coaches and fours to the hearse would have a singular appearance to the neighbours . . .' 'Well, say four!' 'Thank you, Sir. Feathers of course?' 'No, no feathers. They're absurd.' 'Very good, Sir. *No* feathers?' 'No.' '*Very* good, Sir. We *can* do four without feathers, Sir, but it's what we never do. When we buried Mr Grundy, there was feathers, and – I only throw it out, Sir – Mrs Grundy might think it strange.' 'Very well! Feathers!' 'Thank you, Sir.'

Undertakers, now more often than not called funeral directors, rarely use such naked arguments as keeping up with the Grundys, but people are still put under subtle pressure to pay out large sums. Others, particularly pensioners and the unemployed, can find paying even for the simplest funeral financially crippling. In his introduction to *A Death in the Sánchez Family* Oscar Lewis wrote:

> These three stories reveal the difficulties encountered by the poor in disposing of their dead. For the poor, death is almost as great a hardship as life itself. The Danish novelist Martin Anderson Nexo, writing in an autobiography about his early life in a Copenhagen slum, recalls that when he was about

three years old he asked his mother whether his brother, who had recently died, was now an angel. His mother replied, 'Poor people don't belong in heaven, they have to be thankful if they can get into the earth.'

A Death in the Sánchez Family is primarily about the struggle to get Aunt Guadalupe into the earth. In Britain, with the simplest funeral costing in 1987 from £300 upwards, for many it is still a struggle to get someone into the earth. Recognising that struggle, an undertaker from Manchester advised in the programme 'After a Death', 'Never ever go without food or heat or anything else in order to save up for the funeral,' and stressed that 'Nobody has yet not been buried. So if the DHSS, the social services or the local authority conduct a funeral it will be done with absolute dignity.' There is considerable common consent about the desire to have decent and dignified funerals, but these qualities are still all too often equated with cost. Some undertakers genuinely try to meet people's wishes and not pressurise them into paying for what they cannot or do not want. Others have changed little from the days of Charles Dickens, except that now they are selling the size and number of cars rather than horses decked with feathers. Members of the British funeral industry have been, during this century, restrained compared to their American counterparts whose profit-making zeal was so well recorded by Jessica Mitford in her book *The American Way of Death*.

Choosing what kind of funeral to have involves all kinds of pressures. There are the pressures of cost. These can mount up very fast and people should try to choose what they really want and not what they feel they ought to have. For many people it is extremely important that no expense is spared, for they find consolation in doing this final act for the person they loved. Others can feel pressurised into spending what they do not have and feel they do not need.

The type of funeral service can also present great difficulties of choice. If the dead belonged to a particular religion the type of service will naturally be of their religion, and if that religion is shared by family and friends there will be an unquestioning acceptance that that is the right, in all senses, service to have. Of course an individual's religious beliefs or non-beliefs are not always respected at their funerals. Many a non-believer has been given a religious funeral because the relatives thought that more decent and proper, or were unaware that there was any alternative to a religious funeral. In a society where a large number of people are not practising believers in any religion, or are atheists, there is a need to create meaningful non-religious funeral services. Sadly, many religious funeral services are now carried out by clergy who never knew the deceased and do not or barely know the bereaved. The service is thus impersonal, the clergy being able to offer little except their status and ability to conduct the service. Such services often leave the bereaved dissatisfied with the manner of the final leave-taking. If a service is also conducted in a manner in which the mourners feel they are just another party passing through that day, then the whole funeral is reduced to an experience that does little to meet the emotional needs of the bereaved.

Christopher Leach in his book *Letter to a Younger Son* described the funeral of his eleven-year-old son Jonathan. In spare, bleak words he captures the impersonality, the feeling of being part of a production line, the total emotional emptiness of many modern funerals. Arriving at the crematorium, Christopher Leach noted that 'behind us another hearse, a little earlier than arranged, stopped and cut its engine'. Once inside, his funeral party 'lifted our faces to the priest, whose name I knew, but whose church I had never visited. He said the customary things. We sang the old hymns, remembered from childhood.' Outside again, there was the human warmth of people shaking hands and speaking words, but this was marred by 'the engine of the second hearse [which] came to life and purred. Wheels inched forward over gravel. Another priest came out of the small chapel to meet the next death, his finger marking the place.' After reading that description one cannot help thinking that we should be able to create methods of burying our dead that give much greater and deeper emotional solace. Sadly, it is often in situations like that of Christopher Leach where, through sudden death, the bereaved are totally unprepared and, in the case of the death of a child, deeply numbed and shocked that they are least able to arrange a service that meets their needs. No funeral of a lost, deeply loved person can be anything but emotionally painful, but feeling that the final good-bye can be said in a personal way can make a great difference.

Non-believers have for almost a century been able to have secular funeral services, though many people are still unaware that this is an alternative. During the latter part of the nineteenth century the idea of secular funeral services began to be put forward as a more fitting service for non-believers. Annie Besant and Austin Holyoake both drew up secular burial services to be used as guidelines for others wishing to conduct such a service. People ask why, if there is no belief in a religion and no legal requirement for a service to be held, there is a need for a service at all. The National Secular Society, who will arrange, if requested, secular funerals, advise that: 'It is worth bearing in mind the psychological value of holding a funeral ceremony, even of the simplest kind. It is an occasion on which those deeply grieved may share their feelings, and sharing their feelings can be of great relief especially at times of emotional shock.' Above all, they go on to point out: 'It is an occasion when the finality of death has to be faced – an important part of mourning and, according to psychologists, a necessary process in eventually re-establishing and continuing life after bereavement.'

Long before psychologists were ever invented, human beings recognised the importance of funeral rituals, and every known established society has had some form of ritual marking the finality of death. Getting someone else to help arrange a secular funeral can greatly help those who do not know how to go about it or who are in a state of too much shock to organise one. It is worth either obtaining help or organising it oneself, for the benefit of feeling that the funeral service is in harmony with one's beliefs are very great. We spent much time between the death of our son and his funeral service planning it. It was in fact extremely simple – the reading of a poem, some words said by a close friend and some silence. It felt right. We were not involved in impersonality, hypocrisy or compromise. Looking back, the only thing I would have changed would be that I would have chosen some music to have started and finished the service. Others who have attended such services created personally to mark and mourn the passing of an individual, and what that individual had meant to the mourners, have commented on how the service met their emotional needs with humanity, decency and dignity.

It is possible to do everything relating to the disposal of the body and the funeral service oneself. Legally, it is not necessary to use an undertaker. It may not be a choice most people would want to make, but doing so can make the whole process much more personal. One can buy a coffin, make arrangements with a crematorium or place of burial and take responsibility for the funeral. The benefit of doing so was described by Jane Warman in 'After a Death' as, 'Apart from being cheaper for me it was actually an extension of caring, right to the very end.' Besides buying the coffin and making her own arrangements with the crematorium, Jane Warman and other family members and friends organised their own form of service for her mother. They had a gathering at home the evening before the cremation which she described as a 'very beautiful time when all her family and friends and some of her relations got together and we had music and poetry that had meant a lot to all of us during her life'. Having taken the body to the crematorium themselves, they then had a service of readings and music which they had chosen.

One choice some people make is to have a small private service – private to the immediately bereaved – after the death and a memorial service for a larger number of people

After a Death

later. This tends to be more common when famous people die, enabling the family to have some privacy at the funeral but also enabling others to share later in paying tribute and mourning. This combination of public and private services is not reserved for the famous, however, and increasingly others also choose it. In choosing it one has to be aware that, whilst it can be a great source of support to share in a memorial service one's memories and grief, it does mean going through a stressful situation twice.

Many other decisions also have to be made with regard to the funeral besides those required by the undertakers or relating to the type of service. Informing people of a death and of the date and time of a funeral service has to be done. Decisions have to be made about whether to announce it in a newspaper, and if so what to say. People ask whether flowers are wanted or black worn. Rarely now is the wearing of black expected by mourners, and often people ask that money is donated to a chosen charity instead of being spent on flowers – that charity usually being one involved with the cause of death. We asked that instead of flowers people made donations to the Down's Syndrome Association, for our son was a Down's Syndrome baby. Others ask that donations be sent to hospices, research charities for different diseases or other organisations. Because we have no one accepted ritual these all become choices, and the benefit of this is that the individual's need can be met. The need to make choices can, however, add considerable stress. Although the decisions are best made by the bereaved, for they have to live with the decisions, others can give much emotional support and practical help in respecting and effecting the decisions. For instance, if the bereaved wish to make an announcement in the newspapers others can organise it for them.

The other major decision relating to the funeral is whether to have a funeral gathering afterwards. Geoffrey Gorer in his book *Death, Grief and Mourning in Contemporary Britain* found that, 'Apart from the religious rites accompanying the disposal of the body, this [family gatherings] is the most widely spread ritual of mourning in Britain today.' Although his study was done in the sixties there is no evidence to suggest that this has ceased to be the 'most widely spread ritual of mourning'. Gorer found some regional and class variation, but he commented that 'in general the distribution of this custom is much the same for people of all ages, of all social classes and of all creeds'. The fact that most people choose to do it reveals that it is more than an expected social ritual. It meets the deep human need to be surrounded and supported. Usually the funeral gathering is held at the home of the bereaved, where food and drink is served. This may be simply tea and biscuits or something much more elaborate. The Irish wake is perhaps the best known of the more ritualised and elaborate funeral gatherings. The bereaved, particularly women, can sometimes find arranging such a gathering useful emotionally as it gives them something to do when life seems suspended. In other cases the bereaved may well not feel up to the work but would like to have such a gathering, and in those cases friends and neighbours can offer real practical help in organising it and clearing up afterwards. Some choose not to have any gathering at all, and no one should be forced into it. Most find the ritual, although stressful, important.

Sometimes the bereaved may choose not to attend a funeral or not to have a funeral gathering because they fear they will break down and lose control. This was the choice made by Geoffrey Gorer's sister-in-law Elizabeth, who chose not to attend the funeral of her husband. Gorer explained that the decision not to go to the cremation herself was because, 'She could not bear the thought that she might lose control and other people observe her grief; and she wished to spare the children the distressing experience.' The consequence of her decision, Gorer commented, was that for the children, 'their father's death was quite unmarked for them by any ritual of any kind'. It is a sad reflection on our society that someone should feel unable to attend a funeral because they fear that loss of control would be socially unacceptable.

Other cultures, even European ones, accept and allow expressions of grief. People are allowed to wail and to weep. It was noticeable to anyone who saw the television coverage of the funeral of Princess Grace of Monaco that her husband, Prince Rainier, was clearly overwrought with grief. He walked behind her coffin physically supported and in tears. At the funerals of British Royals or other important people it is rare to see anyone even brush away a tear. The pressures are very great, particularly on men, not to show emotion. There is of course no harm in people feeling that their way of coping in public is to control their emotion; often in the first few days or weeks of grief many people are kept going by a basic survival instinct. That survival instinct makes people get up in the morning, keep going and cope in public; it is their way of dealing with the shock. The harm is if people feel that they *have* to control their emotions, creating the fear that if they can't they must hide away. Funerals are primarily for the bereaved, and those attending should make it possible and acceptable for anyone to show emotion without fear. Even the simple gesture of offering a handkerchief or tissue can be a sign that 'it is all right to cry'.

It is the close relatives of the deceased who are at the centre, who have to make so many decisions and who have to live with the consequences of those decisions. They cannot avoid the situation. Things have to be done, said, written and signed. They have to dispose of the dead and face living. For those not immediately bereaved there are also choices to make. The decisions taken can make a great difference to the ability or not of the bereaved to confront the reality of death and build their lives again.

Supporting roles

Immediately after a death the bereaved need all kinds of help and advice. If it is a first bereavement most do not know what to do. If the death occurs in a hospital or hospice then the doctor or nurses will or should inform relatives of what to do. Although deaths happen regularly in hospitals, and although they have set procedures, little informational help to the bereaved is offered. Hospices give in every way much more information and support. At home a doctor is usually the first person to be called and consulted, and in most people's experience doctors offer little information and/or support. Unless, which is nowadays rare, doctors know the family well, they are unlikely to be able to deal with the situation in any other way than in their professional capacity of examining the body and offering formal condolences to the bereaved. The only other thing they offer is tranquillisers or sleeping pills. It is quite normal for people to be deeply stressed following a death and to be unable to eat properly, to be untranquil and to be unable to sleep. This is not a condition that needs treating with drugs, and indeed drugs may inhibit emotional and physical responses that are a necessary part of grieving. This is not the same as saying that suffering pain is ennobling. It is to say that grief is a process that has to be worked through in order to reach a state of being able to live with the loss. Sometimes short-term help in the form of drugs can enable the body and mind to get a much-needed rest, but their long-term use almost always hinders rather than helps healing.

After the doctor has certified someone dead, whether the death has occurred in the home or a hospital, a nurse or district nurse rather than an undertaker can be called in to perform 'the last offices' – the laying-out of the body. Women, whether professionals or not, have always performed these 'last offices', which involves washing the body and laying it out, closing the eyelids and, if necessary, putting a bandage around the head and jaw to keep the mouth shut. The body is generally tidied up, the hair combed, nails cleaned and a plug of cotton wool inserted into the rectum. Geoffrey Gorer described the visit of two ex-nurses whom the doctor had asked to come in to lay out his brother.

> They imparted a somewhat Dickensian tone; they were fat and jolly, and asked in a respectful but cheerful tone,

After a Death

'Where is the patient?' One of them was out a couple of minutes later to ask if he had a fresh pair of pyjamas; I could not bring myself to go through his clothes, and showed them his suitcase. Some half hour later their work was done, and they came out saying, 'The patient looks lovely now. Come and have a look!' I gave them a pound for their pains; the leader, pure Sarah Gamp, said, 'That for us, ducks? Cheers!' and went through the motions of raising a bottle and emptying it into her mouth.

It is not necessary to call in a trained nurse to lay out the body, though most people would prefer, if it needs doing, to have it done by someone else. In a hospital it will automatically be done before the body is taken to the hospital or hospice mortuary.

The other professionals usually called in, if the death has occurred at home, or contacted soon after the death if it has occurred outside the home, are the undertakers. These are the people who are most useful in providing immediate practical advice about all the things that need doing and the arrangements that need making. It is more often than not the undertakers who explain to people the need to register the death, how they do it and where they have to go. The undertakers will remove the body from the home and will then arrange for it to be embalmed if that is required and, if desired, for the body to be returned to the home prior to the funeral or for relatives to visit the chapel of rest to view it. Likewise, they will liaise with the hospital or any other mortuary either to collect the body immediately before the funeral or to lay it out before the funeral. If the coroner is involved they will liaise with the coroner's office. It is part of the service they offer to arrange all these things and to give the bereaved the information they need. Undertakers, like nurses and doctors, all have a job to do, and they can do it in a way that is not only respectful but humane. One funeral director quoted in Ian Crichton's book *The Art of Dying* said, 'My attitude to clients is not professionally gloomy. Obviously you can't be jokey, but to pretend to be mourning someone you've never even met is wrong. You've got to show respect, though.'

After a death other professional advice can be sought. Citizens Advice Bureaux are one source of help and information that people regularly turn to. In the programme 'After a Death', one woman who works for a Citizens Advice Bureau said, 'Quite often I've picked up the phone in the morning and people have rung up and said, "My mother [or my husband or my wife] has just died and I just don't know where to start." And then they come in and we can literally go through the whole system with them, starting with whatever is their most immediate problem.' Citizens Advice Bureaux are well placed to advise people to shop around for undertakers, give them information relating to registering a death, the DHSS benefits and how to choose a solicitor if necessary.

For many people practical help, information and advice come from friends and relatives who know what to do from having had to do it before. This kind of practical help is one way in which those not immediately bereaved can give much needed support. Although it is important for the bereaved to say what they like, others can do much of the running around to organise everything. They can also help in many other practical ways: offers to shop, cook, clean, look after any dependants can all be welcomed. One of the problems of the breakdown of accepted and known rituals surrounding death and funerals is that those who are not immediately bereaved often do not know how to behave. There are no set guidelines about whether to visit the bereaved or not, phone them or not, or write to them or not. If we visit, phone or write we do not know how to behave or what to say, and indeed whether to say anything.

A death cannot and should not go by unacknowledged. For life to go on and relationships to continue that acknowledgement has to be made, and it is easier to make immediately than to leave. The bereaved can draw on much emotional support through feeling that those around them acknowledge their bereavement, sympathise with them and express that sympathy in words and in deeds. Our embarrassment when confronted with someone who is mourning

After a Death 113

often inhibits any expression of sympathy. We should forget *our* embarrassment and think more of the needs of the bereaved. If they want to talk we should listen. If they want to cry we should let them. If they want to be silent we should respect their wishes but know that their silence is their choice and not one socially imposed on them. If they are at a distance we should phone or write. The latter is often easier for the bereaved as a letter can be opened when they feel like opening it, read and re-read as a source of support.

Many people do not write because they feel that they are unable to express themselves in a letter of condolence. We can all be reassured that even the greatest writers feel inadequate when confronted with writing such a letter. In *A Book of Condolences*, a collection of letters of condolence written by some of the greatest writers, we discover, as the editors comment in their foreword, that, 'We are all in the same predicament: there is nothing to say except, "I love you, and I care."' We learn that writers are also unable to find the words to express their love, disbelief, anger, care and pain when confronted with a death. Edith Sitwell, in writing to Wilfred Owen's mother after his death, ended her letter, 'I cannot write more, because words are so little; before the face of your loss and your grief, they sound too cold.' The feeling of the littleness and coldness of words in the face of grief and loss is something which all share when writing a letter of condolence. Many centuries earlier the younger Pliny, writing to Colonus after the death of Pompeius Quinctianus, shows that he is well aware that Colonus will find the letter upsetting to read. 'Why do I aggravate your affliction by reminding you of his merit?' Pliny asks, but adds, 'I know your affection for the memory of this excellent youth is so strong, that you had rather endure that pain than suffer his virtues to be passed over in silence.' Nothing can be so hurtful to the bereaved, whether in A.D. 104 or in 1987, to feel that their deceased loved one is, by friends and relatives, 'passed over in silence'.

The excuse most people use for not writing, visiting or

saying anything is that, 'I didn't want to upset them.' This excuse is usually because the maker of it fears being upset themselves, being unable to handle someone else's pain and the embarrassment of the situation. The bereaved *are* upset. Bereavement *is* upsetting. Pretending that there is no upset makes, through isolation, the pain even worse.

There is much that all those involved with the bereaved can do to help. Many bereaved do find that in the period immediately following a death they are supported and given practical help, information and emotional comfort. Although most people in our society do not have set rituals for coping with a death, there is still a recognition of the need to rally round immediately after a death and help. However, the socially recognised period of mourning is very brief. Most bereaved people say that they found everyone wonderful at first, but then . . . The 'but then' is when society turns its back on those in mourning, taking the attitude that they should get on with their lives and let others get on with theirs, unembarrassed by the presence of someone in mourning in their midst. Mourning is a long process with many stages, and we can do much to help others – and ourselves, for bereavement strikes everyone – by recognising it.

CHAPTER FIVE

Grief

> Blessed are they that mourn; for they shall be comforted.
> (Matthew 5:4)

> After the funeral and burial comes mourning in the true sense of the word. The pain of loss may continue to exist in the secret heart of the survivor, but the rule today, almost throughout the West, is that he must never show it in public.
>
> (*The Hour of our Death*, Philippe Ariès, 1977)

The statement by Philippe Ariès about contemporary attitudes to mourning is a far cry from that expressed by Jesus when he said: 'Blessed are they that mourn: for they shall be comforted.' Mourning the loss of a loved person is not a phenomenon new to the twentieth century. For at least as long as people have written about being human mourning has been part of that experience. Because people witnessed more death in the past, there is no evidence that they did not grieve. People were portrayed grieving in the Greek tragedies as they were in the plays of Shakespeare. In the fourth century St Augustine, after the death of a friend, found that, 'At this grief my heart was utterly darkened.' Many centuries later, in 1755, Samuel Johnson wrote, after the death of his wife, 'I have ever since seemed to myself broken off from mankind; a kind of solitary wanderer in the wild of life, without any direction, or fixed point of view; a gloomy gazer on the world to which I have little relation.'

Although there was clearly a level of acceptance about the death of babies and children, their loss was keenly felt. The fact that people did not expect their children to live did not mean that they did not grieve over their death. In her autobiography the seventeenth-century Lady Warwick described how, at the news of the death of their son, her husband had 'cried out so terribly that his cry was heard a great way; and he was the saddest afflicted person could possibly be'. The American diarist William Byrd, though not upset himself about the death of his two-year-old son, did record on 3 June 1710 that after the funeral 'my wife continued to be exceedingly afflicted for the loss of her child, notwithstanding I comforted her as well as I could. I ate calf's head for dinner.' One of the most tender observations of parental grief is to be found on an eighteenth-century gravestone to a nine-year-old girl, Penelope Boothby. One can only wonder at who wrote the following lines summing up so poignantly a family tragedy. 'She was in form and intellect most exquisite. The unfortunate parents ventured their all on this frail bark and the wreck was total.'

There is nothing new about the fact that people mourn. What has changed is the attitude to those in mourning: mourners are rarely comforted for long but are frequently shunned. I had been at the receiving end of that social reaction myself, and the documentary series *Merely Mortal* grew out of my desire to make a film about it. Five years after the death of my first child I wrote a book called *Will, My Son*. In the first few years after his death I had, over and over again, been writing it in my head. Putting it down on paper was an attempt to work through my feelings and question the reactions of others to the birth and death of a handicapped, Down's Syndrome child. Looking back, the writing of the book was for me just another stage in my grief, a stage when I could only express my feelings in words. The process of writing is a private occupation, even though the product may become public. With time, although writing had satisfied my need to say the things about the life of Will that I had wished to say, it left many things unsaid about my grief. The book dealt briefly with it but said little of the way society shuns those in mourning. I

Grief

had to write the book to be able to 'talk', but having worked through that stage I felt there were still many things that needed saying. Ready to go public, a series of programmes seemed a way of exploring the wider issues based on a range of people's experiences.

As I began to read books on grief I noticed that much of the work done by others in trying to change our attitudes to mourning had also been triggered by personal experience. One of the first studies in grief was that done by Geoffrey Gorer in the early sixties. It has become a classic, not just for the attitudes and experiences revealed but because of the human and understanding way in which the material is presented. In his introduction he describes how, after the funeral of his brother, 'We all went for a few days to friends in Frome; and then life had to be resumed. It was the experience of the following months which suggested to me that our treatment of grief and mourning made bereavement very difficult to be lived through.' This realisation led him to study *Death, Grief and Mourning in Contemporary Britain* to find out whether the lack of support in the professional middle classes in southern England, which he had experienced, was typical. He found, with little variation, that it was. Having done a wide survey he concluded that 'The majority of British people are today without adequate guidance as to how to treat death and bereavement and without social help in living through and coming to terms with the grief and mourning which are the inevitable responses in human beings to the death of someone whom they have loved.'

Geoffrey Gorer did much to raise the issue, but there is little evidence to show that social behaviour has changed significantly since the early sixties. What has changed since then has been a recognition that social attitudes create problems for the bereaved; this has led to the development of a number of support groups in which mutual experience can be shared. Many bereaved feel that no one else understands, and to be with others who have been through the same kind of bereavement (e.g. loss of a spouse, loss of a child) can provide much-needed understanding and support. Bereavement counselling has also been recognised as a need.

The other noticeable change since the sixties is that grief has now become recognised as a source of mental ill health, due in great part to the work of Colin Murray Parkes. Writing on bereavement in 1972, he pointed out that although grief was a known 'psychiatric disorder' it was so neglected by psychiatrists 'that it is not even mentioned in the indexes of most best-known general textbooks of psychiatry'. Increasingly, it has become recognised by psychiatrists. They have started to study the problem and treat those unable to work through their grief. There is no denying that some people need help of a professional kind, though the danger of emphasising the need for psychiatric recognition is that mourning can become regarded as abnormal behaviour. Freud himself wrote in *Mourning and Melancholia*: 'Although grief involves grave departures from the normal attitude to life, it never occurs to us to regard it as a morbid condition and hand the mourner over to medical treatment. We rest assured that after a lapse of time it will be overcome, and we look upon any interference with it as inadvisable or even harmful.' Freud recognised the normality of grief, and it is interesting to note that he regarded any intervention as inadvisable. However, it has to be remembered that he was living in a period when mourning was regarded as normal. It was recognised and ritualised. Most people's grief still does not need *treating*, but needs recognising. It is its non-recognition as normal that can lead, in some people, to mental ill health.

Knowing about the normal reactions, feelings and common stages of grief can help to increase understanding both of our own grief and that of others. Understanding leads to greater help and support being given. It can reassure the bereaved that although they are in pain they are quite normal. Most importantly, it can help the bereaved to work through the experience and be able to rebuild their/our lives again.

Grief

The first shock

The medical definition of shock is, according to the *Oxford Dictionary*, a 'state of prostration following overstimulation of nerves by sudden pain as of wound etc. or violent emotion.' Learning that someone deeply loved has died is perhaps the most violent shock we ever receive to our emotional systems. The more unexpected, the greater the shock. People vary in their immediate responses to such a shock. Of my reaction I wrote: 'The first stage of grief is total – the mind and body are totally consumed in one emotion. The mental shock is a physical shock. I felt cold, very cold, and kept adding layers of clothing. I felt sick as though I had been kicked in the stomach and couldn't eat. . . . People had talked of heartache but only then I realised it is a physical sensation.' In a way I was like someone who had been in a violent accident and needed a blanket wrapped round me (emotionally and literally) and a warm drink.

Later I found out that others suffered physical reactions. C. S. Lewis opens his book, *A Grief Observed*, with the statement: 'No one ever told me that grief felt so like fear. I am not afraid, but the sensation is like being afraid. The same fluttering in the stomach, the same restlessness. I keep on swallowing.' Although in novels and films people, usually women, are portrayed as fainting when receiving such news, I have not met or heard of anyone who has literally fainted. People frequently talk of the news of a death as a 'blow', and the body reacts to emotional blows as well as physical blows; the body frequently crumples or collapses.

James Agee in his autobiographical novel *A Death in the Family* described how Mary received the news that her husband had been killed in a car accident. Andrew, her brother, having broken the news and embraced her, then, 'feeling her become heavy against him, said, "Here, Mary," catching her across the shoulders and helping her to a chair, just as she, losing strength in her knees, gasped, "I've got to sit down," and looked timidly towards her aunt, who at the same moment saying, in a broken voice, "Sit down, Mary", was at her other side, her arm around her waist and her face as bleached and shocking as a skull'. Just as a physical blow stops people in their tracks, so does an emotional blow. Some people are too numbed and stunned by the news to register any immediate observable reaction.

Christopher Leach in *Letter to a Younger Son* observed the young doctor's distress who, after being called out in the middle of the night, arrived 'only to find death; and to have to lift a helpless face to parents who were waiting for a miracle'. Having described the doctor's reaction, he wrote of his own: '(Always the writer's detachment: that feeding upon every happening, however desperate; catching glances, interpreting the set of a face; building the lives of others – always the observer. Now it angered me: telling myself I ought to feel more – not knowing that, like your mother, I was in the first stages of shock, which was to last for days.)' That shock can often lead observers erroneously to think that someone has 'taken the news very well'. Their non-reaction may well be because the shock is so great that they have not assimilated the news at all. In such a state people go into a kind of auto-pilot, going through the motions without really being aware of what they are doing. James Agee wrote of this reaction: 'When grief and shock surpass endurance there occur phases of exhaustion, of anesthesia in which relatively little is felt and one has the illusion of recognizing, and understanding, a good deal.'

These immediate physical reactions are but the beginning of a range of physical disorders. Loss of appetite is very common, as is the feeling of having a lump in the throat and a dry mouth. Colin Murray Parkes in a study of twenty-two widows found that, besides loss of appetite, 'Insomnia was mentioned by seventeen widows and was severe in thirteen; difficulty in getting to sleep at night and a tendency to wake early or during the night were also reported.' The other symptoms his study found quite common were headaches, palpitations and muscular aches and pains.

Grief

These reactions are all quite normal and some or all will be felt during the first few weeks, and possibly during the first year.

Occasionally the physical reaction to the emotional blow of bereavement can be extreme. A seventeenth-century doctor, Dr Heberden, listed the number and causes of death in 1657 in London. The vast majority of deaths were caused by 'Flox and Small Pox, Griping and Plague in the Guts'. A few died from 'French Pox and Gout', twenty-four 'Hang'd and made away 'emselves' and nine were 'Found dead in the streets etc.' The only other cause of death Dr Heberden listed was 'Griefe'. What is not explained is whether those deaths were an immediate reaction to the death of a loved one, or the result of long-term sorrow and the loss of the will to live following a bereavement.

Lily Pincus in her book *Death and the Family* cites the case of a Mrs Green who had a stroke immediately after the funeral of her husband. This first stroke was followed by two more in quick succession and she died five months after her husband. This case is by no means unique. Most people know or have heard of the death of a spouse following soon after the death of the other. Mortality statistics reveal that there is, in the first year of being widowed and particularly after being made a widower, a higher than average death rate. A study carried out in 1963 found an increase in the death rate among 4,486 widowers over the age of fifty-four of almost 40 per cent during the first six months of bereavement. Other studies have confirmed these findings. What is interesting is that of those deaths a very high percentage were from heart disease; death from a broken heart can and does happen. Those that survive the first year of bereavement are out of the danger group and have the same average mortality rate as the non-bereaved. Although grief is no longer recognised as a cause of death, it quite clearly can and does cause the onset of disease that leads to death. Grief in itself does not literally kill, but it can lead to the loss of the will to live.

Lily Pincus cites the case of Tony who, after the death of

his wife, 'went to pieces'. He had a serious relapse of TB from which he had once suffered, and 'was readmitted to hospital, and was again on the danger list'. Tony survived to re-build his life for himself and his children, but his case shows how the body can react to grief. Colin Murray Parkes, in a study of widows and widowers, found that 'four times as many bereaved as non-bereaved had spent part of the preceding year in hospital'. Illness or injury triggered by grief is a common experience. Lily Pincus, after her husband's death, decided to go to Israel for a break. A few days after her arrival she fractured her ankle and while she was being treated asked her orthopaedic surgeon 'whether people often fracture bones after bereavement', to which 'he said, without even looking up from my injured foot, "Naturally, people lose their sense of balance."' Lily Pincus commented in her book that, 'Perhaps some have to fracture limbs or hurt some other part of themselves before they can acknowledge what has happened to them.' Besides the more dramatic injuries and ill health requiring hospitalisation, the bereaved also have a higher rate of minor illnesses.

The physical reactions to shock are well known and are taught to anyone doing even the most basic first-aid course. However, most people are unaware that the emotional shock of bereavement needs treating in exactly the same way as any other traumatic experience. Like anyone in shock, the bereaved need to be coddled physically and emotionally. Lily Pincus wrote: 'For physical shock, rest and warmth are the recognized methods of treatment, yet the most frequent advice given for the emotional shock of grief is to "keep going", "get busy".'

I was at first too shocked to 'get busy' and fortunately no one advised me to do so. The days between Will's death and the funeral we both spent drinking cups of tea and coffee that other people made for us. My mother cooked and cleaned, my father shopped and helped with funeral arrangements, and our friends and other relatives also did many things for us. We were lucky in that we had family and friends around and we had each other. Unlike many, we did not have the pressure of having to keep going for other children or dependants. We also did not at first, though I did very strongly later, feel that we had to be busy to keep going. In contrast, Lily Pincus after the death of her husband felt she must yield to the pressure of keeping busy. 'I know,' she wrote, 'from my own experience and that of others the frightening and exhausting results of the innumerable blunders of those first busy days — the things mislaid, lost, wrongly addressed, and so on, and the agonizing attempts to retrieve them.' It was only when she fractured her ankle that she was forced to take rest.

Part of all the busyness stems from a desperate need to fill one's life with something when it has suddenly become totally empty. Keeping busy can often be, as Geoffrey Gorer pointed out, a reaction to 'the belief that giving way to grief and mourning is "morbid" and "unhealthy", and that psychological health will best be maintained by endless trivial distraction — by continuing to be as active as possible'. Some people use the remedy of busyness from the outset, while others allow themselves to be cared for in the period immediately after the death but use it as a remedy to cope with the isolation following abandonment after the funeral.

The process of grief

Margaret, are you grieving
Over Goldengrove unleaving?
Leaves, like the things of man, you
With your fresh thoughts care for, can you?
Ah! as the heart grows older
It will come to such sights colder
By and by, nor spare a sigh
Though worlds of wanwood leafmeal lie:
And yet you *will* weep and know why.
Now no matter, child, the name:
Sorrow's springs are all the same.
No mouth had, no nor mind, expressed
What heart heard of, ghost guessed:
It is the blight man was born for,
It is Margaret you mourn for.
(Gerard Manley Hopkins, 1844–89)

From birth we lose things, pets and people we love. We often lose people through separations – divorce or emigration, for example – and these are particularly painful if unwanted. They are all losses which we mourn over, yet there is a difference between other losses and loss through death. In death there is no possibility of a comeback, and it is this finality which the bereaved have to face. In some cases, facing the reality starts before the death. Most children, as their parents age, begin to wonder what life will be like when they are dead. This is not the same as the small child fearing the death of parents, but a natural reaction to the fact that parents who approach seventy-five or eighty will not go on living for ever. That process of imagining is the beginning of facing the realisation that parents do not live for ever. It is both a preparation for the eventuality and the beginning of mourning. Other people are forced into starting the process of mourning by the knowledge that the person they love is dying; that knowledge leads them to imagine what life will be like without the person around. Although in such situations the actual death still comes as a shock, the process of confronting that reality has usually already started.

Simone de Beauvoir, after learning that her mother was dying of cancer, 'went home', and then wrote that she 'talked to Sartre; we played some Bartok. Suddenly, at eleven, an outburst of tears that almost degenerated into hysteria.' She was amazed by her reaction, not having cried when her father died. Of her feeling of impending loss she wrote: 'I had understood all my sorrows until that night: even when they flowed over my head I recognised myself in them. This time my despair escaped from my control; someone other than myself was weeping in me.' Others will recognise that uncontrolled pang of grief which is one of the normal reactions to loss or to the knowlege of impending loss. My experience, however, is that in situations where someone *might* die it is hope rather than reality which is the driving force of the imagination. We knew that the heart operation which they performed on our son carried a high risk that he would not live. Despite that knowledge, I never really considered or imagined that he could die. I lived until the moment of his death in hope.

The ways in which people learn to cope with the reality of someone's death are very varied. The immediate and harshest reality that confronts the bereaved is simply that the person is not there. The bed is empty of the partner, the chair by the fire is no longer filled, the child's bedroom is quiet and still. Christopher Leach 'went alone into Jonathan's room' shortly after his death and later wrote: 'Now every crease in sheet and blanket, every dog-eared book, every picture in danger of falling, every broken pencil and dried-up colouring stick, spoke of absence.'

Some respond to that absence by removing very quickly every trace of the person; they find the reminders too painful and think removing them will help. Later, that action is often regretted as in a more calm frame of mind it becomes possible to decide which things to keep and cherish and which to get rid of. This reaction of total removal can even extend to verbal removal, whereby the name of the dead person is never mentioned. Somehow, by denying their existence, there is a hope that their death too can be denied. Others keep things exactly as they were in an attempt to freeze life before the moment of death. It is another way of refusing to acknowledge the death. Many keep a whole house or one room in a house unchanged. Following the death of John Lennon, Yoko Ono kept their sitting-room for years just as it had been when he had died. Whilst it is quite normal and wise to leave everything untouched or hidden for a period of time, leaving it untouched indefinitely does inhibit the process of rebuilding one's life. There is a profound difference between keeping things to remember someone by and keeping things unchanged.

Clothes are the most personal of objects. One remembers someone wearing them, they still bear the smell of that person, they are the cruel reminder that they were once worn by a live, warm body. Of all of the material things left by someone, clothes are the hardest to confront. Other things associated with the dead person are also painful reminders. Slowly, in their own way and in their own time, people do let go of those personal effects. Doing so is an important part of recognising that someone is dead; this is not to be confused with forgetting them – it is part of the process of learning to live with the memory.

Personal belongings are very often the things which trigger a pang of grief. Seeing someone's slippers, or hearing their favourite piece of music, or seeing the teddy bear once clutched every night can cause a welling up of acute feelings of pain and anguish. At first nothing specific may trigger the pang, though later it is usually particular things that jolt the bereaved's assumed calm. Colin Murray Parkes defines a pang of grief as 'an episode of severe anxiety and psychological pain. At such a time the lost person is strongly missed and the survivor sobs or cries aloud for him.' Pangs of grief are an experience had by all survivors. They may start a few hours after the loss or some days later when the numbness wears off. Returning to everyday life after the funeral brings with it the pressure and expectancy that the bereaved will behave 'normally', but pangs of grief will cause the bereaved to go out of control, often breaking into floods of tears or sobbing uncontrollably. Describing these pangs, C. S. Lewis wrote: 'Then comes a sudden jab of red-hot memory and all this "commonsense" vanishes like an ant in the mouth of a furnace.' Other people are frequently embarrassed by such behaviour and therefore, to avoid triggering an outburst of emotion, they refrain from mentioning the dead person or anything to do with them. This is in the interests of the feelings of those not bereaved, but denial by silence does not help the bereaved to confront their pain.

I remember dreading that something would suddenly trigger me and that I would break down in situations where people would either not understand or be deeply embarrassed by my behaviour. Because of that, when I was 'in public' away from the safety of close friends and relatives I tried to keep an iron control on myself. I remember, too, wishing that mourning ritual would allow me to wear a black armband. In public I wanted to wear some symbol of my inner fragility that would both warn those that didn't know and would explain such irrational behaviour as bursting into tears. Until then I had thought the wearing of black an old-fashioned practice which we modern people had liberated ourselves from. The wearing of mourning apparel became excessive in late Victorian times when social etiquette, not emotional need, dictated who wore what kind of mourning clothes and for how long.

Katharine Moore remembered what she called 'the Victorian Parade' of death, with its required mourning clothes often supplied from special shops like Jay's of Regent Street. She also remembered that it was the First World War which

> broke the habit and ended the fashion really, because almost everybody that I knew lost somebody. The massacre of the young men was terrific and you couldn't keep up the same parade. You hadn't got the people there, they were killed overseas. It was really a holocaust of the youth and it was impossible to keep up the same degree of formality about death then. I think it certainly broke the fashion and I don't remember it after the First World War.

Now the only time mourning clothes are worn is at funerals, and even then many do not wear the traditional black. Most people would not wish for a return to the social imposition of mourning clothes, but their absence means that no one knows, apart from family and friends, that someone is in mourning.

Mourning clothes gave the wearer an outward symbol of their emotional vulnerability and were also a recognition of the fact that mourning lasts for a considerable period of time. Most bereaved people are now only special for a brief period of time, usually for only the first few weeks and sometimes only until after the funeral. During this period of specialness the bereaved are treated differently – as important people. They get phone calls, visits, gifts and letters. Other people interrupt their lives for the bereaved, who are the centre of attention. 'This special treatment,' Judy Tatelbaum wrote in *The Courage to Grieve*, 'is enormously supportive. It may be the only thing that bolsters us as we face the pain of our grief.' However, as Judy Tatelbaum points out, that period of specialness usually ends abruptly when, 'People seem to pull back from the bereaved suddenly and arbitrarily, as if the time for grieving were over and we were expected to resume our usual lives.' That abrupt end was once cushioned by the wearing of mourning clothes which signalled that mourning was not yet over.

Different societies have imposed the wearing of mourning clothes for different lengths of times, but the commonest is to wear them for a year. This custom was not based on some arbitrary canon of social etiquette but on a recognition that a year is an important milestone. With the abandonment of the outward symbols we have lost the understanding of the reasons for those symbols. Getting through each and every anniversary is an emotional hurdle to be approached with fear, lived through and passed on. People find their own ways of dealing with anniversaries. On the first anniversary of Will's death we visited his plaque at the crematorium and then went away for the weekend. Staying in a hotel in November on the East Coast we could cling to each other and our memories. The bleak coastline and the emptiness all around echoed our mood and helped us work through the pain of the anniversary. Besides the personal anniversaries, almost all find Christmas particularly empty and hard. In the course of the first year many feel that they are coping well and indeed may well be doing so. However, those who have travelled the long road of grief know that it is at least a year before normality can really be resumed. Those who have lost a child frequently say that the second year is the hardest. People should not underestimate how long it takes to work through the complicated emotions of bereavement.

Bereavement is not one emotion but a whole range of mixed emotions. Like Simone de Beauvoir, in her amaze-

Grief

ment at her almost hysterical tears when she found out that her mother was dying, most bereaved people are surprised at some point by their emotional reactions. Christopher Leach discovered, through grief, that 'there exists in myself acres of my nature which are still undiscovered'. Sorrow and pain are accepted and recognised reactions but anger, guilt, relief, frustration, depression are all also very commonly felt, though not as commonly recognised. The blow of the death of a loved one leaves people not just physically but emotionally unbalanced. That emotional unbalance causes people to manifest all sorts of behaviour often quite out of character. The usually rational can at times be thrown by their irrationality.

Many feel at some time or another anger. It is an anger at life that ends in death. The anger may express itself outwards towards other people or it may be turned inwards. The bereaved may lash out with blame. The blame may be directed at specific people – the reckless car driver, the company that allowed a faulty aeroplane to fly, the employer who didn't insist on stringent enough safety precautions or the doctor who failed to arrive. Martha Weinman Lear blamed the doctors, not for causing her husband Hal's death, but for the way they had treated him during a long period of heart disease. In her book *Heartsounds* she wrote that, 'I have spent much of these months trying to come to terms with bitter feelings. They are corrosive. I want to be rid of them.' Of her bitter feelings about the doctors she conceded 'that much of the anger I felt was simply, primitively, because they could not do the impossible: they could not make him well'. Believers can feel very angry with God for letting death happen.

Anger and resentment that others are alive when a loved one is dead can be very strong. The resentment is at those who still have a spouse, a child, a parent or a close friend and is usually directed at specific people, often those who are the closest, rather than at people in general. Such waves of resentment are not harmful and only become harmful if long-term. Two adults I know felt that their mothers resented them for being alive when, in each family, their brother had died. Interestingly, this kind of resentment has been explored in children's fiction.

The Secret Garden by Frances Hodgson Burnett is the most dramatic portrayal of the effect of such resentment. The story starts when a young orphaned girl, Mary, is sent back from India to live with her uncle, Mr Craven, in Yorkshire. He too is bereaved, his wife having died ten years before the story begins. During those ten years Mr Craven has never managed to confront his grief. He is unable to form relationships and, in particular, cannot accept his son Colin. Colin, aged ten at the beginning of the story, is bedridden and believes he will die before reaching adulthood. He knows that his father resents the fact that he is alive when his mother is dead. The secret garden of the title had been Mrs Craven's favourite place, but in it a branch of a tree had fallen on her, causing her death. After the accident Mr Craven locked up the walled garden and threw away the key. Mary finds the key, unlocks the garden and, with time, unlocks the father and son who are trapped in grief and the repercussions of that grief. In the secret garden Colin slowly becomes normal and healthy, able to walk and run. The father one day, finding the garden unlocked, goes in. In that action he confronts his grief and in doing so finds a future. He embraces his son Colin and, instead of selling the house and garden in Yorkshire, agrees that they should all stay there. The book ends with them all beginning to rebuild their lives.

In general I didn't resent people for having children, but I resented a friend of mine who had given birth to a son some six weeks before Will was born. To this day I still have ambivalent feelings about him which are absolutely nothing to do with him but everything to do with me. The other time I felt resentment was a considerably delayed reaction. After my second child, Jessie, was born, contrary to my expectations that I would be finally through grieving, I found myself plunged into a second period of mourning that not only took me by surprise but about which I felt

Grief

guilty. I felt guilty because instead of feeling joyful and thankful I was grieving. In my book I wrote: 'I felt even more guilty because there were times when I resented Jessie because she was in those first few months so difficult and demanding. Her brother, I would think, never demanded anything and yet here she was demanding all the time.' Quite quickly my feelings of resentment disappeared altogether, enabling me to feel deep joy about her life. Judy Tatelbaum wrote that after the death of her brother David at the age of twenty she 'envied intact families, now that we were three instead of four'. Others just resent and envy all others around them who still have their loved ones.

Sometimes the anger is turned into constructive anger. Many a crusade to change things has come out of the anger of someone bereaved. The campaigns to make such things as cars, places of work and children's toys safer have received much of their impetus from anger at the fact that lack of safety had led to death. Anger that someone has died unnecessarily can also be turned into campaigning to make sure no other similar deaths occur. For the bereaved, using their anger constructively not only helps others but helps them. It is a way of creating meaning out of a death that may have seemed meaningless. Anger is expressed too at quite innocent parties. One of my expressions of anger was at a plant. When we returned home from the hospital after Will's death I saw a plant I had bought for Ed on St Valentine's day – the day of Will's birth. On seeing the plant I grabbed it and, sobbing, ripped it out of its pot and threw it away. It had, I thought, no right to live when my son was dead. Angrily the bereaved ask, 'Why me?' and lash out at a world that has delivered this cruel blow.

Phases of seemingly irrational irritability are also very common. They are partially due to the fatigue of grief, but are also due to being emotionally off balance. It is very like the irritability many women suffer in the days preceding a period. Such anger and periods of irritability usually come and go; it is not a case of going through an 'angry' phase but, like the other emotions of bereavement, these feelings well up, subside, only to well up again until grief is worked through.

Another strong emotion is that of guilt. With grief there can be much guilt. Those who have time to prepare for someone's death through knowing and sharing that knowledge with the dying person rarely feel guilt. They have the chance, if they take it, to say the things they want to say, which can benefit and console the bereaved greatly. Martha Weinman Lear, who had a long period of knowing that her husband Hal would die, expressed well the strength she gained from the openness of their relationship: 'It must be that grief is more bearable in the absence of guilt. And I, who was always addicted to guilt, feel comfortingly little of it now that he is gone. There is nothing that was not said between us. There are no if onlys. There are few regrets. We knew and said that we gave each other joy.'

Unfortunately, some people are unable to use the time and knowledge they have. Others do not have any time – sudden death deprives them of it. People can feel guilty about what they did not do and did not say before the death. This can give rise to much self-questioning and self-blame: blame that they were not there at the death, that they didn't get more medical advice and help, that they didn't stop an adult going out in a car on a dark foggy night or a child from playing somewhere dangerous. Mostly, this self-blame has no rational base but occasionally it is justified. A person in that situation may well need a lot of help in coming to terms with themselves. Some people never get over blaming themselves and turn inwards in a self-destructive way. Others try to assuage their guilt by working through it. Drunk drivers, for instance, may devote their lives to campaigning against drink and driving; it does not resolve the guilt but at least gives it a positive and constructive expression. Feelings of guilt are very frequent following bereavement caused by suicide.

Guilt that one is alive and someone else dead haunts the bereaved and can lead to suicidal thoughts. The depression that goes with grief and the feeling that life has lost all meaning can undermine the will to live; death appears as a welcome end to the pain and a way of joining the dead person. 'There was a time, a black moment,' Christopher Leach wrote, 'when I thought of following Jonathan: the child alone, out there in the totally unknown. I wanted to share the dark with him, stand by. It passed.' Of such suicidal thoughts it is important to know and remember that they are only thoughts and that, as they did for Christopher Leach, they pass. It is important to know that such thoughts are common and that they do slowly disappear as life regains its meaning.

The bereaved often feel that their misery makes them an unwanted person to have around, and they feel guilty that their presence spoils other people's fun. A classic fictional portrayal of such guilt is that felt by the widow Mrs Gummidge in Charles Dickens's *David Copperfield*. She is frequently sure that her bouts of weeping, depression and contrariness spoil things for those around her. Despite constant reassurances from those around her, particularly Mr Peggotty, she remains convinced that she makes 'the house uncomfortable' for all. Mrs Gummidge's guilt at doing so leads her to suggest that: 'I had better go into a house and die. I am a lonelore creetur, and had much better not make myself contrairy here. If thinks must go contrairy with me, and I must go contrairy myself, let me go contrairy in my parish. Dan'l, I'd better go into a house, and die and be a riddance!' After that speech Mrs Gummidge leaves the room. 'She's been thinking of the old 'un!' Mr Peggotty says to David by way of explanation for her behaviour. Although Mrs Gummidge, throughout the book, feels guilty for her 'contrairiness', those around her, as David observes, treat her with nothing but the 'profoundest sympathy'. With that kind of sympathy most people find that their contrariness disappears and they can, once again, be good company.

Guilt frequently accompanies the feelings of relief which bereavement can in some cases bring. Those who witness a loved one suffering through a long terminal illness can, understandably, feel relieved when the death occurs. They often feel guilty that they feel relieved, but there is no reason why they should do so. It does not imply that they had not loved or cared enough for the person whilst they were living. Others feel relief because death has liberated them. John Dryden clearly felt relief, which he succinctly expressed in the following 'Epigram-Epitaph For His Wife':

> Here lies my wife.
> Here let her lie!
> She is at rest
> And so am I.

Sons and daughters can feel relieved and liberated after the death of a parent, particularly if they felt their lives were oppressed by that parent. Sometimes the emotional reaction is complicated — love and oppression are not always mutually exclusive — but in some cases the response is one of uncomplicated relief. Grief is usually for the loss of a loved one, but sometimes it is for the fact that the love had never been. Death can bring home not only the realisation of what never was but what, through death, can never be.

Another type of guilt is that of those people who feel they should mourn more or for longer. It may seem strange that, whilst for most their need is to be allowed to mourn and for as long as it takes to work through their grief, some need to be allowed to stop. There is no set length of time for the healing process. People feel guilty if they enjoy themselves when they think they ought to be mourning, and guilt can be particularly associated with finding another sexual partner. The bereaved may think that to be intimate with another person is both an act of infidelity and a betrayal of their dead loved one. Indeed, being able to lead a normal life again can inculcate feelings of guilt. Immedately after a death one wonders whether a day will ever go by that you do not think of the dead person. Then one day you realise that a day has gone by without thinking of them and you feel guilty. It can sometimes be hard to

Grief

realise that being happy again is not a sign of disrespect to the dead.

Mourning is a period of time of irrational behaviour, emotional complexity and fatigue. Because of this irrational behaviour major decisions should be left for as long as possible. Impulsively, a bereaved person may decide to change jobs, get a new partner, have another child, or sell the house. The latter is often considered as a way of helping people to get over grief by leaving behind all the daily reminders contained in a house. But, as so many people find, running away from the physical reminders does not make the mental anguish easier. Those considering moving house would be wise to think of the words written by Daphne du Maurier to a bereaved friend. She advised:

> Stay in your own home with the familiar things around you. . . . If at first the silence may seem unbearable, it is still the home you shared, which you two made your own. As time passes something of tranquillity descends and though the well-remembered voice will not call from the room beyond, there seems to be about you an atmosphere of love, a living presence. As though you shared in some indefinable manner the freedom and peace of another world where there is no pain.

Others can help, like Daphne du Maurier, in counselling the bereaved not to take impulsive action but to wait until they are feeling more emotionally balanced.

Another reason for not making important decisions impulsively is that the ability to concentrate is also usually much diminished. The mind is obsessed with replaying over and over again the events of the death or remembering the past. I remember watching entire television programmes and being totally unable to say at the end what they had been about. Equally, I remember conversations going on around me that I could not concentrate on or engage in. C. S. Lewis wrote, after the death of his wife, 'There is a sort of invisible blanket between the world and me. I find it hard to take in what anyone says.' Because of that inability to focus outward, anything that is important and needs concentration should be avoided.

Much of the fatigue is a product of the emotional strain and of eating and sleeping disorders. Very often the bereaved do not eat properly, picking at meals, neglecting to eat or eating comforting but unnourishing food. Sleeping disorders mean not only getting less sleep because of insomnia, but also having disturbed sleep. Nightmares and bad dreams are very common. One woman told me that at first, after her son died, the days were hell as every single waking moment was a reminder of his death and absence. Sleep was her only respite. Then her days became bearable but the nights hell. In her sleep she dreamt about him and searched for him. Then her dreams turned to nightmares about his death. Geoffrey Gorer wrote that during the three months following the death of his brother he 'lost about twenty pounds in weight and my sleep tended to be disturbed. I had frequent dreams about Peter, many of them about our early childhood; waking from them was very distressing.' I too had distressing dreams and about six months after Will's death the dreams turned into nightmares which were so bad that I would wake up and try very hard to keep myself awake. I feared that sleep would bring another nightmare, which it invariably did. That was the point when I began to think I was going crazy, losing touch with reality and with my ability to cope.

Others, I later found out, also had periods when they thought they were going crazy. People can go rushing off down the streets thinking they have seen their loved one, only afterwards to think they were crazy to have such an irrational relapse. Judy Tatelbaum found that 'months after my brother died, I was at a large family gathering when someone greeted one of the relatives at the door with "David" – said with a great deal of feeling. I simply assumed my brother had come back to join us (from the dead) and was shocked to remember that I also had a cousin named David.' Another American woman, Zora Neale Hurston, in her autobiography *Dust Tracks on a Road* described how, after the death of her mother, she saw whilst on a walk from school 'a woman sitting on a porch who looked at a distance like Mama. Maybe it *was* Mama! Maybe she was not dead at all. They had made a mistake. Mama had gone off to Jacksonville and they thought that she was dead. The woman was sitting in a rocking chair just like Mama always did. It must be Mama! But before I came abreast of the porch in my rigid place in line, the woman got up and went inside.' These relapses are often ways of testing out reality. After the 'relapse' the reality of the person's death is reaffirmed. Slowly that reality becomes permanent and the relapses stop. For Zora Neale Hurston the process involved giving up 'the hope that the woman was really my mother' before she 'accepted' her bereavement. Accepting the death does not mean that one forgets the person. One just remembers that they are only a memory.

All these oddities of behaviour are quite normal. They only become abnormal when they persist. In such situations people can become trapped in their grief; like Mr Craven in *The Secret Garden*, they have locked themselves up in grief and thrown away the key. It was the children in *The Secret Garden* who found the key, unlocked the garden and finally Mr Craven's grief, and those trapped usually need, like Mr Craven, the help of others if they are to be able to confront and work through their grief. 'Unresolved grief' is the term used for people who, as it implies, are unable to come to terms with the death of a loved one. People who are unable to resolve their grief find that they are unable to form new relationships or nurture old ones. They may have deep fears that inhibit them from leading normal lives, or they may just cut themselves off from the world about them. People thus locked in need help of some kind, either from a self-help group, from counselling or from psychiatric help. If as a society we knew better how to help the bereaved, far fewer would need to seek help.

Helping

The bereaved can both help themselves and be helped by others. The two forms of helping can and should interact, but all too frequently there is little outside help and the bereaved are left isolated and unsure of how to help themselves. Of the need to help ourselves in bereavement Judy Tatelbaum wrote: 'Mourning may require self-supports different from those we are used to. We may need to be more active or more quiet than usual. We may need to talk more or contemplate more. We may need to express feelings out loud or write feelings in a journal. We may need work or responsibility to bolster our self-esteem, or we may need the freedom to take on less responsibility. Most of all, we need to accept our needs, regardless of what we were like before we suffered this loss.' Often it is hard to recognise our needs and, having done so, even harder to act on them. Confronted with the conventional wisdom that the bereaved can best help themselves by resuming normal life as quickly as possible, it can be very hard to resist such wisdom if one's needs are to withdraw quietly. Those around can be of greatest help if they refrain from giving conventional advice but offer to support the bereaved in their choice of behaviour.

After a death, another piece of conventional wisdom is to advise the bereaved to replace the dead person. The getting of a new husband, a new wife, another child is often advised. In the long term these new relationships can be important, loving and fulfilling, but in the short run the desperate attempt to fill the emptiness with another person neither resolves grief nor provides a good basis for the growth of a new and loving relationship. This kind of advice is most frequently given after the death of a child. It is as though the advisers believe that one child can replace another, but human beings cannot be replaced. Widowers are also urged and encouraged to find another wife, though in the last century the advice was rarely given to widows. Unless rich, widows were not regarded as desirable potential marriage partners, and they were expected to live out their widowhood showing devotion to their dead husband. Queen Victoria set the example, and there was much pressure for other respectable widows to do likewise. Whatever the pressures or advice, the bereaved would do better to form new relationships or create new lives when they have worked through their grief. The forming of new relationships may then well be a very important part of rebuilding a new life.

Many bereaved find their own private ways of helping themselves. Writing is extremely common, its therapeutic value having long been recognised. Dr Johnson suggested to his publisher, James Elphinstone, after the death of Elphinstone's mother, that, 'There is one expedient by which you may, in some degree, continue her presence. If you write down minutely what you remember of her from your earliest years, you will read it with great pleasure, and receive from it many hints of soothing recollection when time shall remove her yet further from you, and your grief shall be matured to veneration.' Whether James Elphinstone followed Dr Johnson's advice is not known, but others have found writing all that they can remember of great help.

At a meeting of Compassionate Friends (a self-help organisation for bereaved parents) one man brought out a thick hard-backed exercise book. He then told the meeting of how, after the death of his son, he had secretly written in his car parked in laybys over a period of time everything he could remember about the life of his son. He had done it secretly because he feared that people would censure him as being morbid for doing it. In writing his book he found that he worked through some of his grief. The sad thing was that it was only in the protective and understanding atmosphere of Compassionate Friends that he could reveal and talk about his writing.

As a writer it was perhaps not surprising that Christopher Leach should have chosen this means to work through some of his grief; because writing was his profession he did not feel the need to hide his occupation and could make public the result. His profoundly moving book, *Letter to a Younger Son*, no doubt helped him, but in sharing through words his experiences it helps others too. The list of those known to have, one way or another, used writing as a way of coming to terms with grief and loss is quite long. Of the well known, C. S. Lewis (*A Grief Observed* about the death of his wife), Simone de Beauvoir (*A Very Easy Death* about the death of her mother) and Vera Brittain (*Testament of Youth* about among many other things the deaths of the man she loved, her brother and many of the young men of her generation) are just three. Many others write not for publication but to fulfil their own need. It is not a morbid occupation but constructive therapy.

Other people find different forms of self-help. One can be reading books like those mentioned above, and gardening, walking, painting, listening to or playing music are just some of the many occupations people use as therapy. Work can be a therapy but it can also, only too often, be a form of escape. The bereaved need times of escape, but they also need time to grieve. Those who have faith in a religion can find comfort and solace in their beliefs. This may be through prayer, through attending a place of worship and through the support of fellow believers. Many too find solace and a form of self-therapy in visiting the grave or memorial-place in a crematorium.

What most bereaved find very hard to bear is people's fear of them and the social isolation that results from that fear. All too frequently they find that if, after the socially recognised period of mourning (not more than six weeks), they do not pretend to be well again they are not welcome socially. Geoffrey Gorer resisted this social pressure to hide his wound and refused one or two invitations to cocktail parties, explaining that he was in mourning. 'The people who invited me,' wrote Geoffrey Gorer, 'responded to this statement with shocked embarrassment, as if I had voiced some appalling obscenity. Indeed, I got the impression that, had I stated that the invitation clashed with some esoteric debauchery I had arranged, I would have had understanding and jocular encouragement; as it was, the people whose invitations I had refused, educated and sophisticated though they were, mumbled and hurried away.' He also suspected that they were frightened 'lest I give way to my grief, and involve them in a distasteful upsurge of emotion'.

People can help the bereaved by extending invitations but respecting the response. The offering of an invitation extends the hand of friendship, but should be framed so that the bereaved are made to feel that whichever way they respond is acceptable. Pressured to be sociable with such arguments as, 'Come on, you ought to get out and forget it all', the bereaved are likely to withdraw. An invitation should also be framed in a way that makes it clear that if the bereaved do come they will be accepted if they don't behave normally. If they suddenly burst into tears or want to leave after the soup, they should be made to feel that their behaviour is understood and accepted. C. S. Lewis, after his wife's death, was uncomfortable when invited to join other couples because he felt his presence was 'like a death's head'. Meeting 'a happily married pair' he could 'feel them both thinking, "One or other of us must some day be as he is now."'

Others need comfort and company but have equal difficulty in finding it. Writing in the *Guardian* (21 January 1987), Rebecca Abrams described how, aged eighteen when her father died,

> For a long time I did not think it could be 'lived through'. After the initial feelings of furious impotence, guilt, a profound sense of the injustice of death, I began to notice the world outside again. But the world did not want to notice me. Friends were embarrassed, not knowing what to say. To my amazement I often found myself comforting *them*. 'It's all right, don't worry, I'm fine now,' I'd say, thinking, 'Hang on a moment. Why should I ease their embarrassment, as well as coping with my own problems?' They're supposed to be helping me.

As a result of the social treatment she received, Rebecca Abrams 'felt totally alone' with her grief 'as if I had some kind of disease'. Because she felt that others kept their distance from her she learnt to keep her distance too. Social isolation can be even more extreme than not being invited to go to the pub or out to dinner. People avoid the bereaved literally as though they have the plague, as C. S. Lewis felt. Of his social isolation he wrote:

> An odd by-product of my loss is that I'm aware of being an embarrassment to everyone I meet. At work, at the club, in the street, I see people, as they approach me, trying to make up their minds whether they'll 'say something about it' or not. I hate it if they do, and if they don't. Some funk it altogether. R. has been avoiding me for a week. I like best the well brought-up young men, almost boys, who walk up to me as if I were a dentist, turn very red, get it over, and then edge away to the bar as quickly as they decently can. Perhaps the bereaved ought to be isolated in special settlements like lepers.

Almost all bereaved people will recognise and identify with the experience described by C. S. Lewis and Rebecca Abrams. I have heard more than one person describe how they were aware that people would literally cross the road rather than meet them. One woman worked in a glass-fronted small shop. After her son died she could see people she knew cross the road rather than pass by the shop, let alone come in to offer her some company and comfort. Such 'passing-by on the other side' is selfish and cruel. It stems from a total lack of imagination and consideration for the person who has most need, the bereaved.

To talk or not to talk is a problem for both the bereaved and for those around them. Shakespeare wrote in *Macbeth*: 'Give sorrow words: the grief that does not speak whispers the o'er fraught heart, and bids it break.' Wise as Shakespeare's advice may be, following it in the twentieth century is not so easy. The whole subject is one of social embarrassment, as Rebecca Abrams, C. S. Lewis and many others have testified. The bereaved should try to act on their own needs and talk if they want to talk or remain silent if that is their need. Those around can help by learning to listen for cues. Listening for cues may well be a case of asking, 'How do you feel today?' and then taking the cue from the answer. If the bereaved say, 'Fine,' and change the subject it is clear that they do not want to talk. If, however, they say something like, 'It's a bad day today for me, I can't help remembering this time last year,' then the listener can take that as a cue that they do want to talk. Letting someone talk can be a way of giving great help. Listening is equally important, and also involves listening out for the moment at which they want to stop talking. Friends and relatives can provide different kinds of listeners. Those who were also close to the person that died can share memories and the loss, while others, not so close, can be listeners. Although people sometimes feel made to talk when they wish to be silent, the majority complain of how 'no one will let me talk, no one will listen'. I remember only too vividly the number of times the conversation was changed when I mentioned my son Will, and I remember very tenderly those people who let me talk.

One thing to be remembered is that sometimes others besides those immediately bereaved need to grieve and to have their grief recognised. Close relatives may find they are giving all their emotional strength and practical help to the immediately bereaved and not taking time to recognise their own grief. In the period of a few years my parents suffered the loss of two grandchildren and had to witness the pain of grief in two of their children. I know that after the death of my sister's first child, a daughter called Sarah, and after the death of our first child they spent their time helping and giving to us. They did not take time to grieve. After the death of my niece I was too young and ignorant to understand about their need and, after the death of my son, too wrapped up in myself to consider others. My mother later complained about how people had not let her talk and had not recognised her grief and emotional strain.

The grief of children is frequently ignored. There is a commonly held assumption that, particularly if the child is young, they will 'soon get over it', healing easily and forgetting quickly. Because of this attitude it is assumed that they need little attention, support or open discussion. Another equally commonly held but contradictory view is that children will suffer so deeply if they are told the truth that it is best to protect them as far as possible from that truth. Whichever view is taken the child's grief is likely to be ignored. Children survive much better if their questions are honestly answered so that they share in the truth and in the suffering. Adults, especially men, are often embarrassed to let their children see their tears, or fear that the child may be upset to see them out of emotional control. The child is, in the long term, much more likely to be deeply upset and destabilised by being excluded and isolated.

Children need to grieve just as much as adults, even though they may manifest their grief in different ways. The fact that a child may be able to play quite happily for periods of time soon after the death of someone they had loved does not mean they do not feel the pain of loss acutely. If the child has lost a parent or a sibling, the surviving parent or parents may be too wrapped up in their own grief to be able to offer support and comfort to the child. Daphne Vaughan, talking of her grief following the murder of her son Robert, said: 'Just when you need to support each other you're so sunk into your own grief – I remember wondering where all the tears came from and how come the body didn't dehydrate – that you forget about how the rest of the family are feeling. My other children after all had lost a brother, but it was a long time before I thought to ask how they were coping.' (*Time Out*, 14 January 1987)

Although relatives of murder victims have some particular problems, Daphne Vaughan's comments apply to many a family facing bereavement in which the adults forget the children. For the child that has lost a parent that loss can leave them not only grieving but fearful and insecure. The more sudden the loss, the more frightening and threatening it is to their security. In the case of witnessing someone they love dying, children can prepare themselves for the eventuality if they are allowed to share that experience and have it discussed openly with them. Children can have

Grief

complicated emotional reactions, sometimes blaming themselves for the death or, particularly if a sibling has died, feeling that they should have been the one. Older children may, witnessing the grief of their surviving parent, suddenly become 'grown up', protective and feel that they should not further distress that parent by showing their own grief. Unless these fears and anxieties are expressed and worked through they may well be carried into adult life. Those close to the family can offer much help in recognising the needs of the child or children of whatever age. If the parent or parents are so wrapped up in their own grief, help for the children can and should come from others. Including children in any rituals of mourning is as important as discussing with them as clearly as possible about the death. Children need to bury their dead too, both literally and metaphorically.

In *King Lear* Shakespeare wrote: 'The mind much sufferance doth o'erskip when grief hath mates.' Almost all would agree with him that being able to share grief makes the suffering less. Although some find people around with whom they can share their feelings, many do not. Widows and widowers are often very lonely in that they have not just lost the person they love but are frequently left physically on their own. Others can be on their own for different reasons, perhaps because no one around them shares, listens, or recognises their grief. Non-recognition causes isolation for many different groups of people. Parents of stillborn babies are one group who find their need to grieve unrecognised; the fact that the baby did not live does not, as some people assume, mean they have not lost a human being, with all that that implies. Mothers in particular do have a deep need to mourn the loss of the child which has lived inside them; they need to bury their baby and mourn over its death.

If the dead person was the partner of a homosexual or lesbian they may find their grief unrecognised, particularly if their relationship had been secret. This is a problem homosexuals have had to face recently in increasing numbers. AIDS has not only brought about death but has also left many bereaved. They often have to face the double stress of coping with social attitudes to AIDS as well as to their sexuality. A close friend may mourn deeply for the loss of a friend, but again society does not recognise such grief. Relatives, spouses and fiancés may grieve, but not friends. Some years ago there was an article in the *Guardian* by a woman whose close friend, with whom she had shared a flat for many years, had died. The woman who died, shortly before her death, had become engaged. The writer of the article complained about how her grief was unrecognised and yet the fiancé, of much shorter acquaintance, received recognition and sympathy. Relatives of murder victims suffer a different kind of isolation. Their grief may be recognised but because of the nature of the death they can feel ashamed, however irrational that feeling may be. Of that additional hardship Daphne Vaughan said, 'You sit around all day because you can't face going out – I felt somehow ashamed, I don't know why, and couldn't face even the people on the pavement.' Whatever the circumstances of the bereavement, a loved person has died, leaving those that loved them in suffering and in pain. Their grief should be recognised and help, support and friendship extended to them.

Some bereaved people, recognising the loneliness and social isolation of bereavement, have started self-help organisations (see details on pp. 200–3) in which experiences can be shared and help received and given. Each organisation, whether it be for widows or widowers, bereaved parents, gays or lesbians, parents of murder victims, is there to provide support for others who have experienced a similar bereavement. Interestingly, there is no group for sons and daughters of whatever age. Rebecca Abrams tried to start a self-help group for other young adults like herself who had lost a parent, but explained that, 'I was not trained in counselling, and after only a few months, chronically depressed, I admitted defeat.' But, as she pointed out, the need for such a self-help organisation is obviously there.

The organisations that do exist are based on the knowledge that help and strength can come from sharing experiences. Those who have worked through their grief can help pass on advice, but the very fact that they are there can give hope to those in the first raw stages of grief. For the bereaved can at first feel as though the experience is impossible to survive. I remember meeting by accident an old friend of mine whom I had not seen for years, though I knew that in those intervening years his daughter had been killed in an accident. Our meeting was in a crowded room and he just said, 'It does get easier.' I clung to his words. If he could survive, I thought, perhaps I could. I know now that I too could pass on those words and that comfort.

As well as passing on experience, these organisations offer a variety of ways of helping, advising and supporting their members. They recognise that individuals have individual needs. Often they work by simply informing the bereaved of their existence and leaving an address and phone number to be called if needed. Most find that their need for such help is not in the first stage, but afterwards when they are expected to have returned to normal life. Those close can help by informing the bereaved of the existence of the relevant organisation and giving them an address and phone number. The information is thus there if and when it is needed. Most of these organisations provide one-to-one contact and/or the chance to share experiences in a group. Sometimes the organisation will put people in contact so that they can share experiences and comfort through correspondence. Breaking the feeling that you are the only person in the world that has suffered so, and that no one else understands, can be an important step in the process of recovery. Because these organisations were set up and are run by those who have experienced bereavement themselves, they are sensitive to the needs of the bereaved. Many have found much help, solace and healing through sharing with others.

Help is also available from trained professionals, though it is not often offered but has to be sought. There has been a growth in the recognition of the need to provide counselling, but many people do not know about such services or where they are to be found. In many areas counselling is still not available and in those areas where some provision is made it is often inadequate. Hospices and home care units for the terminally ill see it as part of their job to offer a follow-up service to the bereaved. Christine McGee in the programme 'Born to Die' spoke of the continuing help she had received from her support team following the death of her mother. She explained:

> When my mother died the support team said, 'We're still here, we haven't left you or anything. If there's anything you want to do with child benefits, your social security, things like that we're here to help you.' And as my younger brother, Desmond, lives with us – he's fourteen – they are there to deal with him as well. Any help I need. It is not necessarily the sister that comes to me but the social worker of the support team still comes to me once a fortnight.

Such continuing support and help is a far cry from the hospital doctor who responded after Will's death to my question, 'What should we do now?' with the words, 'I would go home.' No one even asked how we would get home. In fact we drove which, looking back, was clearly highly dangerous. No one in such a state of shock should be allowed to drive, let alone negotiate Hyde Park Corner and Marble Arch. Our home care doctor and sister did both visit to express their sympathy, and their visit was deeply appreciated. However, no continuing help or counselling was offered, and indeed I did not know then, nor did anyone inform me, that such a thing existed. It was some years before I even heard of Compassionate Friends. Besides home care units, health visitors, home helps and social workers are increasingly being made aware of the needs of the bereaved and some train in bereavement counselling. However, there is still inadequate provision of counsellors even for those most in need. Daphne Vaughan said of the relatives of murder victims, 'You need counselling, you really do. Not straight away, because you are not thinking straight, but after about six months. Look at the murderer: he's got doctors, psychiatrists, psychologists – the whole lot. Not one person came to see us.'

Colin Murray Parkes in a paper for the *British Medical Journal* (5 July 1980) entitled 'Bereavement counselling: does it work?' concluded after assessing several studies on the benefit of counselling that, whilst many did not need it, those who did 'seem to benefit from opportunities to express grief, reassurances about the psychological accompaniments of grief, and the chance to take stock of their present life situation and to start new directions'. Those needing counselling may need, Colin Murray Parkes noted, 'permission to grieve' or 'permission to stop grieving'. Obviously the benefit or otherwise of counselling is dependent on many variables, but people are and can be helped by it.

With help and support most bereaved people do in their own time, and in their own way, work through their grief to build a new life. They are changed by the experience. That change brings about a greater understanding of themselves and a re-evaluation of life.

Re-evaluations

Rebecca Abrams in her *Guardian* article divided society into 'the haves' (those that have experienced the death of a loved one) and the 'have nots'. Of these two groups she wrote: 'There is a great gulf of experience which separates the "haves" and the "have nots", and in between lies the waste and wealth of death itself.' The wealth of death is to be found in the survivors, for in the process of surviving much is learnt about oneself, about others and about life.

Surviving bereavement is a triumph for the individual. That survival represents the ability to have coped with one of the greatest challenges we meet in our lives. It is the survival of what for many is the unimaginable. Most work through the unimaginable to re-build their lives the stronger for having survived. They find one day that they can laugh and love again. Life can and does go on. It becomes possible to have memories, but not to live in those memories. The anger, bitterness, guilt and pain slowly disappear and their occasional re-surfacing acts as a reminder of the time when it was all much worse. The utter meaninglessness of death and the seeming meaninglessness of life recedes and new meanings are found.

One of the most natural reactions to the death of someone deeply loved is, 'I shall never love again.' The reaction is a combination of idealisation of the dead one and a form of self-protection. Many people scorn obituaries which always say the good about a dead person, but the desire to say and think only the good arises from a deeper need than that of social etiquette which requires that the dead be respected. Thinking only of the good things about a person is a way of giving meaning to the meaningless fact of death. It is also a form of self-protection. Believing that the relationship with the dead person was 'perfect' and that it would be impossible ever to find another relationship that is so good and loving is a way of protecting oneself from being so hurt again. If loving can lead to so much pain, the reasoning goes, then it is safer not to love. Yet the old cliché 'It is better to have loved and lost than never to have loved at all' is true, and with the healing process of grief people find that they are glad that they loved. They learn that life is the richer for having loved, and that new emotional richness can be found again; that loving again may mean finding another partner or may mean learning to cherish and love friends and relatives. The rejection of the possibility of love that accompanies grief can be a rejection of a world that, in its lack of respect for life, appears casual and cruel. Being able to risk loving again is to begin to live and survive.

The last sentence of Vera Brittain's *Testament of Youth* is a testament to the capacity to survive the cruelty and meaninglessness of death and to find the capacity to love and build life again. During the First World War Vera Brittain lost the man she loved, her brother and many of her

Grief

friends. After the death of her brother Edward she wrote: 'I knew now that death was the end and that I was quite alone. There was no hereafter, no Easter morning, no meeting again; I walked in darkness, a dumbness, a silence which no beloved voice would penetrate, no fond hope illumine.' Although the loss of her friends, and particularly her brother, were to be felt and remembered all her life, she did learn to love again. Some years after the war she met another man and agreed to marry him on his return from a period in Europe. To welcome him home she climbed on board the crowded Southampton–Waterloo express train and pushed through the crowds. Of finding him she wrote: 'And as I went up to him and took his hands, I felt I had made no mistake; and although I knew that, in a sense which could never be true of him, I was linked with the past inextricably and forever, I found it not inappropriate that the years of frustration and grief and loss, of work and conflict and painful resurrection, should have led me through their dark and devious ways to this new beginning.'

The First World War showed too the way in which grief can be used as a weapon of war or a weapon of peace. Grief can and does cause anger, hatred, the desire for revenge and the desire to inflict grief on others. As such it can perpetuate wars. However, during the First World War that emotional weapon turned against war as more and more young men lost their lives in what increasingly seemed meaningless slaughter. The desire for life overtook the desire for revenge. The experience of grief can completely change people's attitude to war and violent conflict. It can transform 'the enemy' into 'some mother's son', and in doing so bring about the realisation that despite differences human beings are ultimately the same. Grief can unite. The best expression of that realisation is in the words of Mrs Boyle in Sean O'Casey's play *Juno and the Paycock*:

> Maybe I didn't feel sorry enough for Mrs Tancred when her poor son was found as Johnny's been found now – because

> he was a Die-hard! Ah, why didn't I remember that he
> wasn't a Die-hard or a Stater, but only a poor dead son. It's
> well I remember all that she said – an' it's my turn to say it
> now: What was the pain I suffered, Johnny, bringin' you
> into the world to carry you to your cradle, to the pains I'll
> suffer carryin' you out o' the world to bring you to the
> grave! Mother o' God, Mother o' God, have pity on us all!
> Blessed Virgin, where were you when me darlin' son was
> riddled with bullets? Sacred heart o' Jesus, take away our
> hearts o' stone, and give us hearts o' flesh! Take away this
> murdherin' hate, an' give us Thine own eternal love.

Grief does link one, as Vera Brittain perceived, inextricably with the past but it can also lead to a new future. Before my child died I had unconsciously assumed that grief, like a photo, would slowly fade with the passing of time until it was gone. This caused me to panic, when I was grieving, that one day Will's image would disappear and leave me with a blank sheet in my memory. One goes on remembering, like replaying a film in one's mind, in case one should forget. The long-term experience of grief has taught me that one does not forget. The memories and images of Will have never faded. What happened was that, in the process of grieving, I learnt to live with those memories as memories. C. S. Lewis also found that:

> Passionate grief does not link us with the dead but cuts us
> off from them. This becomes clearer and clearer. It is just at
> those moments when I feel least sorrow – getting into my
> morning bath is usually one of them – that H. rushes upon
> my mind in her full reality, her otherness. Not, as in my
> worst moments, all foreshortened and pathetized and
> solemnized by my miseries, but as she is in her own right.
> This is good and tonic.

Accepting the memory of my son marked the beginning of being able to rebuild my life and, with time, grow to realise just how much he had given to me. He caused me to re-evaluate my life. Will's legacy indeed made me richer – richer in the realisation of the preciousness of time and love. I have risked loving again. The thought of the loss of those that I love causes me literally to go into a cold sweat of terror; that cold sweat reaffirms my knowledge of their preciousness. Life is all we know we have, and we ignore that at our peril.

Many others have found that surviving the death of a loved one has caused them to re-evaluate their lives. Christopher Leach at the end of his book *Letter to a Younger Son* wrote three sections entitled: 'What have I discovered?', 'What have I learned?' and 'What do I believe?'. His answers to his own questions reveal that he discovered and learnt much and found a firm belief. He discovered much about the pain of grief and that 'tragedy needs not diminish those who suffer it'. He found that his belief in life 'is strengthened by death'. His section on 'What have I learned?' is an eloquent testimony to the way the experience of 'a deeper grief than I thought possible' can not only be survived but can cause profound change. Christopher Leach learned 'what is important; that faced with the ultimate, things move to a correct proportion'. He also learned much about himself and about the range of emotions released by grief. Addressing the book to his younger son, he wrote: 'I have learned compassion: I know what it is to mourn. I have learned, too late in one respect, that I have not cared enough. And now it is too late for him. But not for you.' In that process of learning meaning also returned to his life. The person who had contemplated suicide in the dark days after Jonathan's death could write a year later: 'I have been granted a certain time to walk about this Earth, and to take a look at its marvels and its follies – and perhaps contribute to both – and what I do *matters.*'

More than anything, what grief does is remind us of our mortality. Tagore wrote: 'I shrink to give up my life, and thus do not plunge into the great waters of life.' We do shrink from the knowledge of death, preferring to cruise through life in the implicit assumption that we are immortal until suddenly the death of someone we love brings us up with a sharp jolt. Our confidence in the certainties of life are shattered. Despite the fact that we are aware of others dying in wars, in famines, in accidents, in cancer or geriatric wards, we do not relate those deaths to ourselves. It is only when someone we love dies that we realise that others we love can also die – but most of all that we ourselves can die. That realisation of mortality is a realisation of what it is to be human.

Part Two

RACHAEL TREZISE

None of us wish to face the fact that we or anyone close to us may die. We therefore find it hard to assimilate any information about a time in our lives that we dread. Yet it is useful and helpful to know about services for the dying, the laws relating to death and support groups for the bereaved. At the time of confronting dying or death we are least well equipped to take in or seek out such information. We hope that this section of the book will provide the necessary information and ease the pressures when the time comes.

The following chapters are broken down to cover three subject areas. The first is information on sources of help for the terminally ill, the second will give you information on the legal requirements and your options under the law when someone dies, and the third will provide information on bereavement counselling.

In all cases we have tried to provide a range of addresses and information points, but it is impossible to list all the regional branches. The head offices of all of these organisations will be happy to tell you if there is a branch in your area – or look in your local telephone directory.

CHAPTER SIX

The Terminally Ill

There are various forms of help available to the terminally ill and their families; the important thing is to find the help that is most beneficial to you. In the last few years there has been a sharp increase in the number of hospices in this country, as well as hospice-related services such as home nursing, which might provide an alternative form of care which suits your needs better than traditional hospitalisation.

Hospices provide a range of services and should not be considered purely as a place where people go to die. People can be admitted for short stays, either to get the pain-control level established or to give relatives or themselves a break. Most hospices accept short-stay patients. Hospices are funded by various sources and are sometimes established by charities and then run by the National Health Service. Some of the hospices are run by religious organisations; they may still be open to everyone regardless of denomination but may have a religious 'overtone' which is not right for you. All hospices, however, will provide religious comfort to individuals even if they are not run by a religious order. There are new hospices opening up all over the country as it seems that they provide a 'treatment' that suits many people.

The main function of the hospice is pain control, which recognises that most 'patients' are terminally ill and that, regardless of what stage of the illness they are at, there is no need for anyone to suffer pain. Any possible addictive side-effects of this course of treatment, normally opiates, are generally considered to be less important than the intolerable levels of pain that many people suffer when dying from such illnesses as cancer.

Admission to a hospice is normally made through your doctor, either your general practitioner or the hospital doctor, but you can make a direct approach to the hospices in your area to find out the admission details. Most hospices do not charge for your stay, but it is something else to check when asking for information or when considering what kind of 'pay care' might be right for you. Hospices do also sometimes offer day-care facilities which can be used to complement home nursing. The atmosphere in a hospice is usually very different from that of a hospital. The staff-to-patient ratio is normally much higher, with a range of optional activities provided. Once the pain is under control there is no need for people to stay in bed, and often patients are able to go out to the shops or the theatre or just enjoy a game of cards – but there is always someone on hand to provide medical attention. The main difference is that whilst hospitals tend to regard death as a failure, a hospice is there to make that death as pain-free, comfortable and acceptable as possible.

There is a national information service run from St Christopher's Hospice in London which will send you a *Directory of Hospice Services*, incorporating a countrywide list of hospices and information on other forms of terminal care. They also run a bookshop and will send you a list of publications that are available through them. (They will deal with telephone enquiries.)

> Hospice Information Service
> 51–59 Lawrie Park Road
> Sydenham
> London SE26 6DZ
>
> Telephone: 01 778 1240/9252

At the moment they do not receive any funding and are run as a voluntary organisation. Please bear this in mind and enclose a large stamped addressed envelope and/or a small donation.

Your local doctor or health centre should also be able to tell you where your nearest hospice is, as should the Social Services Department in your area. The Citizens Advice Bureaux may be able to help you as well. Check for these in your *Yellow Pages*.

Home nursing for the terminally ill is now provided by both the National Health Service and some charities.

Terminal care and support teams – who work on referral from hospitals and social workers – are run by the NHS and are based within hospitals themselves. They are there to provide back-up for people who wish to nurse those who are terminally ill at home. The home-care 'team' is usually a doctor, nurses and social worker. They not only arrange for pain-control to be taken care of at home, usually in the form of injections or suppositories, but also help the whole family to come to terms with what home nursing really means. They can be called for advice or support when necessary. Their aim is to provide a care that is normally associated with the hospice movement, but in people's own homes, and will often liaise with the local hospices to arrange for short-term stays etc., as well as putting you in touch with other organisations who might be able to offer some practical help with home nursing. Your local doctor or hospital will be able to put you in touch with these teams. Do not think that they want to come in and take over your lives – their aim is to help the whole family unit as much as they can.

The National Health Service also helps administer nurses provided by charities such as Macmillan Nurses and Marie Curie Nurses. These often work in conjunction with the terminal care and support teams, which are also known as the continuing care units.

Macmillan Nurses are funded by the Cancer Relief Macmillan Fund (which is also known as The National Society for Cancer Relief). These nurses will have been either district nurses or health visitors, and act as part of the team of carers. They see their role as not only helping to build up and maintain a continuing care relationship with patients and their families, but also to support and encourage other members of the team who may at times find the situations difficult and stressful. Their workload is deliberately planned so that they have time to spend with, and talk to, the people concerned, which is often not possible with NHS staff. Their goal is to help patients spend their time in comfort and peace of mind, and at the same time to support the family. Macmillan Nurses generally work through the Community Nursing Officer of the local health authority, who you can contact direct for information; or your doctor can advise you if there are nurses available in your area.

> Cancer Relief Macmillan Fund
> Anchor House
> 15–19 Britten Street
> London SW3 3TY
>
> Telephone: 01 351 7811

Marie Curie Nurses are provided in most areas of the United Kingdom by the Marie Curie Foundation. Some of these nurses are part-time and nearly all are either Registered or Enrolled Nurses. They provide day and night nursing, again enabling families caring for the sick person to obtain adequate rest. They are administered by the Community Nursing Officer and, in the first instance, applications for nursing care are best initiated by your doctor, health visitor or social worker.

> Marie Curie Memorial Foundation
> 28 Belgrave Square
> London SW1X 8QG
>
> Telephone: 01 235 3325

Both the Macmillan Fund and the Marie Curie Foundation are registered charities and rely on donations – they make no charges for their services and indeed have limited amounts of their funds available as grants to patients in need. This can be in the form of help with a heavy fuel bill, providing extra blankets or helping with specialist dietary needs. Both run homes or small units either within hospitals or independently run homes. A list of these will be included in the Hospice Information leaflet available as above.

BACUP – British Association of Cancer United Patients – which was founded in 1984 by Dr Vicky Clement-Jones, became fully operational in 1985. BACUP aims to provide information and practical support to patients and their families on a national basis. BACUP is a voluntary organisation which receives some funding from the Macmillan Fund and the Marie Curie Foundation as well as from other sources. Their information service is manned from 9.30 a.m. to 5.00 p.m. on Mondays, Wednesdays and Fridays, and from 9.30 a.m. to 7.00 p.m. on Tuesdays and Thursdays. There is no weekend cover at the moment, but they offer practical information as well as counselling.

> BACUP
> 121-123 Charterhouse Street
> London EC1M 6AA
>
> Cancer Information Service: 01 608 1661

Cancerlink provides information and emotional support for people with cancer, their families and friends. Its information service, staffed by nurses, provides telephone information for the public about cancer from 9.30 a.m. to 5.30 p.m., Mondays to Fridays. It also provides information to medical professionals and others working with people affected by cancer. The Groups Support Service acts as a resource and information centre for cancer support and self-help groups throughout Great Britain, providing information, training and support.

> Cancerlink
> 46 Pentonville Road
> London N1 9HF
>
> Telephone: 01 833 2451

The Chest, Heart and Stroke Association have a range of information available on how to cope with nursing those who have had a stroke or are suffering from a related problem. They publish leaflets, pamphlets, books and a newspaper and whilst these do not normally cover 'terminal care', they will be able to give you help and counselling on various aspects of coping with the problems of speech impairment, loss of mobility and so on, which can make home nursing so much more demanding.

> The Chest, Heart and Stroke Association
> Tavistock House North
> Tavistock Square
> London WC1H 9JE
>
> Telephone: 01 387 3012

The Sue Ryder Foundation is an international foundation established by Lady Ryder in 1953. It runs eighty homes in Britain and abroad, some of which supply terminal care as well as providing some home nursing, although it does have limited resources. It is a registered charity.

> The Sue Ryder Foundation
> Sue Ryder Home
> Cavendish
> Sudbury
> Suffolk CO10 8AY
>
> Telephone: Glemsford (0787) 280252

The Terrence Higgins Trust – AIDS is now a well-known medical condition. As it is, however, relatively new to this country there are constant changes in resources for AIDS sufferers. The Trust is a focal point for information on what is available. There are plans to open hospices solely for those who have AIDS and also to provide home-nursing support teams, but check what is available in your area as these are constantly changing.

> The Terrence Higgins Trust
> BM/AIDS
> London WC1N 3XX
>
> Telephone: 01 242 1010, Monday to Friday 3 p.m. to 10 p.m.
> (On Saturdays and Sundays these lines are manned from 3 p.m. to 10 p.m.)

All these organisations have different sources of information available. If you would like further information on their services, or wish to contact them for specific assistance, they have indicated that they will be happy to help. Please remember, however, that they all rely on voluntary donations to stay in existence.

Do not forget that, whilst these organisations can give you valuable information, you should not hesitate to contact your local health centre or doctor for help and information – they know your area better than anyone.

Other forms of practical help in the way of equipment or facilities are sometimes available through organisations such as the British Red Cross, who have local branches listed in the telephone directory. If you need help in locating specific services outside those listed, ask at your local health centre or doctor's surgery, or ring the Social Services department of your local council.

CHAPTER SEVEN

When Someone Dies

Most of us, because it is considered morbid to discuss these matters beforehand, do not know what the person who has died would have really wanted in terms of a funeral service or disposal of their body. In this chapter we will not only tell you of the *legal* obligations that we have when someone dies, but also of the alternative arrangements that are within the law but that most people may not be familiar with. We will also detail some background to, and tell you what is needed for, the different legal responsibilities that you face and tell you about the information that is usually circulated by doctors etc. in a sealed envelope – i.e. the cause of death.

First things to be done

If the death occurs at home the first thing to do is contact the family doctor unless he or she has told you that, as death is expected, you do not need to notify them until the surgery is open. If the death is accidental, violent or suspicious you must call the police. If this is the case do not touch anything until they arrive.

If relatives need to be contacted at this point, it may be easier to get a neighbour or friend to come in and help you with this, as it is obviously a very distressing and difficult task. It might be that the relevant minister of religion should be contacted, either for your own sake or because the person who has died would have wanted it.

If the deceased has signified a wish for their organs to be donated, your local doctor or hospital should be contacted immediately. If someone has died at home the use of some organs, such as kidneys, may of course not be possible because of the delay involved. Eyes can be removed up to six hours after death, so if in Scotland, England or Wales contact your doctor or nearest eye hospital, and if in Northern Ireland notify the Eye Bank, Royal Victoria Hospital, Belfast (telephone: Belfast 40503, ext. 371), as soon as possible.

If the deceased has asked that their body be donated to a hospital, arrangements should have been made for this. If not, ring (in England and Wales) HM Inspector of Anatomy on 01 636 6811, ext. 3572/3576, or 01 407 5522 if outside office hours; (in Northern Ireland) Department of Anatomy, Queen's University, Medical Biology Centre, 97 Lisburn Road, Belfast BT9 7BL (telephone: Belfast 29241, ext. 2106); or (in Scotland) the Department of Anatomy at one of the following Universities: Aberdeen, St Andrews, Glasgow, Dundee or Edinburgh; or your doctor will advise you on the correct procedure to follow.

If, however, the death has to be reported to the coroner or the procurator fiscal (in Scotland) his/her consent will be needed before the organs or body can be donated.

If the death occurs in hospital or a hospice, you will need to talk to the ward sister, who will know how to proceed if organs or the body are to be donated and will also arrange a time for you to collect the patient's possessions. The hospital will keep the body in the mortuary until arrangements are made to take the deceased away, and can also offer some information on such things as where the registrar is if you need any help of this sort.

The second stage

The Births and Deaths Registration Act of 1874 was the first Act which made it obligatory for a doctor who had seen a person during their last illness to issue a death certificate stating as accurately as possible the cause of death. It was not, however, until the Act was amended by the Births and Deaths Registration Act of 1926 that any real attention to detail was paid. This Act stipulated that a death could not be registered without a doctor's certificate stating natural causes, unless the death was reported to the coroner. It was in the same year, 1926, that The Coroner's Amendment Act introduced in England, Wales and Northern Ireland the requirement that the coroner be a fully qualified medical practitioner, solicitor or barrister of at least five years' standing. This Act also allowed coroners to exercise their discretion as to whether an inquest had to take place if the body showed no signs of violence or unnatural factors following a post-mortem.

Death certificate
(or 'medical certificate of the cause of death')

Doctors who have treated people during their last illness are obliged by law to issue a death certificate, but a problem can arise when the doctor does not wish to accept the responsibility for having treated the 'last illness'. This means that, for example, someone may have had an illness treated at home over a period of time but then be admitted to hospital where very shortly afterwards they die. The question is then whether the hospital doctor or the general practitioner has treated the last illness. The hospital doctor may not have had time to effect treatment or be as conversant with the case as the GP, but technically would be the last doctor involved. In this case it might well be that the death is referred to the coroner's office, or, in Scotland, the procurator fiscal – *not necessarily because there is anything suspicious about the death* but because the wording of the legislation does not define in clear terms who should be responsible for the issuing of the death certificate. When a death is referred to the Coroner's Office (or the procurator fiscal) it does not necessarily mean that either a post-mortem or an inquest (known as a fatal accident inquiry – FAI – in Scotland) will take place.

The law does not require a doctor to view the body before issuing a death certificate, though over the last fifty years the proportion of deaths which have been certified without the body having been seen has dropped from 48.5 per cent in 1928 to 1.8 per cent in 1980.

This is largely due to the rise in the number of cremations – 65 per cent of people are now cremated rather than buried. One of the requirements for a cremation certificate to be issued is that the doctor is required to view the body. This may be done where the death takes place, but can be done at the undertaker's if that is where the body is taken before cremation. As the doctor who issues the death certificate must have treated the patient within the last fourteen days, this is often another cause for delay. With the increase in the number of health centres and group practices it is not always your 'own' doctor who has treated you, and indeed during the holiday period or when a locum has been brought in there are often a large number of cases which have to be referred to the coroner/procurator fiscal purely because of this 'fourteen-day' rule.

The coroner/procurator fiscal at his/her discretion can decline to accept the case, thus referring it back to the doctor, or can issue a form 'A' which enables the doctor to issue a certificate which is acceptable to the registrar. You may well be asked to collect the death certificate from your doctor or health centre and he/she will at the same time issue a 'notice to informant'. The death certificate will have on it: the name of the deceased, the date of the death, the age of the deceased, the place of death and when the doctor last saw the person alive. On the English death certificate he or she will also circle one of the following:

1 The certified cause of death takes account of information obtained from post-mortem
2 Information from post-mortem may be available later
3 Post-mortem not being held
4 I have reported this death to the coroner for further action

The doctor will also circle one of the following:

a Seen after death by me
b Seen after death by another medical practitioner but not by me
c Not seen after death by a medical practitioner

The other information which will appear on the certificate is the 'cause of death', filled in according to the following:

Ia Disease or condition directly leading to death. (This does not mean the mode of dying, such as heart failure, asphyxia, asthenia etc.; it means the disease, injury, or complication which caused death.)
  b Other disease or condition, if any, leading to (1a)
  c Other disease or condition, if any, leading to (1b)
II Other significant conditions *contributing to the death* but not related to the disease or condition causing it.

There is a further section which asks the doctor to tick if applicable if 'the death might have been due to or contributed to by the employment followed at some time by the deceased'. The signature of the doctor then certifies that he or she was 'in medical attendance during the above-named deceased's last illness, and that the particulars and cause of death above written are true to the best of my knowledge and belief'. For deaths in hospital, the certificate also asks for the name of the consultant 'responsible for the above-named as a patient'.

The doctor certifying death will retain a counterfoil with all the information on it for their records, and the medical certificate will then be either sent to the registrar or put in an envelope and given to you or the person designated as 'informant'. A 'notice to informant', which has been detached from the certificate, will be given to the person registering the death.

This 'notice to informant' will be signed by the doctor confirming that he or she has issued a medical certificate as to the cause of death. It will also tell you the 'duties of informant', which are:

Failure to deliver this notice to the registrar renders the informant liable to prosecution. The death cannot be registered until the medical certificate has reached the registrar.

When the death is registered the informant must be prepared to give to the registrar the following particulars relating to the deceased:

1 The date and place of death
2 The full name and surname (and the maiden surname if the deceased was a woman who had married)
3 The date and place of birth
4 The occupation (and if the deceased was a married woman or a widow the name and occupation of her husband)
5 The usual address
6 Whether the deceased was in receipt of a pension or allowance from public funds
7 If the deceased was married, the date of birth of the surviving widow or widower

The form also asks for the deceased's medical card to be delivered to the registrar. It is not always possible to find this immediately, in which case you will be given a stamped addressed envelope in which to send it once you have found it to the NHS Central Register.

On the back of the 'notice to informant' is a description of 'persons qualified and liable to act as informants':

The following persons are designated by the Births and Deaths Registration Act 1953 as qualified to give information concerning a death:

Deaths in houses and public institutions
1 A relative of the deceased, present at the death
2 A relative of the deceased, in attendance during the last illness
3 A relative of the deceased, residing or being in the sub-district where the death occurred.
4 A person present at the death
5 The occupier* if he knew of the happening of the death
6 Any inmate if he knew of the happening of the death
7 The person causing the disposal of the body

Deaths not in houses or dead bodies found
1 Any relative of the deceased having knowledge of any of the particulars required to be registered
2 Any person present at the death
3 Any person who found the body
4 Any person in charge of the body
5 The person causing the disposal of the body

*'Occupier' in relation to a public institution includes the governor, keeper, master, matron, superintendent, or other chief resident

In the case of elderly relatives, or if you are acting for someone who is not a relative, you may not always know all the information required by the registrar. Do not worry – it is not unusual for the notifier not to have all the information available – the registrar will advise you if there are any difficulties.

The registrar

The address of the Registrar of Births and Deaths can be obtained from your local telephone directory, the hospital, your doctor or health centre, the Citizens Advice Bureaux, your local council office, post office or police station. In England and Wales a death has to be registered in the sub-district in which the death occurred, although in Scotland or Northern Ireland it can also be registered in the district of the deceased's usual residence. If you are not sure which is the right registrar to go to, ring up and check before you go; it may not be your local registry office if the death has occurred in hospital in England or Wales – where the death took place rather than where the person lived is the deciding factor.

This does mean that if death takes place whilst temporarily away from home – on holiday for example, or travelling for one's job – someone has to travel to the place where the death occurred to register it. This can obviously cause some problems, but you will find that your local registrar or social services department will be able to advise you on how best to cope with this.

Most registry offices are open during normal office hours, but do check before you travel any distance – some may be open Saturday mornings but closed for the local half-day 'early closing'. It is best to call them and check. Do also check if you have any disability that the office is accessible – they may be upstairs and it can add to the distress if you get there and are faced with a flight of stairs. They will try and accommodate you if you let them know of your problem in advance.

You should take with you the 'cause of death' certificate and, if available, the medical card and birth certificate of the deceased.

You are required by law to register the death within five days in England, Wales and Northern Ireland, or within eight days (fourteen days if it is written notice) in Scotland. No burial or cremation can take place until the death has been registered. If the death has been notified to the coroner/procurator fiscal, the death can only be notified rather than registered until authority has been received from the coroner/procurator fiscal to proceed.

The registrar needs the information as stated on the 'notice to informant', as well as your 'qualification' and address. You are required to sign that the details on the form are correct; these will have been completed on a 'certified copy of an entry' which is 'pursuant to the Births and Deaths Registration Act, 1953'. This information will then be entered into the main registration book. These books are kept in the Registrar's Office until full and then passed on to the main registry office. If you require a copy of this certificate, and you will almost certainly need at least one for your solicitor, you will have to pay for it; it costs £2 in England and Wales, £5 in Scotland or £3.75 in Northern Ireland. Should you subsequently require any further copies, the registrar should indicate at the time of registration how much longer the certificates will be in his/her possession before you have to apply to the General Register Office.

In England and Wales, once the certificates have 'moved

When Someone Dies

on' they cost £5 per copy, but the charges remain the same in Scotland or Northern Ireland whenever you apply. This application can be made in person or by post, but certificates are not available on the spot. In England and Wales they can be obtained from the General Register Office, St Catherine's House, 10 Kingsway, London WC2B 6JP; in Scotland from the General Register Office for Scotland, New Register House, Edinburgh EH1 3YT; or in Northern Ireland from the Registrar General's Office in Belfast.

The registrar will, however, give you a 'certificate of the registration/notification of a death' for which there is no charge. This had sections on the back to fill in to claim the Death Grant, but from April 1987 this has been abolished. You are now only eligible for financial assistance from the Social Fund administered by the DHSS if you are already receiving additional benefits. There are also sections to fill in to make the claim for Widow's Benefit; one section, which applies for the increase in the retirement pension for widows, requires you to fill in the pension or allowance number on the pension book. It is best to take this form to your local Social Security Office so that you can fill in all the relevant forms at one go, but if this is not possible complete the form and send it on to your local Social Security office and they will send you the forms to make the claims. These are all state benefits for which you have contributed for many years – do not hesitate to claim them.

At the same time as you are registering the death you will also be asked for further information for statistical purposes. This is not entered in the register and *you are not required by law to give it*.

The registrar is required to notify the appropriate authority if the deceased was receiving pensions or allowances from government funds, as well as any relevant professional body. This is either done by preparing a full certified copy of the death entry, or there may be a special form of notification to be completed.

The Registrar will give you a certificate for disposal – if the coroner/procurator fiscal has not already issued one –

which should be given to the undertakers if you are using their services. If not, it should be given to the superintendent of the crematorium or cemetery. It is usually the undertaker who makes sure that this form is completed as the 'notification of burial or cremation'; this has to be returned to the registrar to ensure that proper disposal of the body has taken place.

Registering a Stillbirth
If you are registering that a baby has been stillborn – i.e. that a baby has been born dead after the twenty-eighth week of pregnancy (before this time it is considered a miscarriage) – you will need to give the registrar a certificate of stillbirth issued by your midwife or doctor, if present. If neither of the above were present the parents are required to sign a form which is available from the registrar. You will then be issued with a certificate for burial. Do not be upset by the fact that this form does not have specific space to enter a name for the baby – the registrar can enter one for you if you so wish.

Information available from the registrar
You may well find, in the Registrar's Office, copies of various leaflets prepared by the Department of Health and Social Security which give practical advice. One of these is particularly good, 'What to do after a death, D.49'; it is free and gives much helpful advice.

Other leaflets are: 'Income tax and widows, IR23', produced by the Inland Revenue; 'Industrial death benefits for widows and other dependants, N.I. 196'; 'Your benefit as a widow for the first 26 weeks, NP35'; and 'Widows – Guidance about NI contributions and benefits, N.I. 51'. All these leaflets deal with different aspects of state pensions etc., but you may prefer to leave dealings with these things until after the funeral, when it may be easier to confront these sorts of problems. You can then either go along to your local Social Security office or Citizen's Advice Bureau and talk to them about what help you can receive – or your bank manager, if you have one, might be able to help with some of these problems. If you need help with funeral costs it is advisable to talk to the Social Security office or the undertaker before the funeral takes place. Only certain things can be covered by Social Security, although a perfectly adequate funeral can be arranged.

Registering a death which occurs abroad
You need to register the death in accordance with the regulations of the country in which the death occurred. You also need to register the death with the British Consul so that a record will be kept in your home country and copies of that record available at a later date.

The coroner or the procurator fiscal

Most of what we know of coroners comes from reading reports in the newspapers or from television news reports of 'sensational' inquests or post-mortems, or of course from television series like 'Quincy'.

Coroners are drawn from the ranks of those who have been, for five years or more, either a qualified doctor or member of the legal profession – a lawyer, solicitor or barrister. In Scotland the functions of a coroner are performed by the procurator fiscal.

If you are coping with someone's death and are told that it is being reported to the Coroner's Office, most of us immediately think that there must be some indication of foul play – and indeed you are quite likely to have a police officer question you on the circumstances of the death to report to the Coroner's Office. This still does not necessarily indicate that a 'suspicious' death has occurred.

As previously noted, the law demands that the coroner is informed if the deceased has not been treated by a doctor in the last fourteen days or if, for instance, someone has recently been admitted to hospital and dies before a proper diagnosis can be made. It is also true that in some areas of the country people are trying to obtain statistics on causes of death such as hypothermia to provide background information on whether additional social and medical facilities are required. It is also true that sometimes bereaved members of the family themselves wish to know of all elements that might have contributed to the death.

There are various stages that coroners can follow. They can acknowledge that there is no doubt as to the cause of death, even though the deceased has not been seen by a doctor in the last fourteen days. If, for instance, the deceased has been suffering from high blood pressure for which he/she is being treated and subsequently dies suddenly, the doctor will intimate that he/she sees nothing suspicious in this, having been aware that it would be the likely conclusion. The coroner can then either issue a 'form A' which allows registration and disposal to take place, or can refer the death back to the doctor for normal procedures to take place.

The post-mortem

If it is considered necessary for a post-mortem to take place the coroner can proceed without the relatives' permission, although you will be informed. There are no charges involved. A post-mortem involves the body being medically examined and various tests taking place to discover the cause of death. The body is removed either from the place where death occurred or from the undertaker's for the post-mortem to be carried out, usually in a district hospital. The body is then returned from whence it came – although if it was taken from home it can be returned to the undertaker that you are using. Once there has been a 'finding' the coroner can either:

> a) Issue a pink form to the registrar which allows disposal of the body to take place. This will either be sent direct to the registrar or given to you to deliver. The coroner will tell you the results of the post-mortem, but if he/she tries to tell you in language you do not understand, ask for an explanation. They are so used to medical terminology that they often do not realise that the lay person cannot understand it, but will be happy to explain if asked to do so. The Coroner's Office

When Someone Dies

will talk to you on the telephone, but if you do not have one either make an appointment to go and see someone in the Coroner's Office or get a relative with a telephone to take comprehensive messages.

b) Proceed to an inquest or FAI. If the decision is to proceed to an inquest/FAI you can apply for the funeral to take place before this is convened. A letter of 'the fact of death' can be provided by the coroner/procurator fiscal at this stage if it seems that there may be some time lapse so that social security benefits can be obtained or insurance policies dealt with (depending on the insurance company's policy).

You might find it necessary to ask for a post-mortem to take place if you think that there might have been an 'industrial' cause of death so that you can pursue a financial claim. If you request a post-mortem there will be charges involved – the Coroner's Office or your undertaker will detail these for you. It is, however, sometimes advisable to consider a post-mortem solely to help you allay any fears and unanswered questions about the death. One woman I talked to had asked for a post-mortem to be held to find out whether her husband had been suffering from asbestosis when he died – not because she had wanted to benefit financially from that knowledge, but because she had wanted to for her own peace of mind. A post-mortem was duly held and no trace of asbestosis found. She said that this had 'put her mind at rest' and allowed her to begin to accept his death.

The inquest or fatal accident inquiry

If an inquest/FAI is to be held, the body has to be formally identified. Think about this – the next-of-kin does not *have* to do this and you should carefully consider, as is always the case, whether you wish to see the body. Many people do not wish to do so and it may be easier for someone who is a little more removed from the situation to identify the body for you.

An inquest/FAI is an inquiry into the medical cause of

death and the circumstances in which it occurred. It is held if the death was:

- **a** violent
- **b** caused by an accident
- **c** caused by an industrial disease

or

- **d** if after the post-mortem there is still uncertainty as to the cause of death

Inquests/FAIs are public and are sometimes held with a jury. The coroner/procurator fiscal decide how they are to be organised. In Scotland the FAI is held in the local sheriff court and the sheriff presides, with the procurator fiscal examining witnesses. Relatives can attend and, with the coroner's permission, question witnesses who are called. If there is the possibility of a claim for compensation (either against you in the case of a road accident, for example, or by you, in the case of an industrial accident) or any criminal proceedings following the inquest, it is best to have a lawyer present. You cannot claim legal aid for an inquest.

After the inquest the Coroner will issue:

- **a** a free certificate for cremation or order for burial if this has been withheld
- **b** a certificate-after-inquest for the registrar, which states the cause of death
- **c** a letter confirming the fact of death (as above if not previously issued)

Removal of the body from the country

If you wish the body to be removed from the country for burial/cremation elsewhere, then, regardless of whether there is any other reason for the coroner or procurator fiscal to be involved, it is this office who have to give permission for this to take place.

It is also likely that you will need an undertaker to help with the special arrangements – you will need to have the body embalmed and may need a special lead-lined coffin. It is not that unusual a situation, so most undertakers will be able to advise you of shipping arrangements etc.

Returning a body to this country for disposal
If the death has occurred in another country (and this includes England, Scotland, Wales and Northern Ireland) or on a ship or aircraft registered other than in Britain, you have to register the death and comply with the local regulations and get a death certificate. You will also need permission from the appropriate authorities to remove the body from the country of death, and then make your funeral arrangements in the relevant country. You will also need *either* an authenticated translation of a foreign death certificate *or* a death certificate issued in England, Wales, Northern Ireland or Scotland, as well as, possibly, further forms such as the 'certificate of no liability to register'.

It is wise to think of all possibilities before making plans to return the body to this country for disposal. If burial abroad seems inappropriate it might be better to have a cremation before returning the ashes to this country (this might well be a good financial option). However, if you are wishing to arrange a cremation in your *own* country following a death abroad you may require further orders or certifications, depending on the country of death (this does not apply to England, Scotland, Wales or Northern Ireland). If you are in this situation it would be sensible to use the services of an undertaker who is conversant with the requirements of the country concerned, although you could of course ask your local authority or Citizen's Advice Bureau for help.

The undertaker

The first thing to consider is whether you *want* to use an undertaker. Although it is unusual, less so these days than in the past, there is nothing to stop you from making all the arrangements yourself. You can buy a coffin (either from a factory or from an undertaker) and arrange the burial/cremation direct. You can book a time with your local crematorium and arrange the service as you wish, or contact the relevant person in your local council to buy a burial plot (if this has not already been done) and arrange a time for a burial to take place. Although most people do feel that they need someone else to take all the arrangements off their hands, it is another option that you have and one that does mean that you are personally involved all the way through.

Choosing an undertaker can be very difficult at a time when decisions are hard to take. You may find that your local council runs a municipal funeral scheme which provides a good cheap service, or you could look for one in the *Yellow Pages*. The undertaker deals with a great many things for you so it is important that you find the right one.

The undertaker (or funeral director – they are the same thing) can be of enormous help to you at what is always a very complicated and emotional time. There is a governing body for this profession, the National Association of Funeral Directors, who are based at 57 Doughty Street, London WC1.

They, in conjunction with the Office of Fair Trading, have put together a code of practice which outlines how the profession is to conduct itself, and they also run a complaints and grievance procedure. Most funeral directors are members and, as is always the case, it is advisable to use a firm who are. There are, as in all professions, some firms who are not members of the trade association and can be 'cowboys'. Do try and steer clear of them.

One of the requirements of the code of practice is that 'a written estimate of all charges should be given immediately' and, although this may seem distasteful to you at the time, it is something that you should get and look at. It is worth asking friends for advice on who to go to if you have a choice in your area, partly because it is emotionally very important that you do get what you want, or what you think that the person who has died would have wanted.

One of the first things to do is to check if any instructions have been left as to whether the deceased wished to be buried or cremated, and if there was a particular kind of service that they wanted. Many people leave these instructions in their will, so it is worth checking with whoever holds the will whether this is the case. If the deceased have left instructions in writing that they do not wish to be cremated this has to be adhered to by law, whatever the wishes of the next-of-kin, although the coroner or procurator fiscal can overturn this.

Burial
If you want to be buried somewhere particular it is often necessary to buy the plot in advance – you cannot assume that there will be room for you at a particular place at a particular time unless you have 'booked' it. The costs of burial plots vary from district to district, but your undertaker will be able to advise you on these costs (as could your local authority). There are also different types of plots available: there are those which you buy in perpetuity where the plot can never be re-used, there are plots beside the path or in a particular area which may be more desirable and therefore more expensive, there are those which can be re-used at a later date, and those which cannot have a headstone. More and more cemeteries have lawn plots where you are restricted to stones level with the ground. Do check at the time that the plot meets all your needs now and in the future – you might want to buy a double plot so that when the time comes your partner can be buried alongside. Your undertaker will be able to tell you of the alternatives in your area or, if you wish to sort this out in advance, talk to your religious minister or council.

Cremation
If you wish for cremation to take place – as 65 per cent of the population now do – you can decide at a later date where the ashes are to be scattered, if that is what you want to do. This can be in the grounds of the crematorium or in almost any other place imaginable – from your favourite cliffs to your local football ground (as long as you get

permission from whoever owns it!). Most crematoria have a Book of Remembrance or a rose garden where you can have a plaque or suchlike; again these vary in each area but your undertaker or local crematorium superintendent will be able to advise you.

It seems appropriate at this point to raise the fears that many have of cremation. Many people think that all sorts of things take place once the body has passed behind or through the curtains. Stories are always told of coffins being re-used, or bodies kept for a week before being disposed of, or jewellery being taken from bodies. Most of the crematoria in this country are municipally run but, whether private or public, they all operate under a code of practice. The people who do this job take a great pride in their work and gain certificates in proficiency. Many of them are able to officiate or assist at services, though few are actually religious ministers, and try and create a respectful atmosphere – no mean task when, in a lot of areas, there are up to thirty or forty cremations a day. They try and make everyone feel that theirs is the only and most important service of the day.

Once the coffin has passed through into the crematory (where the bodies are actually disposed of), the coffins are *not* opened and indeed two mourners are able, if you so wish, to accompany the coffin. This goes some way to concurring with religious obligations that some people have, such as those of the Sikh religion, but it is an option that we all have and some feel is the final moment of farewell.

Some crematoria hold 'open days', which enable the public to have a look round and ask questions and hopefully allay their fears. For example, cremations always take place on the actual day of the service. If jewellery has been left on the body it may sometimes be left in the ashes; if you had wished to have it returned but forgotten to ask the undertaker to ensure this, you can contact the crematorium supervisor and see if they can identify it and return it to you. If jewellery is not 'claimed' it is buried in the grounds

When Someone Dies

of the crematorium. Flowers are kept at the crematorium for as long as possible and then either passed on to hospitals or somewhere similar or just disposed of. The undertaker will normally ask if you want them to retain the cards for you; if not, you can ask someone else to collect them if you do not feel able to do it yourself at that time. The people running crematoria are as aware as anyone else that they are part of a service which has to be provided but which in a lot of respects we all wish didn't have to exist, and they are as compassionate as any one else involved and as responsible with the charges that we lay upon them.

Undertakers usually provide a twenty-four-hour service and will take the body away, if you so wish, to their chapel of rest. If the death occurs in hospital the body will be removed to the mortuary until you have made arrangements; you do not need to use the undertaker recommended by the hospital – do make up your own mind. The body can be brought home from the hospital if you would prefer that it stayed there until the funeral takes place.

Some areas still have people who will come and lay out the body for you (this basically means cleaning the body and clothing it as you think appropriate), or the undertaker will do this for you. Embalming is not a usual practice these days but can still be carried out, though in most cases an injection of preservative will suffice until the funeral takes place.

Different cultures do of course have traditional methods of preparing the body for disposal; these tend to be based on religion and, if you are not certain of all the processes to be adhered to (for you may not be a practitioner of that faith but know that the deceased would have wanted the traditional methods carried out), the appropriate religious officer will be happy to tell you of the process if it is not one that the undertaker is familiar with (and indeed most faiths do have books which outline the methods).

This is again a time when you might have to make a choice of seeing the body – some find it a great comfort to see the body once it has been laid out as it often resembles the living person more closely than immediately after death occurred. I know of a friend who had seen her father's body in the hospital mortuary and it had seemed to be someone else altogether, but once the body had been laid out the family had felt much happier at 'saying good-bye' to the person they had known. It has to be a *personal* decision, however.

Another decision which has to be taken is whether any jewellery should be left on the body. You might feel that it is more appropriate to leave on wedding rings etc., but do think seriously about this, particularly if cremation is to take place or someone has died in hospital, as the body may be removed from the mortuary to the chapel of rest and the funeral take place with nobody thinking to ask for the jewellery.

One of the first things that the undertaker will need is the disposal certificate which will have been given to you by the registrar, and your decision as to whether burial or cremation is to take place. They will then need to know what else you will require from them before they can give you a quote – how many funeral cars, obituary notices in the papers, flowers or wreaths and what kind of coffin you require. Most undertakers have a coffin which they recommend for use with cremations which is perfectly substantial but relatively inexpensive. Most also have catalogues which show different styles of coffins and choices of interiors (you can choose a particular colour of lining if you so wish), which of course vary considerably in price. You might find that the undertaker only stocks two types of coffin – one for burial and one for cremation – in an attempt to keep costs down, but if you have a particular wish for something else they will be happy to provide it. Everybody has a natural desire to do the best for someone when they die, but I am sure that none of us would wish to have a fortune spent on the coffin etc. if it placed a financial strain on the family, so try and reach a decision which you can cope with in all respects.

Once you have made these initial decisions, the undertaker is in a position to give you a quote. It is advisable to get two quotes from different undertakers and also to establish how quickly payment has to be made. In local communities undertakers will sometimes stagger payments, as most of them genuinely want to help as much as they can – don't be afraid to ask.

Financial assistance with the funeral
If, as next-of-kin, you cannot afford to pay for the funeral yourself and yet there is sufficient money from the estate of the deceased to cover it, it may be possible for some of that money to be released to meet the immediate needs. This does depend on where the money is saved but some building societies, the Trustee Savings Bank and the Department of National Savings or The Ulster Savings Branch can, although they are not bound to, release sums of up to £1,500 on the evidence of the death certificate.

If you think that you cannot afford the sum of money quoted by the undertaker (burials are usually slightly more expensive than cremations, but the overall minimum cost is usually between £350–£450 depending on where you live), contact your local Department of Health and Social Security *before the funeral takes place*, and they will be able to advise you on what *they* can pay for. This depends on your financial circumstances if you are next-of-kin, as well as the circumstances of the deceased.

The usual things that the DHSS will pay for are: any necessary certificates, a plain coffin, transport for the coffin and bearers and one extra car, disbursement fees and tips and sometimes flowers. If the DHSS are paying for a burial *do check on the kind of grave that they provide*, as it may mean that you will not be able to put up a headstone or that there are other restrictions on the plot which may influence your decision on whether burial or cremation should take place. The disbursements referred to are such things as doctor's fees, church and ministers' fees and any fees due to the crematorium. Undertakers do not differentiate in the services that they provide if the Department of Health and

Social Security are paying – as one undertaker said, 'no one need ever fear that the neighbours will notice any difference'. It is not a stigma if you cannot afford these costs yourself – they have escalated over the last few years and many people, particularly the elderly, have not been able to keep pace with inflation and do not have enough money saved.

There are also various other forms of financial help which might be available to you, depending on the circumstances. Again, *check before the funeral takes place.*

Employers, trades unions or associations. Most trade unions and employers will offer financial assistance of a varying degree. Some have a clear sum laid down for this eventuality, while some decide what is appropriate at the time.

War Pensioner's Funeral Grant. The War Pensions Office or your local Social Security office will tell you how to go about claiming the grant, which is payable when someone dies as a result of pensioned disablement or while in hospital receiving treatment for it.

When someone dies in hospital, a local authority home or in temporary accommodation. The local authority has a duty to bury or cremate as above if no other arrangements have been made, and can claim against the dead person's estate. The hospital, home or local authority will be able to give you details.

In the event of a stillbirth. In some parts of the United Kingdom help can be given with the funeral of a stillborn baby, whether born in hospital or at home. This offer will normally be made by the midwife but you should be clear, if you accept this offer, that the baby will be cremated or buried in a common grave, which may not meet your wishes.

No one is ever not buried or cremated – the authorities have an obligation to make sure that some form of service takes place. These are no longer like the pauper's burials of the past – all funerals are conducted with respect and dignity.

Funeral services

Most of us assume that when we die a religious ceremony will have to take place. There is no *legal* obligation for this, only that proper disposal should take place. If, however, you want a religious service to take place the undertaker will sort out a date and time with the relevant minister, subject to any special requests that you might have – for example, if relatives wish to travel from abroad or long distances you might have to allow for this. The undertaker will also have to take into account that if the death has been reported to the coroner or procurator fiscal (as previously outlined) the funeral will not be able to take place immediately.

The religious minister will then liaise with you about what hymns and readings you want within the service – it is nice to have the time to think about someone's favourite hymns or readings and whether they would have liked someone from the family to be involved. The local minister will normally be amenable to some participation by the bereaved; don't be afraid to ask – it is your service. If there is to be a cremation after this service the undertaker will also check that is possible for this to follow on (allowing for any travelling time required). Some people prefer to have just the one service at the crematorium, which can be a religious service. Most crematoria allow twenty minutes per service, so this may determine what you do.

It is customary, if there has already been a religious service, for immediate family only to proceed to the crematorium. Most people choose to put an insertion in the local paper, usually at the same time as the death is notified, telling people what the funeral arrangements are. If you want family only or wish to mention only the religious service, make sure that the undertaker is fully aware of your wishes as well as your decision on whether flowers are wanted or if it is to be family flowers only, with donations to a charity appropriate to the person who died (these can either be administered by the undertaker or sent direct). It is particularly true that at cremations flowers do not always seem to have a 'place', whereas they sometimes seem more appropriate with a burial, but you must make a personal choice on what seems right for you or the deceased.

Most burials now take place in municipal cemeteries as the traditional local churchyards are full, and most of these cemeteries have dedicated chapels which are similar to the chapels at crematoria. This means that any kind of gathering or service can take place which is not necessarily religious-based. There are various secular (non-religious) organisations which will conduct a service for you if you wish, or you can do it yourself. If the person who has died was never religious – and in this day and age a lot of people no longer have an affiliation with a particular religion – you may feel it more appropriate to have something which reflects the way they lived, even if it is not what you would want for yourself. Those who run the municipal cemeteries and crematoria want to help you have the service you want, and are therefore usually only too happy to fall in with whatever plans you make. If you want pop music played, or no music at all, they can usually help you.

The secular organisations – such as The British Humanist Association, 13 Prince of Wales Terrace, London W8, telephone: 01 937 2341; The National Secular Society, 702 Holloway Road, London N19, telephone: 01 272 1266; or The Belfast Humanist Group, 30 Cloyne Crescent, Monkstown, Newtownabbey, Co. Antrim – will be happy to put you in touch with someone in your area who has taken a service before. Your undertaker is also likely to know of a relevant person in your area, and sometimes even the undertakers themselves take services. These forms of services can sometimes seem much more personal and 'right' because they enable you to remember someone specifically with readings, oratory and music. What is most important is that whatever kind of 'funeral' you have, it is right for you.

Memorial services

We tend to associate memorial services with not only religion but also those who might have been deemed to have left 'some kind of mark' on the world, such as politicians. It is, however, something that any of us can have or hold for someone. They really only apply to most of us if we wish to have a private family funeral, or the death has occurred abroad and we know that there are others who would like to commemorate the life of that person. They do tend to be held in the relevant religious 'house', although there is nothing to stop you holding such a service anywhere – a hall, community centre or even your own home. It is of course another alternative that we have but it does need, as all these things do, careful consideration.

It may be that to prolong the ritual process might be distressing and disturbing and seem to not allow the first stages of initial mourning to be completed – on the other hand it may seem only right and proper that the achievements, kindness, charity or social contributions of the deceased be publicly recognised, but at a time when you have had the chance to come to terms with the initial grief and shock. A memorial service can take any form that you choose. For example, music may have been very important to the person who has died, and it might seem appropriate for a group of friends to sit and sing their favourite songs, which might have seemed inapplicable in a religious service. What is most important is that you realise that this is another choice you have.

A permanent reminder

You may wish to have some permanent form of remembrance for a family member or a friend. This is not, of course, one of the things that has to be decided immediately, although if it is to be a gravestone you should consider when buying the burial plot whether a stone of some sort can be erected.

Gravestones
I think we probably all make the assumption that we can choose any gravestone we like and have anything put on it. Unfortunately, this is not the case. Whether you are buried in a churchyard or a municipal cemetery, there will be regulations which govern such things as the height and size of the stone and whether it can be upright or one of the new-style pavement stones. There may also be restrictions on what kind of stone you can use. What is in some respects strangest is that you cannot necessarily inscribe what you wish – some cemeteries do not allow Roman numerals, some do not allow the use of nicknames or names that were a term of affection within the family, some have a limit (sometimes imposed by the size of the stone) on the number of words that can be inscribed, and some religious ministers object to quotations from the Bible or phrases such as 'safe in the arms of Jesus', believing this to be presumptuous!

It is therefore wise to talk either to the undertaker who dealt with the funeral or direct to your local stonemason before becoming too set on a particular form, so that they can let you know of local restrictions.

It is usual for a stone to be erected some months after a burial has taken place – this is for several reasons. The ground needs to settle once it has been disturbed, and in order to ensure that the stone stays in place once positioned some time has to elapse; also, people often need time to come to terms with a death before being able to erect a stone that is, in some respects, symbolic of an acceptance that that person will not be returning. The other reason is often a more basic one, the cost. The cost of a stone will vary according to the kind and size of stone that you wish to be used and the number of letters that are to be carved on it. The cheapest stones usually start at about £100 but, again, it is worth talking to your local stonemason to see how this cost can be spread and what the range of price alternatives are. Some stonemasons have books which show a variety of stones in different styles – some shaped as books, some with rounded edges, some with windows carved into them and some even more elaborate – and they can tell you what the choices are in your area.

Most stonemasons will say that a memorial stone is for the living as much as for the dead – it presents a focal point for people to go to and feel close to the person that they have lost.

Marking the disposal of ashes
Many people wish there to be some permanent reminder of the dead, even if a cremation has taken place and the ashes scattered. This can be arranged in a variety of ways. Ashes can be buried, in an urn, in a cemetery and commemorated as with a burial, or sometimes stones can be placed where the ashes have been scattered – although this obviously depends on where this has taken place. Most crematoria provide different forms of remembrance – some have rose gardens where you can have plaque placed, or you can enter the name in a special book or on a wall. These practices obviously vary from area to area, and again either the superintendent of the local crematorium or the undertaker will tell you of your options.

Alternatives
There are, of course, other less obvious ways of establishing a memorial. Finances permitting, you could endow a children's or hospice ward, but for most of us it is more realistic to think of planting a tree, making an achievement award in someone's memory or buying a park bench.

For those lost at sea
The British Maritime Charitable Foundation have commissioned a book to go on permanent display at All Hallow's Church, Tower Hill in London, in which people who have been lost at sea and have no other memorial can be remembered.

* * *

Sometimes even the things for which people have no further use, such as old photographs of a town or village, can be framed and donated to the local library or suchlike. It does not have to cost much to perpetuate someone's memory. What is important is that it satisfies your sense of what you think is right and what you think the person who has died would have wanted done. I think this is particularly true when the majority of people are cremated – most of us have at some point sought out our family gravestones and feel that with the advent of cremation we might only continue to exist in people's memories, and as they in turn die we will disappear with nothing to mark our existence. Different religions view this in different ways, but it is something to consider if we wish to leave something tangible behind.

Pre-planning a funeral
If it is the first time that you have had to organise a funeral or been involved with the organisation of one, it might make you think about what kind of arrangements of services and so on you want when *you* die (as we all must do), as well as the financial effect on those left behind.

It is of course relatively easy to sort out some things with your family or friends, such as whether you wish to be buried or cremated, but other things need greater planning and thought. It is important, particularly for the elderly, that people feel that they have left enough money to be buried/cremated properly, and it is often the case that elderly people will keep enough money for their funeral when they have very little other cash. This amount 'put by' sometimes mean that they become ineligible for heating and/or supplementary benefits. It would therefore often be sensible to sort out some kind of pre-payment scheme rather than keep the actual cash in the bank.

There are now several kinds of pre-payment schemes available, a range of which are detailed as follows:

Life insurance

There is, of course, the traditional life insurance, which means that during our lifetime we pay in to some form of insurance policy so that on our death there is a lump sum payable to the next-of-kin. This may be a straightforward policy which only pays out in the event of our death – the sum being determined by the amount that we have paid in – or it may be an *assurance* policy, which runs for a specific length of time and, in the event of our death occurring before the policy matures, a specified sum is paid out; if we 'outlive' the policy we receive a lump sum at the end of the agreed timespan. This might be quite inadequate for our needs depending on who is dependent on us. Mortgages, too, usually carry some form of insurance so that in the event of the death of either of the householders the family home is automatically paid for, providing a roof over the family head.

Pre-payment schemes

These are now operated by various (mostly insurance) companies, and it is very important that you check that you are going to get what you want. Some municipal councils now work in conjunction with local funeral directors in providing a pre-payment scheme, so check with your local council. The National Association of Funeral Directors, 57 Doughty Street, London WC1, also run a Funeral Expenses Plan which your local undertaker will be able to give you information about. There are also the Co-operative Funeral Services, which are called different things in different areas but which have been for many years a traditional way to pay for a funeral. It is of course now worth checking whether there is a newer scheme which is more suitable for you.

These pre-payment schemes mainly work in two ways: you either pay a lump sum which guarantees certain things (this is made practical for whoever is running the scheme because they get the interest on your money for the period between investment and death) or you pay in instalments.

If you take on instalments you do, of course, need to make sure that you can afford them – and it may be that you would be better off putting the money aside in a special building society or bank account whereby you or your family would receive the interest that accrues. It is something that you must work out to suit your own circumstances and discuss with either your bank or organisation like the Citizen's Advice Bureau.

Making over your property
There are some schemes in operation now where, if you are a householder, you can make over the property for either a cash sum and certain guarantees with regard to your funeral, or in consideration of certain repairs etc. being carried out whilst you are living in the property. *Please consider these sorts of schemes very carefully and seek independent advice from someone like the Citizen's Advice Bureau before you enter into anything like this.*

Funeral-planning societies
There are now various sorts of planning schemes around which do not necessarily require an outlay of much money. One of these has been established for the people of Salford, Greater Manchester and was originally set up with the help of Age Concern. Here you pay a small subscription and are given details of the local charges for burial plots etc. in your area and provided with a form to fill in. This form details whether you wish to be buried or cremated and asks, if you wish to be buried, if you have purchased a plot (and if not which kind you would prefer if it is available), what kind of service you would like (you can specify certain hymns and readings) and whether you want flowers or donations. These details are then placed on file and when the death occurs the next-of-kin gets in touch with someone from a list of designated contacts, who then acts as the intermediary. He or she then rings round and obtains quotes for the funeral required and puts the family in touch with the relevant undertaker. It does mean that at a time when you

may feel emotionally incapable of coping with ringing round and asking questions someone else can do that for you, and take at least that burden off your shoulders.

There are of course various arrangements that you can make with regard to pre-planning, which may just be a group of you writing your wishes down and agreeing to help each other. Age Concern (England), who helped set up this scheme, are based at 60 Pitcairn Road, Mitcham, Surrey and do issue advice on planning funerals; you may, however, find it better to look up the local branch in the *Yellow Pages* or telephone directory and ask them what advice and practical help they can give you relevant to your area. There may also be other local organisations in your area, so ask at your health centre or Social Services office.

CHAPTER EIGHT

Grief and Bereavement

Once the funeral is over you face the most difficult period of coming to terms with the loss that you have suffered.

If you are working, most companies have a stipulated period of 'compassionate leave' which can be a week or two, a month or in some cases as flexible as you need it to be. It is a time when the harsh reality of financial need often clashes with emotional needs. There are, of course, no hard and fast rules about when you feel able to tackle different aspects of your life, and all sorts of circumstances may dictate when you feel ready to face a work situation. Most companies are sympathetic to the problems that you have to face and may allow you to return part-time to your job for a while – it is something that is always worth talking to your personnel officer about. Some people do find it easier to return to work and have a certain routine imposed on them, rather than have too much time to think immediately after a death, but might need to take some time off later on. Don't be afraid to ask for this kind of consideration – people often do not wish to broach the subject with you and think that you are coping well when in fact you may desperately need some time to re-charge your batteries and put things in perspective.

Immediately after a death, when your emotions are in turmoil, is not the time to make hasty decisions. It may well be that you feel the need to change jobs or move house to avoid the memories that the surroundings bring, but it may also be that after a few weeks or months you realise that it is in fact comforting, rather than disturbing, to have those memories around you and acting too swiftly might cause you more pain later.

Practical financial advice

Any death is likely to bring with it some basic practical problems. These may have been alleviated to some extent by a will which has set out very clearly what is to happen to the possessions, effects and money which belonged to the person who has died – this of course may also cause some problems. If you co-owned a property with the deceased (this might be a husband, wife, parent or another family member) this property is likely to be insured against the death of either party and any outstanding mortgage paid off. If you have a joint tenancy agreement this can usually be transferred to a single name or that of one of the children. If the property was owned, for instance, in the husband's name only, he can leave it to whoever he chooses, although a widow (or widower) and any children (including step-children) can challenge a will that leaves them nothing at all. This is done on an overall percentage basis and is something that you should take legal advice on as soon as the will has been read if you are not happy. A divorced wife or husband who hasn't remarried can also sometimes claim against the estate if this claim was not negated in the divorce settlement.

There can also be claims against the estate for any debts outstanding by the deceased at the time of death – these could be credit card bills, claims for work done or other personal loans. In reality some of these may be 'written off' by people who do not consider either that the amount was sufficient to cause any upset or that there was no pre-knowledge of impending death when the debt was incurred.

A will has executors whose function is to process the wishes and intentions of the person who appointed them. You do not have to be asked if you will be an executor but you can decline to perform this function. The probate office will send you a 'power reserved' letter to sign to signify that you have renounced your role as executor. In some cases the executors named in the will may have already died themselves, or may not be well enough to perform this function, in which case either a substitute executor as listed in the will can be appointed, or a member of the family can take on this task. It is worth remembering when making a will that it may be wise to name at least one executor younger than yourself, as they may be in a better position to cope when the time comes.

If the executors appointed include either a bank representative or a solicitor you will probably have to pay charges. The banks work on a percentage of the estate (and if you are establishing any kind of trust this will be an ongoing charge against the interest accrued) and a solicitor will normally incorporate into the will that you have to pay for his/her time and administrative costs from the estate.

In most cases the executors (who are not paid for their time, although provision might be made in the will for any expenses incurred) will have to apply for grant of probate. This has been described as 'making sure that you have paid all your taxes on earth before going to meet your maker'. It is well worth considering when you make your will whether you can avoid heavy death duties or capital transfer tax.

The grant of probate may take some months to come through and the bereaved may face financial difficulties during this period. If you have a bank manager it is worth talking to him or her about a short-term overdraft. If, in the case of husband and wife, there is a joint account in operation you can continue to draw on it, although money in this account will be considered as part of the estate – in most cases as a 50/50 split. Life insurance policies can usually be paid out more quickly than probate is granted, so it may well be that this money can be applied for and obtained before any bequests. You might also be entitled to a pension from a partner's place of work or union, which can be processed relatively quickly.

As a widow you may be entitled to the state widow's allowance, which runs for twenty-six weeks and then becomes the widow's benefit (which is taxable). Both the widow's allowance and benefit are only paid if you meet the requirements – for example, your husband must have been paying the appropriate class national insurance stamp for the required period and there are certain age considerations.

These are outlined in 'Your Benefit as a widow for the first twenty-six weeks, NP35' and 'Your Benefit as a widow after the first twenty six weeks, NP36'. If you are over sixty you need NP32A, which tells you how your retirement pension is affected. All these leaflets are freely available from some post offices, Citizens Advice Bureaux or your local Department of Health and Social Security office.

You may also be entitled to a widowed mother's allowance if you have a child under nineteen who normally lives with you or for whom you are entitled to child benefit. If you are pregnant at the time of your husband's death you will be entitled to benefit for this child too.

Widow's benefits cannot be paid to a widow who lives with a man as his wife but is not married to him, who remarries later or who is in prison.

Help and counselling

In some cases financial and emotional needs may interrelate. It is certainly a time when you do not want to have to face, or cope with, problems with money, and many organisations provide counselling and information designed to meet a range of needs, both emotional and financial. The organisations listed below provide a bereavement counselling service or can provide information on local groups who do. In some cases they may also be able to offer you further practical advice, and where that is applicable it is indicated.

Age Concern is a registered charity. They have over a thousand independent local groups in England, Scotland, Northern Ireland and Wales, and provide counselling as well as practical information for the elderly. To get in touch with them either look in your telephone book for a local branch or contact one of the main centres as listed below. They will also be happy to send you a list of their publications and leaflets.

> Age Concern England
> 60 Pitcairn Road
> Mitcham
> Surrey CR4 3LL
>
> Age Concern Scotland
> 33 Castle Street
> Edinburgh EH2 2DN
> Telephone: 031 225 2889
> (Open from 10 a.m. to 4. p.m. weekdays)
>
> Age Concern Wales
> 1 Park Grove
> Cardiff CF1 3BJ
> Telephone: 0222 371821/371566
>
> Age Concern Northern Ireland
> 6 Lower Crescent
> Belfast BT7 INR
> Telephone: 0232 245729

The Bereaved Parents Helpline is run on a small basis, and mainly for the London area, but they are happy to talk to parents who have lost a child and to refer you to other sources where applicable.

> The Bereaved Parents Helpline
> 6 Canons Gate
> Harlow
> Essex
> Telephone: 0279 412745

The Compassionate Friends offers a support service to bereaved parents. They do have local contacts throughout the country who all have a particular understanding of the problems facing bereaved parents, whether that occurs through stillbirth or the loss of an older child.

>The Compassionate Friends
>6 Denmark Street
>Bristol BS1 5DQ
>
>Telephone: 0272 292778

Cruse: the National Organisation for the Widowed and their Children was founded in 1959 and is a registered charity. It has over a hundred local branches throughout Britain, which you can find in your telephone directory, and is for both men and women regardless of age, nationality or belief. You can become a member of Cruse at a cost of £4 a year for national membership; the branch membership fee is determined locally. Cruse provides a valuable source of information and help, as well as organising social activities and holidays. They also run training courses for health-care professionals and volunteer counsellors, and conduct research into aspects of bereavement. They also provide individual and group bereavement counselling.

They publish the monthly *Cruse Chronicle* and *Bereavement Care*, a journal for those who help the bereaved, and produce fact sheets at 10p each plus postage, for their members only, which deal with a variety of topics including: 'Obtaining Probate Yourself', Training and Employment for Women', 'You and Your Pension Position', 'Insurance' and 'Social Activities of Interest to the Widowed'. They also have a book list with subjects ranging from *When Children Grieve, Selected Poems, Easing Grief for Oneself and Other People, Holiday List* and *The Cruse Cookery Book*.

Cruse: the National Organisation for the Widowed and their Children
Cruse House
126 Sheen Road
Richmond
Surrey TW9 1UR

Telephone: 01 940 4818/9047

The Gay Bereavement Project was established in London some years ago. They can offer advice and comfort and, although they are mainly based in London, can offer you some assistance for other parts of the country. They are contactable through Gay Switchboard.

The Gay Bereavement Project
c/o Gay Switchboard
Telephone: 01 837 7324 (twenty-four-hour service)

The names of the following organisations indicate their particular areas of knowledge and support with regard to bereavement:

The Foundation for the Study of Infant Deaths
15 Belgrave Square
London SW1X 8PS

Telephone: 01 235 0965 (office hours)

The Jewish Bereavement Counselling Service
1 Cyprus Gardens
London N3 1SP

Telephone: 01 349 0839

The Miscarriage Association
18 Stoneybrook Close
West Bretton
Wakefield
West Yorkshire WF4 4TP

Telephone: 092 485 515

The National Association of Widows
Chell Road
Stafford ST16 2QA

Telephone: 0785 45465

The Scottish Cot Death Trust
c/o The Royal Hospital for Sick Children
Yorkhill
Glasgow G3 8SJ

Telephone: 041 357 3946

The Stillbirth and Neonatal Death Society
Argyle House
29–31 Euston Road
London NW1 2SD

Telephone: 01 833 2851 (office hours)

The Samaritans, who run local helplines throughout the country, will always help and listen to you and will usually be in a position to put you in touch with other groups. Look them up in your telephone directory or *Yellow Pages*.

Nearly every geographical area has an infinite number of small, local groups which have been set up to fill a need. Your local Social Services department or Citizen's Advice Bureau will be happy to advise you on any additional help available in your area. Health centres and doctors' surgeries also have lists of different forms of support groups, and if you have a particular faith you will find that your religious minister will be happy to talk to you and comfort you and put you in touch with other like-minded groups.

If you wish to consider setting up and running a bereavement service yourself, groups such as Age Concern will be happy to advise you. There is also a pamphlet issued through the Hospice Information Service run from St Christopher's Hospice, 51–59 Lawrie Park Road, Sydenham, London SE26 6DZ, telephone: 01 778 1240/9252. There is a charge for this which is in the region of £1.50 – do check before sending off for it.

You may think that no one else knows how you feel, but as bereavement is something that everyone has to face at some stage there are always groups and organisations who can help. I hope that you won't be afraid to ask when you still feel in need of some emotional support and help and the telephone has stopped ringing with friends and family offering assistance. There are people there to help you when you have recognised that need in yourself.

Select Bibliography

For those interested in reading further the following is a list of books which we found interesting and helpful:

Autobiographies
Agee, James *A Death in the Family* (Quartet Books, 1980)
Boston, Sarah *Will, My Son* (Pluto Press, 1981)
Brittain, Vera *Testament of Youth* (Virago, 1979)
Buñuel, Luis *My Last Breath* (Fontana, 1985)
de Beauvoir, Simone *A Very Easy Death* (Penguin Books, 1969)
Graham, Jory *In the Company of Others* (Victor Gollancz, 1983)
Leach, Christopher *Letter to a Younger Son* (Arrow Books, 1981)
Lewis, C.S. *A Grief Observed* (Faber and Faber, 1978)
Lorde, Audre *The Cancer Journals* (Sheba Feminist Publishers, 1980)
Seed, Pat *One Day at a Time* (Pan Books, 1979)
Weinman Lear, Martha *Heartsounds* (Pocket Books, 1981)

General
Ariès, Philippe *The Hour of our Death* (Penguin Books, 1983)
Ariès, Philippe *Western Attitudes Toward Death* (Johns Hopkins Press, 1983)
Ariès, Philippe *Images of Man and Death* (Harvard University Press, 1985)
Crichton, Ian *The Art of Dying* (Peter Owen, 1976)
Enright, D.J. *The Oxford Book of Death* (Oxford University Press, 1983)

Faulder, Carolyn *Whose Body is it?* (Virago, 1985)
Gorer, Geoffrey *Death, Grief and Mourning* (Cresset Press, 1965)
Harding, Rachel and Dyson, Mary *A Book of Condolences* (Continuum, 1981)
Hinton, John *Dying* (Penguin Books, 1981)
Kübler-Ross, Elizabeth *On Death and Dying* (Tavistock Publications, 1985)
Lamerton, Richard *Care of the Dying* (Penguin Books, 1980)
Morley, John *Death, Heaven and the Victorians* (Studio Vista, 1981)
Murray Parkes, Colin *Bereavement* (Penguin, 1981)
Pincus, Lily *Death and the Family* (Faber and Faber, 1976)
Tatelbaum, Judy *The Courage to Grieve* (Lippincott and Crowell, 1980)
Toynbee, Arnold *Man's Concern with Death* (Hodder and Stoughton, 1968)

Index

Abrams, Rebecca, 141, 142, 149
'After a Death' programme, 112
Age Concern, 194, 195, 199–200, 203
Agee, James, *A Death in the Family*, 119–20
AIDS, 42, 146, 164
Aikenhead, Mary, 57–8
anger felt by bereaved, 129, 131–2, 150, 151
Anthony, Sylvia, *The Discovery of Death in Childhood and After*, 25
Ariès, Philippe, 56; *The Hour of our Death*, 26, 41, 77, 115; *Western Attitudes Towards Death*, 52, 53
artists' impressions: of death, 32–6; of skull and hourglass as symbols of mortality, 42–4
atrophine, 65
Auden, W. H., 'Birthday Poem', 44
autopsies, 69, 80

Bacon, Francis, 37; 'On Death', 6–7, 25–6, 68–9
BACUP (British Association of Cancer United Patients), 162
Baker, Richard, 12
Baudelaire, Charles, 40
Baulch, Clive, 49

Beauvoir, Simone de, *A Very Easy Death*, 99, 124, 128–9, 140
Belfast Humanist Group, 188
bereaved, bereavement, 10, 13, 91–114, 196–204; counselling, 11, 118, 148–9, 199–204; disposal of body, 99–100, 173–4, 178–85; emotional reactions, 128–36, 145; funerals, 100–9, 185–9, 192; help and advice, 109–14, 137–9, 142–3, 147–9, 199–204; homosexuals and lesbians, 145–6; legal requirements and options, 95, 165–95; letters of condolence, 113; murder victims' relatives, 144, 146, 148–9; mourning clothes, 127–8; new relationships, 138–9, 150, 151; practical financial advice, 197–9; registration of death, 95, 166–75; self-help, 137–40, 146–7; social isolation, 116, 140–2, 145–6; surviving and re-evaluations, 149–54; viewing the dead, 92–4, 183–4; *see also* grief
Bereaved Parents Helpline, 200
Besant, Annie, 105

Birth and Deaths Registration Act: (1874), 166; (1926), 166–7; (1953), 170, 172
Booker, Christopher, 'Prepared for the End', 78–9, 83, 100
Boothby, Penelope, gravestone of, 116
Born to Die programme, 7, 49, 59, 63, 75, 79, 94, 148
Boston, Sarah, *Will, My Son*, 93, 116
brain death, 31–2
British Humanist Association, 188
British Maritime Charitable Foundation, 191
British Red Cross, 164
Brittain, Vera, *Testament of Youth*, 140, 150–1
Brontë, Charlotte, *Jane Eyre*, 53
Brookwood Cemetery, London, 97
Brown, Audrey, 49
Buckman, Robert, 'Breaking bad news: . . .' 70–1, 73
Buñuel, Luis, *My Last Breath*, 47, 67, 76, 86–7, 89
burials, 95–8, 100, 174, 179–80, 181, 185, 187, 194; buying plot in advance, 181; cost of, 181 185, 194; gravestones, 189, 190–1
Burnett, Frances Hodgson, *The Secret Garden*, 130, 137
Byrd, William, 116

Cancerlink, 162–3
Cancer Relief Macmillan Fund (National Society for Cancer Relief), 160–1, 162
capital transfer tax, 198
cardiac oscilloscopes, 27
Catholic Church, 86, 89, 99
cellular (molecular) death, 29–30

cemeteries/churchyards, 96–7, 181; city/municipal, 96–7, 188, 190; *see also* gravestones
certificate for disposal of body, 95, 100, 173–4, 184
certificate of the registration/ notification of a death, 173
certified copy of an entry (registration of death), 172–3
Chapman, Dr Roger, 27
chemotherapy, 84
Chest, Heart and Stroke Association, 163
Chicago Tribune, 73–4
Chichester, Robert, gravestone of, 16
child benefit, 199
childbirth, 54; death of women after, 56–7
children: death of, 5, 9, 54–5, 104–5, 115–16, 138, 139, 145, 174; grief of, 143–5; impressions of, 33; and language of death, 19–21; learning/understanding about death, 23–6, 94
Christianity, 6, 14, 18, 42, 46–7, 96, 97
Christie Hospital, Manchester, CAT scanner for, 82
Citizens Advice Bureaux, 112, 160, 171, 179, 199
Clement-Jones, Dr Vicky, 162
clinical death, 29, 30
coffins, 94, 102, 106, 179, 182, 184, 185
Community Nursing Officer, 161
Compassionate Friends, 139, 148, 200–1
compassionate leave, 196
Co-operative Funeral Services, 193

Index

Coroner's Amendment Act (1926), 167
coroner's office, deaths referred to, 95, 111, 166, 167, 168, 172; inquests, 177–8; post-mortems, 176–7
counselling, bereavement, 11, 118, 148–9, 199–204
cremation, 80, 95, 96, 97–9, 100, 106, 108, 168, 174, 179–80, 181–3, 184, 193; cost of, 185; funeral service, 187–8; jewellery left on body, 182–3, 184; marking the disposal of ashes, 191
Cremation Society of England, 98
Crichton, Ian, *The Art of Dying*, 12–13, 111
Cruse: National Organisation for the Widowed and their Children, 201–2

Dawson of Dean, Lord, 87–8
death, medical definitions of, 26–32; brain, 31–2; cellular, 29–30; clinical, 29, 30; somatic, 29
death benefits, 101, 112, 186
death certificates, 28, 69, 95, 110, 166, 167–71, 172; cremations, 168; foreign, 179; fourteen-day rule, 168, 175; and notice to informant, 168, 169–71, 172
death duties, 198
death grant, abolition of (1987), 173
'death rattle', 65
'Deep River' (negro spiritual), 39
depression felt by bereaved, 132–3

De Vries, Peter, 91
Department of Health and Social Security (DHSS), financial assistance with funeral, 103, 185–6; information leaflets, 174, 199; Social Fund, 173
Dickens, Charles, 103; *David Copperfield*, 15, 53, 82–3, 133; *Household Words*, 102
Diplock, Lord, 85
disbursement fees, 185
disposing of the dead, 95–100, 173–4, 178–85; legal requirements, 95, 100, 106, 111, 112, 165–95; removal of body from the country, 178–9; returning body to this country, 179; *see also* burials; cremations; funerals
doctors, 165; communications between patients and, 69–74; death certificate issued by, 28, 69, 95, 110, 166, 167–71; and informed consent, 83–6; support for bereaved by, 91, 110
Dodderidge, Sir John, gravestone of, 16
Donne, John, 15
donor cards, 30
donations of organs or body, 30, 165–6
Down's Syndrome Association, 107
drugs used for pain control, 55, 63–5
Dryden, John, 134
Dumas, Alexandre, *Memoirs*, 20
Du Maurier, Daphne, 135
Dunton, John, 33, 38
Dürer, Albrecht, 34
'The Dying Man Prepared to Meet God' (lithograph), 34, 35

Eden Hall (Marie Curie home), 59–60, 63
electrocardiogram (ECG), 29
electroencephalogram (EEG), 29, 31
Elias, Norbert, *The Loneliness of Dying*, 47, 90
Elphinstone, James, 139
embalming, 111, 183
Enright, D. J., 81
estate of deceased, claims against, 197
euthanasia, 83, 86–90; voluntary, 88–9
Evelyn, John, 96
Everyman, 36
Exeter Cathedral, gravestone in, 16, 17

FAI (fatal accident inquiry), 167, 177–8
Faulder, Carolyn, *Whose Body Is It?*, 85
financial advice for bereaved, 197–9
First World War, 17, 40, 45–6, 127, 150-1
Foundation for the Study of Infant Deaths, 202
Freud, Sigmund, 37, 40; *Mourning and Melancholia*, 118
Funeral Expenses Plan, 193
funeral gatherings, 102, 107–8
funeral-planning societies, 194
funerals, funeral services, 79, 80, 99, 100–9, 127, 165, 185–95; cost of, 101–3, 185–6; expressions of grief at, 108–9; financial assistance with, 185–6; making over your property to pay for, 194; memorial and private services, 106–7, 189; personal arrangement of, 106, 179–80; pre-payment schemes, 193–4; pre-planning, 192–5; religious or secular services, 103–6, 187–8; *see also* burials; cremations; undertakers
Furtenagel, Lucal, 'The Burgkmaier Spouses', 43

Gay Bereavement Project, 202
General Cemetery Company, 97
George V, King, death of, 87–8
George VI, King, funeral of, 100
Goldbrom, Hazel, 59–60, 63–4, 79; 'Then and Now', 49–50
Gorer, Geoffrey, *Death, Grief and Mourning in Contemporary Britain*, 54, 55, 73, 105, 107–8, 110–11, 117, 123, 136, 140–1
Grace of Monaco, Princess, 109
Graham, Jory, 52, 65; *In the Company of Others*, 60–1, 79–80, 85
gravestones, 102, 185, 189, 190–1; cost of, 190; regulations governing, 190; wording on, 16–18, 25, 116, 190; *see also* cemeteries
Gray, Thomas, 'Elegy Written in a Country Churchyard', 96
grief, 4, 92, 109, 110, 115–24, 196–204; and attitudes to war, 151–2; children's, 143–5; expressed at funerals, 108–9; the process of, 123–37; sharing, 145; shock effects

Index

of, 92, 103, 119–23; as source of mental ill health, 118; *see also* bereaved
Grimms *Fairy Tales*, 36, 67
guilt felt by bereaved, 129, 131, 132, 133, 134–5, 150

Hals, Frans, 'Young Man Holding a Skull', 42–3
Harding, Rachel, and Dyson, Mary, *A Book of Condolences*, 113
Hardy, Thomas, 'Friends Beyond', 15; 'Her Death and After', 15
heart transplants/surgery, 41, 49, 55
Heberden, Dr, 121
Henley, W. E., 35
Heron, Mabel, 75
Highgate cemetery, 97
Hinton, John, 70, 87; *Dying*, 65, 77
Hoban, Russell, 36
Holbein, Hans, the Younger: 'Ambassadors Jean de Dinterville and Georges de Selve', 43; 'The Dance of Death', 33–4, 36
Holden, Patrick, 7, 49
Holyoake, Austin, 105
home-care units, 60, 148
home nursing, 158, 160, 164
homosexuals and lesbians, bereavement of, 145–6
Hopkins, Gerard Manley, 123
Hospice Information Service, 159–60, 203–4
hospices, hospice movement, 11, 48, 57–61, 62, 65, 75, 83, 86, 93, 109, 158; AIDS patients, 164; day-care, 60, 159; help and support to bereaved, 110, 148, 166; short-stay, patients, 158, 160
hospitals, death in, 47–8, 54–5, 59, 93, 109–10, 111, 166, 167, 169
hourglass, as symbol of mortality, 42, 43–4
Humphrey, Derek, *The Right to Die – Understanding Euthanasia*, 88
Hurston, Zora Neale, *Dust Tracks on a Road*, 136–7
hypothermia, 175

informed consent, doctrine of, 84–6
inquests, 95, 167, 177–8
'In Sure and Certain Hope' (BBC Radio 4), 71, 74
Irish Sisters of Charity, 58
Irish wake, 108
irritability felt by bereaved, 131–2

James, P. D., *An Unsuitable Job for a Woman*, 17
jewellery left on dead body, 182–3, 184
Jewish Bereavement Counselling Service, 202
Johnson, Dr Samuel, 115, 139
joint tenancy agreement, 197

Kamikaze pilots, Japanese, 39–40
Kastenbaum, Robert, and Aisenberg, Ruth, *The Psychology of Death*, 34
Kensal Green cemetery, 97
Kotaluk, Ronald, 73–4
Kübler-Ross, Elizabeth, 76, 82

Lamerton, Richard, *Care of the Dying*, 48, 55, 62, 63, 69, 83, 86
laying-out (of dead), 92, 94, 110–11, 183, 184

Leach, Christopher, 125, 129, 133, 139; *Letter to a Younger Son*, 104, 105, 120, 139, 153
Lear, Martha Weinman, 132; *Heartsounds*, 129
legal requirements for disposal of the dead, 95, 100, 106, 111, 112, 165–95
Lennon, John, 125
letters of condolence, 113
Lewis, C. S., 126, 142; *A Grief Observed*, 119, 135, 140, 141
Lewis, Oscar, *A Death in the Sánchez Family*, 102–3
life expectancy, 24–5, 46
life insurance, 193, 198
life-support systems, 31–2
London Necropolis and National Mausoleum Company, 97
Lorde, Audre, *The Cancer Journals*, 50–1

McGee, Christine, 94, 148
Macmillan Nurses, 160–1
Macmillan Service, 60
Malraux, André, *The Royal Way*, 41
Mann, Thomas, 91
Marie Curie Homes, 13, 58, 59
Marie Curie Memorial Foundation, 55, 58, 60, 161, 162
Marie Curie Nurses, 161–2
Marvell, Andrew, 'To His Coy Mistress', 44–5
Masereel, Frans, 35
medical card of deceased, 170, 172
medical information, control of, 72–4
memorials, 189–92
memorial services, 106-7, 1879

Mental Health Films Council seminar, 10
Miscarriage Association, 202
misdiagnosed deaths, 26–8
mirror image theme, 43
Mitford, Jessica, *The American Way of Death*, 103
Moore, Claude, 49, 61, 79
Moore, Katharine, 49, 67, 68, 80, 101, 127
Morley, John, *Death, Heaven and the Victorians*, 101
mourning clothes, 102, 107, 127–8
Mozart, Wolfgang Amadeus, 50
Mundane, Rory, 42
murder victims, bereavement of relatives, 144, 146, 148–9
Murray, Len, 41

National Association of Funeral Directors, 180, 193
National Association of Widows, 203
National Health Service (NHS), 60, 85, 158, 160, 170
National Secular Society, 105, 188
Norris, John, 37–8
notice to informants, 168, 169–71, 172
notification of burial or cremation, 174

O'Casey, Sean, *Juno and the Paycock*, 151–2
old age, aging, 69, 80
'On Ilkley Moor Baht'at' (song), 46
opiates used to control pain, 63–5
organs or body, donation of, 30, 165–6
organ transplants, 30–1, 41, 49

Index

Owen, Wilfred, 113; 'Anthem for Doomed Youth', 40
Oxford Book of Death, 'Last Words', 81

pain, pain control, 55, 56, 57, 61–7, 158–9
Parkes, Colin Murray, 118, 120, 122, 126; 'Bereavement counselling' (*BMJ*), 149
personal effects (of dead), 126
Pincus, Lily, *Death and the Family*, 121–3
Pliny the Younger, 113
post-mortems, 167, 176–7
pre-payment schemes, 192, 193–4
procurator fiscal (Scotland), 166, 167, 168, 172, 175–8
property, 197; co-ownership with deceased, 197; making over your, 194

Rainier, Prince of Monaco, 109
regeneration, belief in, 46
Registrar of Births and Deaths, 95, 171–5; information available from, 174
registration of death, 95, 100, 111, 166–7, 171–5; death occuring abroad, 175; stillbirths, 174
reincarnation, 46
resentment felt by bereaved, 129–30, 131
Rethel, Alfred, 'Death as a Friend', 35
rigor mortis, 30
Robinson, Paul, 41
Rolling Stones, 45
Rouault, Georges, 34
Rousseau, Jean-Jacques, *Emile*, 24

St Augustine, 115
St Christopher's Hospice, 58, 65, 81; national information service, 159–60, 203–4
St John Stevas, Norman, 89
St Joseph's Hospice, London, 58
St Matthew, 115
Salford funeral-planning society, 194
Samaritans, 203
Saunders, Cicely, 58, 62–3, 66, 72; 'On Dying Well', 75
Scottish Cot Death Trust, 203
Seed, Pat, *One Day at a Time*, 69–70, 80, 82
self-help, 137–40
self-help organisations, 146–7
Shakespeare, William, 14–15; *King Lear*, 29, 145; *Macbeth*, 142
Shelley, Percy Bysshe, 15, 98
shock of bereavement, 92, 105, 119–23
Shorter, Edward, *A History of Women's Bodies*, 56
Sidaway, Mrs Amy, 85
Sidney, Sir Philip, 'A Farewell', 14
Sitwell, Edith, 113
Sitwell, Sir Osbert, 3
skull, as symbol of mortality, 42–4
Social Fund (DHSS), 173
social isolation: of bereaved, 116, 140–2, 145–6; of dying, 57, 74
Social Security office, 173, 174, 175, 185, 186
somatic death, 29
'Some Mother's Son' (film), 49
Stanhope, Anna Eliza, gravestone of, 17
Start the Week (BBC Radio 4), 11–12
Steward, Samuel, 96

Stillbirth and Neonatal Death Society, 203
stillborn babies, 5; financial help with funerals, 186; mourning loss, 145; registering death, 174
Stoppard, Tom, *Rosencrantz and Guildenstern are Dead*, 40
Strasbourg, Musée de l'Oeuvre Notre Dame: statue of death, 33
sudden death, 76–7, 81, 105
Sue Ryder Foundation, 163
suicide, 38, 39–40, 86, 89–90
Suicide Act (1961), 86

Tagore, Sir Rabindranath, 153
Tasma, David, 58
Tatelbaum, Judy, 131, 136; *The Courage to Grieve*, 128, 138
Taylor, *Principles and Practices of Medical Jurisprudence*, 27
Terrence Higgins Trust, 164
Thompson, Sir Henry, 98
'Time is on my Side' (song), 45
'Time Waits for No One' (song), 45
'The Tired Woman's Epitaph', 39
Tolstoy, Leo, *The Death of Ivan Ilych*, 57
Toynbee, Arnold, 37
Toynbee, Polly, 88
trade unions, death benefit provided by, 101, 186
Twain, Mark, 39

Unamuno, Miguel de, 83
undertakers (funeral directors), 92, 94, 104, 105, 106, 107, 111, 112, 168, 174, 179–86, 190, 194; burials, 181, 184, 185; code of practice, 180; coffins, 184; cost of, 13, 102–3, 180, 184–6; cremation, 181–3, 184, 185; funerals, 180–9; laying-out, 92, 94, 110, 183, 184

Vaughan, Daphne, 144, 146, 148–9
Victoria, Queen, 138
viewing the dead, 92–4, 183–4
Voluntary Euthanasia Society, 88

Warman, Jane 'After a Death', 106
War Pensioner's Funeral Grant, 186
Warwick, Lady, 116
widow's allowance, 198–9
widow's benefit, 173, 198–9
wills, 6–7, 99, 197–8; challenge to, 197; executors, 197–8; grant of probate, 198
writing, therapeutic value of, 139–40

Yoko Ono, 125